Euroglass

Lika Vetra

Dedication i

Acknowledgments.. ii

About the Author... iii

Chapter 1: Arrival... **1**

   Entrance 1

   Team lead 4

   Newcomers' lunch.. 10

   Executive Director 18

   Maxim to Veronika. На Север поедет один из вас, на Дальний

   Восток - другой 22

   Friend.. 25

   Senior Counselor 30

Chapter 2: EU Agency Grind **39**

   My progress 39

   Maxim to Veronika. Barenik 46

   Chinese delegation 51

   Reverse of the corporate Fortuna.................................... 61

   Appraisal... 67

   Christmas party 74

   European fairness 87

Chapter 3 The Diadem Project **93**

   New year begins 93

   Maxim to Veronika. Cosmopolitan Christmas 97

   Trip to Heidelberg 102

   Unicorn hunt 107

   Brain twister... 120

   Dancing with Alice 125

   New mission of Karolina 135

Chapter 4 U-Turn... **143**

   On the Philosopher's Walk 143

   Maxim to Veronika. A risky guess 151

Feedback from Carlos 156

Girl with contacts 163

Conspirator 171

Detection begins 177

Audit mission 185

Chapter 5 Investigation **189**

In Cristina's office 189

Barcelona 194

Maxim to Veronika. Need help 198

Ian's headquarters 201

Who is "De Goya"? 205

Cleaners 211

Carlos 217

Chapter 6 Showdown **226**

Silvia 226

Isabel makes a phone call 231

New task from Carlos 238

At Alice's home 244

Shadowing and robbery 254

In the cinema 260

Maxim to Veronika. A whistleblower 263

Chapter 7 Conspiracy **266**

Philipe 266

Rock around the work 273

Ian's concert 282

Computer diagnostic 291

Carlos changes his mind 296

Striking out Blue Stripe 301

Epilogue 307

Maxim to Veronika. See you? 313

Dedication

To Jens and Sascha

Acknowledgments

I am deeply indebted to Regina S. and Wiktor K. for a chance of a lifetime.

I am endlessly grateful to Carla H., Noemi S. and Charlotte G. for the moral support, our therapeutic conversations and for our friendship.

I am thankful to my family and my friends for standing by me in the dark and happy years.

When writing, I was inspired by Sam Brown, Jökull Júlíusson, Mark Knopfler, Ambrosia Parsley, Stealth and The Beatles.

About the Author

Born in 1978 to a Jewish mother and Sri Lankan father, Lika Vetra grew up in Moscow and graduated from MGIMO, the main Russian school for diplomats.

At 13, she wrote a "Star Wars" fanfic. After graduation, she worked as a journalist for The New Times weekly and as a press officer for the Russian central bank. She published a contemporary fiction novel in Russian entitled "Mead of Poetry".

In 2008, Lika moved to Frankfurt to marry a German writer, Tom Kahn, with whom she has a son. In Germany, she has worked as a speechwriter and communication expert.

Lika, whose great-grandfather was executed during Stalin's Purges in 1937, is a political activist. She supports Ukraine and Israel and fights against Putin's regime and antisemitism in Europe.

Chapter 1: Arrival

Entrance

I waded through the crowd flavored with rambling. Dozens of vehicles of all kinds massaged the wide back of the road in front of the Main Train Station. I turned right to make three hundred steps down to the River Main. A harmonica of a street musician on the bridge was singing something anxious but familiar. And finally, here it was. A bottle green cylindrical tower proudly postured between the shiny water of the river and the bright blue sky of Frankfurt. It was going to be my new working place.

I stopped to cool down. After a long walk, my newly bought business suit seemed too warm and tight. The green tower arrogantly showed me its sloping glass hip. The revolving entrance door was casually swallowing and spitting out people. A large terrace of a restaurant next door was quietly awaiting guests. The River Main exhaled a cool blow into my face. The harmonica on the bridge got louder, and I suddenly recognized the melody, "I'm just a soul whose intentions are good, oh Lord, please don't let me be misunderstood!"[1]

I took a deep breath and entered.

---

[1] "Don't let me be misunderstood" by Bennie Benjamin, Horace Ott and Sol Marcus

"European Agency for Innovation Support," I proudly announced to a receptionist, a young man wearing the same dark blue tie as mine.

"27th floor, elevators on the right-hand side." He answered, uninterested, and smiled automatically when I politely thanked him.

The elevator alarmingly beeped and sped up. My excitement grew proportionally to the numbers on the display. With the orange "27", I pushed myself out and stiffened. 3-meter-high glass walls everywhere offered a splendid view of the city. The famous Frankfurt skyline from tourist booklets self-contentedly glanced at me. Transfixed, I stared back. My first moment in a European agency was like a dream.

"Hellooo," somebody screeched. I noticed another reception desk with a ginger-haired female head on top. "Can-I-help-you-Sir?" the head said.

"Good morning. I would like to see Fadila Ribeiro Villescas."

The receptionist curiously looked at me. "A-newcomer-right? Your-passport-or-ID-please."

"Yes, a newcomer. How do you know?" I held my passport ready. (It still felt strange to identify myself with this newly printed purple pass).

The head flourished with a wide smile. "All-newcomers-ask-for -the-head-of-HR! I'm-Etna-nice-to-meet-you." She found my name somewhere on her computer and held out a visitor badge.

"One-floor-down-office-one. Welcome-on-board-Sir!"

"Thank you."

Each sentence of hers sounded like a single word. Only in the elevator, I caught up with what she had said and finally understood why she accompanied her words with a military salutation. Since I arrived in Germany a couple of weeks ago, I have been saying "thank you" every time I couldn't understand what people were telling me. This time, it paid off.

The office door was open, which, in my experience, meant that nobody was inside. Yet a miniature young woman was in. With a slightly rasping voice, she was talking on the phone. She waved and beckoned me to take a seat. Looking around, I thought glass walls could make every office impressive, even this one. Rather small, furnished with a faceless desk and drawers, it was full of light and morning energy. Finally, the woman put down the phone. Her oval face brightened with a white-teeth smile.

"Hello, Ian. I am Fadila, head of HR. Welcome to the agency."

"Hello, Fadila, nice to meet you. I am Maxim." I hoped she didn't get embarrassed by wrongly naming me.

The crescent of her smile turned into a full moon. "Oh, yes." She sat down at her computer and typed something. "Wait a moment, I am getting there. You come from Ireland, right?" she declared happily.

"Actually… Romania."

She wrinkled her nose. Now she didn't look so young anymore, the beginning of her forties maybe. She thumbed through a pile of papers on her desk from right to left. "I am sure I have it in my files here. Oh, yes, you are our new IT expert?"

"Huh…project analyst."

She thumbed through the same papers in the reverse order. Then goggled at the monitor again.

It's a mistake; they never recruited me, flickered in my head a second before Fadila exclaimed, "Oh, yes, Maxim Reut, our new project analyst from Romania. Welcome to the family!"

Team lead

Fadila accompanied me to my office, her rasping voice showering my ears. "InSup (it took me time to understand it was the abbreviation of our agency's name, "European Agency for Innovation Support") is a very young institution. Just six months old. It's our baby and we all are a little family of this baby. But we are very ambitious. We are going to make Europe innovative. We'll improve the life of every EU citizen… You, Maxim, are our employee number fifty-six, and by the end of the year, we will be sixty-five. Many more staff will join next year. It's a hard job for HR. Hundreds of start-ups from the whole EU apply every day for funding. We need superb experts to cope with such a workload…"

In the elevator, her thread of thoughts changed. "It's a luck InSup rents space in this tower. The view from the 27th floor is splendid, isn't it? Wait until you see our big meeting room; it's awesome, too. It was like a Christmas dream. Initially, we were supposed to sit far away from here. But in December, a big construction company suddenly closed its Frankfurt office in this very skyscraper. We were lucky to get their office space. The building is privately owned. The owner was so glad to quickly get a new tenant that he even offered us a discount. Now InSup occupies floors 25, 26, and 27. We in HR want our employees to work on good premises with an aesthetic view from their windows."

"What is on the other floors of this building?" I asked when Fadila took a breath.

She splattered with renewed energy. Dozens of other companies rent the rest of the skyscraper. That's a usual practice with high-rise buildings in Frankfurt. On each floor, there are two staff kitchenettes and toilets, of course. Many offices are still empty. It depends on HR who and when will finally sit here. HR is the busiest area without exaggerations, honestly. We have a new recruitment campaign every second week."

"And here is your office," Fadila announced. She stopped in front of an open door and addressed somebody inside. "Karolina, may we enter? I brought you a new colleague."

A prickle of trepidation ran through my body. Whoever and whatever I find in this office next moment might be decisive for my next years here.

"Yes, sure, I am waiting for you," answered a velvet voice inside.

Fadila let me enter first. "This is Maxim," she said when I had come in.

I froze. Instead of the Frankfurt skyline, this office overlooked a residential area with light-cacao-colored houses and scattered trees.

"Welcome, Maxim; I am Karolina Schiller, your team lead," said a tall woman in her fifties.

She had a firm grip, short black hair, and anthracite vivid eyes. "Now there are two of us in the M-Unit, and you can't imagine how glad I am to have you with us!"

"Thank you, Karolina. Nice to meet you. I look forward to working with you," I pronounced the sentence that I had been preparing for this occasion for a long time. I meant it because Karolina sounded whole-hearted, too.

"Will you show Maxim his desk?" Fadila asked.

"We have two working desks and I think both are equally good, isn't it?" Karolina addressed me.

I couldn't agree more. Both desks were positioned next to the window so that people sitting at them would face each other at a couple of meters' distance. Desks were equipped with a set of shelves each. One desk was piled with books, colorful carton folders, and plastic files swollen with paper sheets. The other one was neat and rather empty. I pointed at it. "I think I know exactly where I'll sit."

"Actually, it's vice versa," Karolina said with embarrassment. "I was storing the archive on your desk because it's so convenient, and desperately failed to arrange it before your arrival. Then I thought we could clean it up together as a kind of introduction."

I was relieved to start with something easy: putting papers on the shelves was precisely the right task. I approached the crowded desk and noticed bright blue folders labeled "A-D", "E-H", and so on up to "X-Z". The books "European Law" and "EU Institutions" were worn out with many stickers that Karolina obviously used as bookmarks. "It would be useful to get familiar with our archive," I said, taking from the top of the highest pile a yellow file entitled "Curious info".

"Watch out!" Karolina screamed.

While taking "Curious info", I hindered the inner balance of the pile, and some folders on top slid down. I rushed to hold them and kicked with an elbow another pile, which lurched in a different direction. I desperately tried to catch everything and instead, like in a bad comedy, found half of our archive on the floor.

"I am sorry," Karolina and I said simultaneously.

Fadila smirked. "I see you are going to be very busy. Perfect time for me to leave you alone. Have a good start in InSup, Maxim." Her white teeth twinkled for the last time, and she ran out of our office.

Karolina and I looked at each other and burst into laughter. In a couple of hours, we perfectly arranged our archive, and I was mesmerized by my team lead. Slim, with chunky silver hoop rings, walking quickly on stilettos, from behind, Karolina hardly looked older than twenty-five years old. Yet twenty-five years was the age of her career, which she carried with remarkable lightness. After we were done with the archive, Karolina declared "a tour-de-floor". To my horror, she meant it literally. We entered every office, where Karolina introduced me to whoever was in. She effortlessly embraced the corporate tradition, making small talk and jokes with our office neighbors. Out of my newcomer embarrassment, I failed to remember a single face or name of my new colleagues. Luckily, the tour-de-floor wasn't long since many offices were still empty.

Afterward, Karolina showed me how one should start a career in an EU agency. First, she told me to get a laptop, which our IT unit had pre-set for me. Next, she sent me my very first email in InSup. It contained no messages but the link to the Official Journal of the EU, which published the EU Regulation establishing InSup. Describing InSup mandate, tasks, and obligations, this regulation was supposed to become my Bible as long as I was working here.

The following document, which Karolina called "our New Testament," was a thick white brochure entitled "InSup business rulebook". The brochure described how to approve documents, request holidays, and other things the daily working life comprises. Karolina warned that the business rulebook was a "living document" and would soon be a new edition.

Finally, she explained my tasks. Start-ups were sending InSup their business plans, and my job was to assess whether they deserved EU funding. In my previous job, I used to analyze companies, too. Just there was one difference. After my analysis, those companies faced unexpected troubles.

"What kind of funding do start-ups receive from us?" I asked.

"There is a complicated methodology behind it," Karolina said, pointing at the InSup business rulebook. "It depends on their size and the potential impact on European society. But money is not decisive. Once start-ups get InSup funding, they can boost private investments. Our ok is kind of a seal of excellence."

After having posed Karolina all sorts of questions the whole morning, I felt like I've got an elder sister. At the same time, I prepared to work hard. Karolina wasn't a leader who would forgive laziness or negligence. She believed in the higher mission of our agency and seemed to expect the same from others. Otherwise, how could she collect such an extensive archive just in six months of InSup's existence?! I looked closer at her workplace. Behind her desk on the wall, Karolina hung a poster with three words *"Home sweet office"*. *Does she feel in InSup at home? Or does she feel at home only when she is working?* I wondered, but didn't dare to ask.

"Get ready, Maxim, the newcomers' lunch is about to start," Karolina suddenly said, without taking her eyes off the monitor.

I was happy to stop swallowing tons of information and get some actual food. "Are you joining?"

I was hoping she would say "yes".

"No, I am behind schedule and need to finalize something," Karolina glanced at me. Then she added apologetically the sentence that, as I understood later, always meant "I'm too busy to waste my time lunching": "Maybe I'll join you for a coffee."

Embarrassment belongs to the first working day, I reminded myself and left alone.

Newcomers' lunch

Newcomers' lunches in InSup invariably took place in a big pizzeria opposite our tower. Hardly did I say "Agency for Innovation Support," as the waiter already beckoned me to follow him. We walked past the buzzing hall full of business lunch eaters; past the kitchen full of cooks, tossing pieces of fresh dough into the air, savored with hot tomato sauce. Finally, we entered a room with a single long table, an area for corporate events obviously.

A dozen of people were already sitting around. I recognized Fadila. She saw me, too, and waved. "This is Maxim, our newcomer," she announced.

"Hello," I said, abashed that everybody was going to stare at me. To my relief, hardly anybody paid attention to my greeting. Some focused on studying the menu, others were talking to each other. Only a couple of people nodded to me affably and turned away. The official part of the newcomers' lunch seemed to have just ended.

I cautiously placed myself at the closest available seat.

"Nice to meet you, Maxim," said a girl next to me. "I am Isabel." I shook her firm, dry hand. "So, in which unit are you starting?" she asked.

"Uhm... I forgot. I work together with Karolina Schiller. I am a project analyst."

She nodded. Her auburn hair was fluffy and slightly curly. "I see. It's M-Unit because you guys are dealing with medical start-ups."

"Indeed, M-Unit, thank you. And in which unit are you?"

At this moment a man with a remarkable hawknose sat down at an empty chair opposite to me. The wily glance of his dark eyes was so infectious that I smiled back.

"Ian?" he asked, pointing his finger at me.

"Maxim!" Isabel and I said simultaneously.

He grinned. "Sorry. Wrong guess. I am Philipe."

"Strange," I said, shaking his hand, "for the second time, somebody calls me Ian today."

Isabel laughed, "Oh, that's easy. Fadila always informs all staff about newcomers, and this month, we've got an email from her with just two names: yours and Ian's."

"Yeh, I missed my fifty-fifty chance!" Philipe said joyfully. "Now, let's talk business. Why don't we quickly order something and then introduce ourselves to each other properly? Otherwise, we'll stay here for ages, and I'll be late for my next meeting."

"He is right; let's order first," Isabel immediately confirmed, leaning over to me and opening the menu in front of both of us. Her perfume reminded me of wet grass after rain and maybe of moss. Her short, glancing fingernail quickly moved across the menu items. "This, this, and this is very good and is served quickly. Risotto is delicious but takes much too long. Minestrone is usually very spicy. Finally, pizza canzone and lasagna are too greasy; you'd better not try at all."

"Bravo, Isabel," Philipe laughed, "a perfect summary of their menu. No wonder that everybody is fighting to get you for their assessments!"

"I am from R-Unit, Research," Isabel explained. "We are supporting you, project analysts." She turned to Philipe, "After six months of working in InSup, I know this menu by heart."

Apparently, there was no canteen in our agency: the architect of our building planned only offices, but no space for cooking. As a result, all the inhabitants of the tower lunched in the nearby cafés, including this pizzeria.

"And what are you doing?" I turned to Philipe after the waiter collected our orders.

"Communication."

"With whom?"

"Media relations, stakeholder relations, staff relations. You name it."

"This is a lot!" I said respectfully.

Philipe tilted his head, his hawknose making him look like a smiling eagle. "Everything that we in InSup do can be called 'communication'. That is a blessing and a curse simultaneously. Blessing because I won't lose my job. This agency can't poke its nose into the outside world without me."

"And why is it a curse?" I asked discreetly.

Philipe puffed, "Exactly, for the same reason. They want my approval for every vacancy notice, every tender announcement, every email to a professional association, and God knows what else… Since I started here, scarcely a day goes by when they don't run after me with kind requests to draft something. What about yourself? Where are you from actually?"

"It's complicated," I wasn't sure that I should talk about my biography at all on the very first working day. "I have a Romanian passport, but I never lived in Romania. I am Russian."

Philipe distrustfully smiled. "How is this possible?"

"You are from the Republic of Moldova then," Isabel concluded rather than asking. She sipped water, and suddenly, her eyes above the water glass became piercing.

"You are right; it's Moldova that I must thank for my Romanian passport. But how do you know it, Isabel?"

"Isabel, knowing something unusual, doesn't surprise me at all," Philipe smirked.

Isabel shrugged her shoulders. "Just observations... I used to work in the European Commission. There, I encountered several colleagues with Romanian citizenship who were originally from Moldova. If I remember correctly, Romania offers its citizenship to people whose ancestors lived in Bessarabia, the territory that once belonged to the Romanian Kingdom before it became part of the Soviet Republic of Moldova."

"Ok, so you are from Moldova," Philipe said.

"No, I never lived there either." I took a sip of water.

Isabel raised one eyebrow. Her face reminded me of an antique statue with fair skin, a marmoreal nose, and pale lips. Only her vivid brown eyes seemed to live a separate life on her face. Philipe was about to say something, but the waiter brought our orders: gnocchi gorgonzola for Isabel and myself, risotto con porcini for Philipe.

"How come you get your risotto so unusually quickly?!" Isabel exclaimed.

Philipe chuckled. "I came here in the morning and ordered it beforehand, my dear researcher. Now, Maxim, tell us your story. I feel it's going to be interesting."

I suddenly felt flattered by their kind curiosity and sincere interest in me. "The story of my family starts in the last century…"

I tried to be short, not to bore them. In June 1941, upon the order of Stalin, thousands of inhabitants of Bessarabia were deported to Kazakhstan and Siberia. My grandfather, a talented carpenter and owner of an atelier, was among them. In the deportation's course, his wife and newborn son died. Maybe they were lucky not to end up in a correctional labor camp.

"GULAG?" whispered Isabel, her eyes filled with horror.

"GULAG indeed. To be more precise, the South-East Railway Correctional Labor Camp. After a 5-year sentence, my grandfather was set free but decided that it was safer to stay in the region. That's how he ended up in Birobidzhan."

"Google speed me, where is Birobidzhan? Near Azerbaijan?" Philipe asked.

"No, it's near China, in the Far East of Russia. Capital of the Jewish Autonomous Oblast," Isabel said.

I started getting used to Isabel being aware of unexpected things.

Birobidzhan had a big workmen's association producing furniture, which my grandfather joined. He made quite a career there and died as a respected citizen, never wanting to return to Bessarabia. In Birobidzhan, he met my grandmother.

She was the daughter of an engineer who worked for the Chinese Far East Railway. Her family lived in Harbin when, in 1935, the whole family was arrested together with dozens of other railway workers. On the night of the arrest, my grandma was visiting her friend, so chekists[2] took everybody who was at home - her parents and two elder brothers but didn't bother to check whether anybody else was left. Only in the 1990s, after she had already died, we could get the information from the KGB archive that the whole family was brought to Moscow, shot dead soon afterward, and buried in a mass grave on the Kommunarka firing range[3].

The family my grandma visited that fatal night advised her to run away. She took a train to Russia and, at one stop, pretended she lost her family and didn't know where to go. Nobody got suspicious. So she ended up as a worker in the same furniture fabric as my grandfather, just some years earlier than him. According to the family legend, they never had to buy any furniture; everything was

---

[2] Members of Cheka (All-Russian Extraordinary Commission) that later on became the KGB

[3] Used for secret executions in 1937-1941 Kommunarka represents a memorial containing over 6500 names of identified victims

produced by my grandfather according to his designs. At home, we still have one bentwood chair from those days. My dad keeps it as a confirmation of this legend.

When Romania began offering citizenship, I could just show the documents proving my grandfather's birth in Bessarabia and his forced departure from there. Getting a Romanian passport was easy.

"So, you come from Birobidzhan, then?" Isabel asked.

"Also, not. My dad had left the city to study first in Khabarovsk and then in Moscow, where he met my mom."

"And how did your mother get to Moscow?" Philipe asked.

"That's less exciting. Mom is a three-generation Muscovite, a typical representative of the intelligentsia. A daughter of a Moscow State University professor, a granddaughter of a dentist, and a grand-granddaughter of an archpriest in the Moscow Cathedral of Christ the Savior, the one that Bolsheviks destroyed in 1931."

For a while, Isabel and Philipe remained silent and serious. Not without pride, I felt I had impressed them.

Finally, Philipe said, "Well, compared to what you have just told us, the story of how my French mom met my Spanish dad sounds like a bus schedule."

"And how did they meet?" I asked.

Philipe snorted. "Studied together in Madrid," he said in a deliberately monotonous voice. He paused and, since I kept looking at him, added, "That is it, end of story."

Suddenly Isabel's mobile rang. She picked up the call, said, "Of course", hung up, and turned to me. "Maxim, Karolina reminds you that in ten minutes, you have a welcome talk with Carlos, our executive director. You'd better come a couple of minutes earlier. Carlos loves German punctuality."

"Yeh, when he doesn't have to wait for others. Not vice versa," Philipe chuckled.

Executive Director

In my Outlook calendar, the invite entitled "Introductory meeting with Carlos de Santos Gomez, Executive Director of InSup" was set to last fifteen minutes.

"Do I need to prepare for it?" I asked Karolina right after I had come back from the newcomers' lunch.

"Not really," she smiled. "Carlos just wants to greet you and wish you a nice start. But be prepared that your next meetings with him won't be so easy; he is very demanding."

I opened the website of InSup to read Carlos' biography in the section "About" – "Organization". A relatively young man in the picture was looking above the camera lens with the face expression of a sea captain observing the horizon. The picture caption mentioned Carlos was a lawyer with an economics diploma, who had worked in various Spanish public institutions before joining InSup.

I arrived at Carlos' office five minutes before the meeting but found there a petite girl wearing Harry-Potter-glasses that suited her oval-shaped face.

"Hi, Maxim," she stood up and energetically shook my hand. "I am Cristina, the personal assistant of Carlos. We have just seen each other at the newcomers' lunch but Isabel and Philipe stole your attention. Take a seat; Carlos will be with you in a minute."

While talking to me, Cristina was filing documents. Her movements were quick and precise. She was in InSup from day number one, knew everybody, and could answer any question a newcomer like me might have. I couldn't help asking about Carlos. She readily replied that Carlos was a great boss, willing that everybody feels at home in InSup. Cristina looked at her dainty silver wrist watch, "Give me a moment; I will ask Carlos whether you can come in yet."

She cracked open an inner door next to her desk, which I hadn't noticed before, and said something in Spanish. The next moment, she threw the door open with the promising smile of a circus conferencier, "You may come; Carlos is waiting."

At the first moment, I didn't see anybody. The large working desk was piled with colorful paper folders. Two big monitors in the middle of the desk looked like the funnels of a steamboat. The wall behind the desk was dazzled with diplomas and photos of kids. Only a moment later, I noticed a small, round-headed man rising from behind the desk. He wore round glasses and a scarlet tie.

"Hello. Please take a seat," he whispered, looking somewhere at my underarms and pointing at the enormous meeting table in the sunny corner.

We sat down. Through the glass walls of this office, one could see not only the skyline but also the twinkly River Main and the vibrant green of a park.

"Wonderful view," I couldn't help saying.

"Thank you," he was almost whispering. "I am Carlos de Santos Gomez, executive director of InSup. I didn't have a plezur to attend the newcomers' lunch, but I always peersonally meet our new staff because we all ur one family. On behalf of all of us, I would like to wehrmly welcome you."

I was about to say that I was also happy to be here, but Carlos already went on.

"I am surr you have all the professional skills that are necessary and useful for InSup. Otherrwize, we wouldn't have selected you." He looked at me, this time definitely waiting for my reaction.

"I'll do my best."

Carlos nodded and put his hands on the table with a loud clank of his cuff-links. "I hope you will be trying harrd," he said (the roll of his "r" sounded especially loud). "Now, let me ask you. What do you expect from me?"

"Given that I started this week, I am afraid I will not give you a meaningful answer right now," I laughed.

He not only didn't smile but winced. I felt chokey.

At once, my former Russian boss, Sergey Vladimirovich Kamarinov, popped up in my memory. Before meeting any new counterparts, he used to instruct me and other junior colleagues with one sentence: "If no words are left in your dumb heads, just say 'for the sake of our mutual goals'."

"I expect you to support my efforts for the sake of our mutual goals," I hummed, sweating cold.

This time I hit the target. Carlos graciously nodded and stretched his lips in a rubber smile. "You can count on me," he said and extended a hand as a sign that the meeting was over.

His handshake was listless, and the glance was unseeing. The past drew up with me. I always tried not to annoy big bosses but never could stay in nice relations with them.

Maxim to Veronika. На Север поедет один из вас, на Дальний Восток - другой[4]

Nika, privet,

So, our split is firm and final. I am in Frankfurt, and you are in Hong Kong. If last summer anybody had told me we would be so far away from each other, I would have never believed. "Distance kills love," everybody told me after you had left for China. They just forgot to add the word "slowly." Or I just turned out to be love-permeable and can't help thinking of us.

How bitterly stupid, I never confessed it to you... Did you know that when we worked together in the Centrobank[5] I used to have many thrills per day? Every time I noticed admiring glances at you, I recalled it is with me, and not with one of them, this splendid girl has just made love in the morning. And it's to me, to our little apartment near Prospekt Mira metro station, this girl will return tonight. Yes, I was proud that you had chosen me, and I wanted to make you happy. If only I knew what I did wrong. Could you explain it?

Ignore this question. I know we agreed not to talk about it anymore. But you anyway deprived me of seeing and speaking to you. No video calls, no phone calls, just emails. And in writing, I

---

[4] "On the North will go one of you, in the Far East – the other" (quote from the Russian song "There were two friends serving" by S.Germanov, V.Gusev)

[5] Central Bank of Russia

can ask you anything because you don't need to reply to each line. Sorry for being melancholic. While writing you this email, I have my usual "Sunday mood."

Sunday is my loneliest day of the week. As I read in one German traveler's guide, on Sundays, nothing should distract Germans from being with their families. So true. Sundays hollow out Frankfurt shops and restaurants and empty the streets of Germany's financial capital. I live in a cute area on the left riverbank called Sachsenhausen. It's full of small houses, trees, and beer restaurants, which Germans call "beer gardens." The tourist information says Sachsenhausen is one of the most populated districts of Frankfurt, but today it's so quiet as if I were in the middle of a forest. Sometimes, I feel like dropping everything and returning to Moscow, back to our crazy never, sleeping megapolis life. Or maybe you would be happy to see me in Hong Kong?

Relax, that was a joke. I wanted to become a European, and I guess this is what a European life looks like. I made so many efforts to get a Romanian citizenship, to pass the job interview in InSup, to arrive here and I don't intend to let it go so quickly.

Actually, the job is something that inspires me. You can't imagine how they greet newcomers here! Everybody is so warm-hearted. So far, no one looked at me top-down or indifferently. In the Centrobank, newcomers can't expect such a truly warm welcome. (Ass kissing towards new bosses doesn't count).

An enormous cultural difference compared to Russia is that everybody calls each other by first name. In the beginning, I tried to call my team lead Karolina "Ms. Schiller," but she explained that EU institutions adapted the American corporate style. This is so democratic! And nobody is waiting for you to make a mistake. On the contrary, they want to help you be successful because they are successful themselves. Probably this is what it means to work in Europe... I hope one day I will also be as bright and kind as the people I have met here.

Take as an example Karolina, with whom I share the office by the way. She comes from the former Eastern Berlin and by age she is close to our senior Centrobank colleagues. Remember how they were teaching us: don't argue with a boss because the boss is always right; don't dispute with more experienced – they know it better; don't be too active otherwise you will get more work; don't do things too quickly otherwise nobody will believe that it was a hard job. And remember how they were getting ready to leave at six o'clock sharp, not to spend a single additional minute in the office?

Well, Karolina is a far cry from our Centrobankers. She unconditionally believes in what she is doing. She works late hours, constantly improves something and she never speaks to me as if she is my senior and knows it better. I must admit, she infected me with her attitude. I want to be like her: a European expert with a mission in the heart.

Now when I am writing this, my mood has improved, and I will leave my apartment for a long walk along the river.

P.S. Nika, forgive my asking, are you together with anybody?

Friend

Summer turned out to be the best time for a start in a European agency. In July and especially August InSup got lethargic. Employees went on holidays, and the flow of meetings and emails dried out. And by the end of this lonely summer, I got a friend. Our friendship started with hate. During my first week at InSup, I suddenly lost connection to the corporate server.

"Happens to newcomers," reassured Karolina without stopping to type on her keyboard. "Just call our IT help desk, and they will fix it."

"IT Helpdesk," a male voice in the receiver swished.

"Hi, it is Maxim Reut from M-Unit. I can't access our server anymore. Yesterday everything was fine; I don't know where the problem is."

The voice in the receiver swished something, and by the tone, I understood it was a question.

"Sorry, I didn't understand your question. Could you repeat, please?"

"Have-you-recently-changed-your-password?" the receiver said louder and slower.

"No, I started in InSup a couple of days ago."

"I see. Did a rally chat?"

"Who did a chat?" I asked, totally embarrassed.

"Did-you-try-to-restart?" the receiver said serenely.

"Oh, yes. Yes, I did."

"Elsi remotely. Your red nation, humble, please."

"My nation? Do you mean my nationality?" For the first time, I asked myself whether I was really capable of working in an English-speaking environment.

"Re-gi-stration-number-please," the receiver said disdainfully. "You-find-it-in-the-top-left corner-of-your-desktop."

I dictated my number diligently, pronouncing every digit and every letter.

"Low as sex, please."

"I am not very familiar with your operational system," I said after a second of intensive thinking about what I had just heard.

"Just-click-yes," the receiver said listlessly.

I noticed a new window in the middle of my screen stating, "Do you want to allow remote access to your computer?" Angry with myself, I pressed "Yes."

A couple of seconds later, the receiver started talking again. My heart dropped, for I didn't understand a single word, not even approximately. But before they fired me for my poor English, I decided to speak out.

"I beg your pardon, Sir," I said so loud that Karolina took her eyes off her monitor. "I really cannot hear well what you are saying. Should I come to your office? Maybe it's more comfortable for you?" The receiver ignored me and kept talking. "I simply don't understand you." I got ready to resign even before my six-month probation was over.

"I wasn't talking to you," the receiver said in a tone that one uses to say "you, dude." "What's your office number? I'll come over."

A couple of minutes later, a skinny and pale young man entered the office. "Hello, I am looking for Maxim Reut," he said.

"It's me."

"Am Ian Murphy from Helpdesk. We spoke a minute ago. May I?"

I jumped out of my seat, relieved he didn't look like the fancy and elegant monster I imagined when we had spoken on the phone. Ian said "hello" to Karolina, timidly sat down at my desk, and started typing something. *A guy with such fluffy ginger eyelashes and baby-like plump lips can't be bad*, I thought after Ian bent over and started manipulating the cables on the other side of the desk.

"It's ok," he said finally. "The connection was distorted; maybe a cleaner moved the cables. I've fixed it now."

"Thank you very much," I said, happy that I understood him.

He ran his hand over the soldier-like ginger haircut. "Sure thing. Cause ship ticket."

"Pardon?" I asked, feeling distressed again.

"I-will-close-the-job-ticket," he repeated and smiled shyly.

Once he left, Karolina giggled. "I also have problems with understanding colleagues from Ireland."

My self-judgment started crawling up. "I wish I could prohibit English natives from talking English to me," I said.

Karolina simpered, "I am afraid Ian and other English natives in EU institutions can say the same about us. How would you feel if 90% of people every minute try to address you in Russian?!"

Ian had no problem with it or better to say, he never thought of it. "Am just amazed by how fluent in English you all are," he told me once I finally dared to ask him.

Ian Murphy was the very same Ian who joined InSup simultaneously with me. After the incident with my laptop, I started encountering him in the shops and on my way home. Soon, we discovered we lived in the same house. Ian and his girlfriend rented the same apartment as mine just one floor higher. By the end of summer, the girlfriend suddenly declared that she couldn't stand being far away from friends-parents-colleagues and returned to her usual life in Ireland. Soon after her departure, Ian and I established a ritual: every morning, we met at the café next to our house, drank a cup of milk coffee with a croissant, and walked to the office together.

Nothing and nobody could throw Ian off balance. I observed him in different circumstances: suffering after the break-up with his girlfriend, watching the defeat of his favorite football team, talking to a drunken trouble-maker at the bar, getting a tight deadline from his manager. But every time, he remained unshakably peaceful. In response, people around him, myself included, automatically lowered their voices and lost the desire to dispute.

In September, InSup woke up to life with the next newcomer's announcement. Everybody wondered what kind of work the newcomer was going to do. Karolina insisted the newcomer would promote our agency in the European industry. Philipe argued that we could only process the start-up applications we were already flooded with by building relations with local governments, and that's what the newcomer would do. Isabel was sure that the newcomer's job would be to obtain more budget from the European Commission. And only Ian said, "Why this chitchat? Isn't it great that one more person will help us out?"

As for me, I only wondered how such unflavored lines could give the others so much food for thought:

From: Fadila Ribeiro Villescas

To: All_InSup_staff

Subject: Newcomer

Dear colleagues,

Please welcome to our little family Hilde Rosenbohm, who will take the position of a senior counselor to the Executive Director and as of now will advise Carlos on our strategic development and way forward.

Invitation to the newcomers' lunch will follow.

Kind regards,

Fadila on behalf of Carlos

Senior Counselor

I took off my eyes from the screen to see a tall man lurking in. His long legs, booted in black loafers, were soundless. His eyes above the long nose and behind the glasses looked straight at me. Something in him was weird.

"Maxim, right?" he asked in a surprisingly high-pitched voice.

"Yes, Maxim Reut."

I understood what was strange: the man didn't wear a tie. Moreover, the shirt under his gray suit had two buttons unbuttoned.

Quite a contrast to the penguin-like outfit of all male colleagues in InSup.

"We didn't have a chance to meet." He showed big yellowish teeth in a smile. "My name is Hilde Rosenbohm."

"Oh yes," I exclaimed, "you are the mysterious counselor who is going to advise us on our future!"

Hilde kept his gaze fixed on me with an unchanged yellowish smile.

"Nice to meet you," I hastily switched to the wording that Karolina used for newcomers, "Welcome to InSup and have a good start. I am working in M-Unit together with Karolina Schiller, my team lead. Unfortunately, she is off sick today."

Hilde's handshake was soft. "I have just sent you an invite, in half an hour, to my office. Would it suit you?" he asked.

"Yes. Where is your office?"

"On the same floor as yours, opposite the restrooms."

"I'll be there."

Hilde kept smiling at me. I was frantically looking for the possibility of filling in the pause.

"I think Fadila is going to organize a newcomers' lunch for you," I finally said.

Hilde nodded. "I asked her to postpone it. I prefer bilateral talks first. Are you running in the mornings?" he suddenly switched the topic.

"No, in the mornings I am actively sleeping and eating."

Hilde ignored my answer with an unchanged smile. "I am going to have morning runs along the river every day under any weather. Feel free to join."

"Thanks a lot, it's a nice idea," I tried to sound polite and grateful without promising anything.

"I am quite ambitious, you know. I aim to participate in the Frankfurt Iron Man one day," he added.

After Hilde had left, I looked in my inbox. Indeed, there was an unread invitation, which he had sent minutes before coming to my office.

From: Hilde Rosenbohm

Required attendance: Maxim Reut

Subject: Kick-off meeting

Location: My office

Dear Maxim,

We need to hold a meeting with the Chinese delegation. I understand that M-Unit is already taking care of it.

In order to have a substantial discussion,
please prepare all the details.

Best,

H.

I had fifteen minutes left before the meeting, which I used to run to Isabel. To my relief, she was in her "small-but-single" office, as Philipe called it, not without jealousy, for he shared his office with two others. Calm and concentrated, Isabel sat in front of the monitor. She had AirPods, in which, as I already knew, she was listening to the playlist entitled "Music of my life". This list was permanently updated and already contained hundreds of items that once were her favorite.

She glanced at me and immediately took off the AirPods, "Did anything happen?"

While I was reporting about my encounter with Hilde, she stood up and grabbed a big carafe of water with floating slices of lemon. (She used every free minute to drink). In response to my last exclamation, "Karolina didn't involve me in that visit. What should I tell this guy?!" Isabel handed me a full glass.

"Exhale and drink," she said. Her deep-forest-green pencil-dress and the lemony water cooled me a bit. Isabel took a big sip from her own glass, "Let's start with a key point: stop calling Hilde Rosenbohm 'this guy'; she's a woman."

I gasped. "Wait a moment, he said he was preparing for the Iron Man."

"Iron Man is a triathlon for both men and women." Isabel looked at me reproachingly, the way she often looked at Philipe. "It's natural for Hilde to look like a man, you know, but I would still use 'she and her' when talking about our new counselor."

"Is Hilde a female name then?"

Isabel nodded. "It stems from the old Hochdeutsch[6]. I think nowadays nobody calls girls like this." She knavishly smiled, "Her full name is Brünhilde, like in the Song of the Nibelungs. But she hates it and prefers everybody to call her 'Hilde'."

"Hilde has just joined us; how do you know that?!"

"From a friend of mine in Brussels. Hilde worked for several years in the German ministry of finance and often accompanied her minister to Brussels." Isabel became serious, "Time's running; we have only five minutes before your meeting. I can brief you on what I know about the Chinese."

The "Chinese delegation" Hilde inquired after, were the representatives of the Association of Chinese traditional medicine in Europe. Carlos was going to meet them in two weeks. Karolina already started preparing the meeting and had it under control.

---

[6] Standard German language as compared to regional dialects

34

Isabel swayed her chin from side to side to relax the neck muscles. "Chinese medicine is very popular in Europe, and they might have many ideas for start-ups. Just tell Hilde that this meeting is a top priority for you and Karolina. It should calm her down."

Next moment, I was running back to my floor. Hilde has got the same kind of small-but-single office as Isabel. That's where the similarity stopped. By Isabel, one could find different geographical maps, all kinds of fact books and dictionaries, pictures from holidays, and a collection of pencils that her friends kept bringing her from all over the world. Contrary to Isabel, Hilde was sitting among naked walls and empty shelves. The only personal possession I noticed was a plate of chocolate on a little round "negotiations" table next to her desk.

"Please take chocolate." Hilde switched on her buttery smile.

I longed for another glass of Isabel's water. "No, thanks, I don't eat chocolate."

"Oh, really? Do we have a real sportsperson here?" Luckily, she didn't wait for my answer and went on. "You know, many colleagues would love to have a nice little snack. That's why I always keep some cookies or chocolate in my office. You can come and get them any time."

By the end of our ten-minute talk, I felt asmear and sticky.

"Carlos considers this visit crucial for the agency."

"Karolina is fully aware and makes the necessary preparations. This meeting is of top priority to us."

Hilde decisively shook her head. Her short, grizzled hair looked greasy.

"Carlos asked me to take over from Karolina because this visit requires strategic thinking."

"We shouldn't deal with it anymore?"

"This meeting will stay within M-Unit. You will work on it together with me."

I jerked as if she was threatening me. "It would be fair if you worked with Karolina. She is already in contact with the delegation," I cautiously said.

"I am afraid we can't take her on board. The quality of preparation should be different."

"Karolina does everything with a lot of care. I never met a person working so thoroughly."

She showed again her big teeth, "Are you refusing to work on the visit?"

"Uh...No."

"Then please start immediately; we don't have much time."

"What am I supposed to do?"

"We should benefit from this meeting from a strategical viewpoint."

"What is our strategy?"

"You've worked here longer. You are supposed to know it better than me. My understanding is that we should establish good cooperation with China."

"Through the Association of Chinese traditional medicine in Europe?"

"I don't see any reasons for doubts, but if you have some, feel free to clarify it with Carlos."

I looked outside. The day was gloomy. Under the cloudy sky, the light-cacao-colored Frankfurt became dreary.

I sighed, "What should I start with?"

"I thought only trainees ask such questions. I don't micromanage people. You can start with whatever you prefer."

"Can you at least explain what's wrong with Karolina's preparations?"

"I can't be more precise than I already was. If you disagree with Carlos' view on the quality of preparation, please ask him directly."

Soon, I felt like walking in a labyrinth, missing the exit and passing the same places instead. When I finally returned to my desk, another outlook invite for tomorrow was already waiting for me.

From: Hilde Rosenbohm

Required attendance: Maxim Reut

Subject: Chinese visit

Location: My office

Dear Maxim,

I would like to meet you on a daily basis to be updated on your progress.

If this invitation coincides with other appointments in your calendar, please move them away.

Best,

H.

The new meeting on "my progress" was scheduled for nine o'clock in the morning. I clicked on the "accept" button, feeling that I had just accepted to never be friends with Karolina again.

Chapter 2: EU Agency Grind

My progress

At first glance, the work in a European agency differed little from the office work in any other place. A circular motion of desk work, meetings, and emails within four walls. Except for one thing. In Russia, I was frequently told I was doing wrong and in my turn never hesitated to say so to others. In InSup blaming somebody for not knowing what they do turned out a taboo.

You let your feet run wild[7]

During our joint breakfasts with Ian, my stomach was already turning like a washing machine, awaiting to meet Hilde first thing in the morning. Our "update-on-my-progress" meetings were a Groundhog Day. Still sweating from her morning runs, Hilde offered me sordid sweets. Then she bombarded me with suggestions, always using a modal verb "should": "should we think again about the participants list?"; "shouldn't we have a stronger introductory statement?"; "shouldn't we be more diplomatic when talking about Europe-China relations?"

I replied, "This is a good idea." Afterward, she constructed an unblinking face expression, which I called "So-I-Am-Listening-Very-Attentively." At these moments, her face made me so sick that

---

[7] "Way down we go" by Jökull Júlíusson.

I had nothing but vomit out the words, "I'll make a new proposal." This brought relief, for she stopped staring at me and started scribbling something on a lonely piece of paper on her desk.

When it was my turn to ask her questions, Hilde was losing interest in our conversation. Her colorless eyes lost focus, and her answers got vague. She often ended our meetings with the sentence, "I hope we have more clarity tomorrow." Well, our tomorrow didn't look a single bit different from our yesterday.

Our most recent meeting left me bemused. The fruit candies perfectly matched Hilde's acid-pink masculine shirt. With her first question, she was zealous as usual. "So, Maxim, where do you stand?"

"I failed to send out the meeting agenda yesterday because Carlos didn't approve it. Was going to chase him today."

Her smile became as wide as it was unnatural. "Stupid, I forgot to tell you. Yesterday, Carlos told me he is fine with your proposal for the meeting agenda."

To stifle a surge of fury, I jumped out of my seat and went to the glass wall. Because of her forgetfulness, I missed a deadline and had to offer the Chinese delegation my apologies for the delay. Behind the glass, underneath, autumn chestnuts were encouragingly eyeing the dozy River Main. It calmed me down. "I will immediately send the agenda out," I mumbled through clenched teeth, without looking at Hilde.

She stood up and approached me soundlessly. I knew it because the sweaty smell got stronger. I turned to her.

"Sure, but before proceeding, we need to do one more thing. Carlos wants us to shift the focus of the meeting and make the discussion more strategic."

I stared at her in disbelief. Her gaze behind the glasses was like a concrete wall, bereft of color and life.

"The agenda is not final, then? Did Carlos specify what does he mean?" I finally interrupted the pause.

Hilde shook her flea-bitten head. "The agenda of this meeting should serve the strategic objectives of InSup. We must be efficient and effective in every step, including such visits," she replied, looking somewhere over my head.

I wasn't even sure she was talking to me. At such a point in our conversation, I always felt she didn't hear me.

"I have no idea what I am supposed to do," I said louder than I should.

She brightened up. Every time I lost my temper, Hilde, on the contrary, was gaining ground. "Are you saying you don't understand why we should be more strategic?" she said softly.

"I don't know how to make a meeting on Chinese medicine more strategic," I spat out.

"There is no reason to get upset," Hilde showed a row of big teeth, a little crooked though.

"I simply want to send out this damn agenda in time."

"This is in your hands. If you are not sure, please approach experts in research and communication. They will be happy to help. We all are one team and always support each other."

A mobile phone on her desk rang. She turned away. I acted instantly. Without considering what I was doing, I pushed under her feet the sports bag that was lying on the floor. She stumbled over it. Next few seconds, like in slow motion, I watched her long body falling on the floor.

My heart clenched with dread, not for Hilde, but for what I have just done. I jumped on my knees.

"Are you…," I asked with sincere worry, but the question died in my mouth.

She turned her face to me, and I saw a squint in her left eye. Obviously, she wore special glasses that camouflaged it somehow. Without glasses, her sight was spooky. I twitched away and saw her glasses on the floor. I picked them up.

"Your glasses are unharmed; that's already good," I said in a repulsively caring tone. "Let me help you."

She was already getting up by herself. "That's nothing. I'm having swimming training later today and was too lazy to put my bag away," she mumbled.

Without looking at me, she took glasses out of my hand and hooked them on. Optically fixed, her face looked almost pleasant now, only for a second.

"Maxim, make the new agenda your priority for today. I am sure you can be quick," she picked up her smile.

My bad conscious instantly faded away. But instead of dropping an irreversibly rude reply, I recalled her long body grotesquely falling, her dreary squint eye, and went out without saying a word.

Every time Hilde mentioned "experts in research and communication," I wondered whether she knew I would run to Isabel and Philipe. These two became my "collective brain". Against the usual corporate ethics, I didn't need to send them Outlook invites before asking my questions. Usually, I came to Isabel's office, and she summoned Philipe by phone.

"What kind of mission impossible does Broomy have for you today?" Philipe asked straightaway, entering Isabel's office.

My mood rose every time I saw him. Dressed in impeccable suits, Philipe always made me feel that I'd be fine as long as he was on my side. At the same time, he never seemed to take work too close to his heart. Probably, that was the reason for his permanently good mood.

"Why 'Broomy?'"

"Our little Brühnhilde, of course!"

Isabel sighed. "I carelessly told him about Hilde's real name, and he simply can't stop making fun of her."

Philipe beamed. "It is not her name I am mocking. The name is just lovely. I am fostering my mental health. Yesterday she pussyfooted in my office to say, 'Carlos would like you, dear Philipe, to coordinate the preparation of the InSup annual work program. Please make the first draft and share it with all business areas tomorrow." Philipe swung his gaze from Isabel to me, "Wonderful deadline for something like an agency's annual work program, isn't it?" However, he looked amused rather than upset. "I asked Broomy, 'How come that somebody who doesn't decide about our work should design the work program?' And her answer was just scorching: 'the work program is our tool for communicating with stakeholders. That's why Communication should prepare it."

Philipe grinned, which made him look like a joyful eagle who had just lunched a souslik. "By the same logic, whatever this institution produces is its communication to stakeholders; who needs all the other experts?!"

"Karolina says that in young institutions, everybody is doing everything; this is a typical phase," I said cautiously.

"I am afraid Karolina is the only everybody of this kind in InSup," Philipe replied. "Others prefer to do what they were hired for and what they are good at. By the way, where is Karolina? Why is she not running with a dynamite stick in the pants like we all do?"

"Hilde doesn't want to involve her. Don't ask me why," Isabel answered for me.

"So much about everybody working everywhere," Philipe steered, loosening his icy-blue tie with a tiny silver snowflake pattern. "Never mind, let's look at it."

Isabel drew him the papers that I brought earlier. "The Association of Chinese traditional medicine in Europe wants to introduce itself to Carlos. No specific issues, just who they are and the scope of their activities in Europe. I think Maxim took a good, symmetric approach and suggested that Carlos tell them about our mission, objectives, decision-making process, et cetera."

"Makes sense," Philipe agreed.

"And today, Hilde asked me to make the agenda more strategic."

Philipe's smile became wily. "Oh, God, strategy is Broomy's Siam twin; it follows her everywhere and doesn't let the poor girl move freely."

Isabel looked at him reproachingly, "Reviens à nos moutons s'il te plaît,[8]"

Philipe raised both hands in a surrendering gesture. "Apologies. So let's save the iron ass of our non-advising counselor." He became concentrated and serious when reading my notes. Without his usual

---

[8] Let's go back to our business (translation of the French say)

smirks, he looked older and tired. "Bon,[9]" he said finally, "I suggest you go one level higher so-to-say. I mean, add general topics such as recourse to Chinese traditional medicine in Europe, or I don't know - interest of Europeans towards alternative medicine."

"I was also thinking of existing exchanges between European and Chinese doctors?" I said.

Philipe nodded. "Very good, although the facts about it might be difficult to find."

"I will liaise with the European Medicines Agency," Isabel said, writing something down in her notepad. "They will give me some tips, I am sure. My counterpart in the Health directorate of the European Commission should have some interesting information as well."

Philipe regained his usual eagle smile, "Then you are fine. Au travail[10]!" He was about to leave but halted. "By the way, Maxim, don't forget to put these new topics on top of the agenda; otherwise, Carlos will never notice that you made it more strategic."

And way down we go…

Maxim to Veronika. Barenik

Nika, privet,

---

[9] Well (French)
[10] Let's get to work (French)

Thanks for the pictures. What can I say? Halfway around the world, you changed your preferences. He doesn't seem to fit the taste you had in Moscow. But we are alike. Here, in Frankfurt, I changed my liking too.

My girlfriend is an artist, can you imagine? I never thought I could enjoy being together with somebody like her. Her mood changes like the sky in Frankfurt: a crystal-clear blue in the morning, which turns into a gloom by lunch and winkles you in the night with a couple of stars. I have already visited as many exhibitions in the Frankfurt region as I have never had during my life. Her name is Gayane. Born in Nagorno-Karabakh, she studied in France, like many Armenians, and then moved to Germany. Unlike you, she is irrational and unorganized, but she admits it in a disarmingly charming way. And she is an owl, you know. Unless she has to work in the morning, which is really rare, we never have breakfast together. Therefore, in the nights, she is full of delightful energy, she often wakes me up to make love. I simply can't and don't want to resist it.

But let me tell you about the place where I met Gayane because it has become my power place in Frankfurt. I found it on my own, without tips from anybody! One August evening I had an easy working day. Ian was on holiday in Ireland, so I wandered alone across the city with no plan and purpose, which since my arrival became a habit of mine. From the office, I see a postcard-view of

Frankfurt – too far, too perfect. Zooming in Frankfurt's green streets and truffle-colored buildings has become my new way to get relaxed and disconnected.

On that evening, I ended up in the district called Nordend. One house attracted my attention because it looked unusually narrow. Suddenly, I saw a small blue signpost, "Barenik." The wrong first letter in the Russian word "varenik[11]" disturbed me, so I decided to look for it.

After straying around, I spotted a similar signpost in front of a faceless panel house of the 1960s. I entered its courtyard and saw a door with the already familiar door plaque leading to a basement level. But what struck me was the door itself: wooden, carved with gingerbread ornament, it was simply too beautiful to belong to this depressing concrete building. Puzzled even more, I pushed it and stopped petrified.

The basement had bright illumination, allowing me to see pictures and paintings generously covering its walls. It was full but surprisingly quiet; everybody looked in the same direction. I followed their gaze and noticed a stage at the back, from which a young man was declaiming something in English, a poem maybe. I examined the public: our age, some looked like hipsters, others - like bohemians. Somehow, I became certain that I would be accepted

---

[11] Вареник (Russian) – filled dumpling, typical for Ukrainian and other East Slavic cuisine.

here. *On the other side of the basement, I saw a counter in front of the shelves full of glasses and bottles. The reciter on stage got his applause, and the place started buzzing and moving. I approached the counter. Behind it, a tall guy with a long blond ponytail said something in German to me.*

"Uhm, do you speak English?" I asked.

He gave me a level stare of electric blue eyes and then said, "Может, сразу по-русски?[12]"

"А можно сразу вопрос?"[13] I asked. "Why 'Barenik'?"

"Because it's a snack kiosk that dreams of becoming a bar!" he grinned.

The lad at the counter was Kirill Kiner, the owner and self-perpetuating barkeeper of Barenik. A descendant of Volga Germans, Kirill was born in Kokshetau in the Northern Khazachstan. His grandparents were deported there from Saratov in 1941 after the start of the German invasion of the USSR and spent years in the forced labor camps.

Kirill is a real cosmopolite. He told me once that his parents always complained of being foreigners: in the USSR they were considered Germans although both spoke Russian perfectly and used it as much as possible with Kirill and his brother. In fact, only

---

[12] Shall we speak Russian right away? (Russian)
[13] Can I ask you a question right away? (Russian)

in the presence of elder family members, they switched to German, which was not Germany's "Hochdeutsch" but a specific "German Volga Dialect." In 1994 Kirill's family repatriated to Germany, where everybody started seeing them as... Russians! So Kirill's parents felt the same mistrust just from a different community.

Was it the parents' disappointment or the feeling of not really belonging to any corner of the planet that made Kirill create a place where nationality and spoken language don't matter? That's what Barenik is. Here, you can taste Ukrainian dumplings, Russian pies, Kazach manti, and German beer. But besides fast-food "Barenik" offers much more: concerts, meetings with writers and poets, exhibitions, art performances and plenty of talks in all possible languages and about all the topics you wish.

I must say, compared to Moscow, Frankfurt doesn't have such an intensive cultural life, but Barenik alone compensates it all right. I think in Russia I never met as many musicians and artists as I did in the first three months here. When Ian returned from Ireland, I brought him to Barenik as well. I wasn't sure whether Ian would feel good in this patchy place. Well, my concerns evaporated when Kirill switched with him to fluent English, found out that he and Ian liked the same music, and immediately introduced Ian to his friend, a young musician from Portugal. Ian chatted with this guy the whole evening while I could spend time with Gayane.

Nika, at the moment, I am not sure that working in InSup is the best that could happen to me, but being part of the "Barenik society" definitely is!

Chinese delegation

Every time Hilde tried to be all over, she ended up nowhere.

She created such an activity whirlpool around the Association of Chinese traditional medicine in Europe that I felt like preparing minimum an EU summit. Instead of one "update talk" per day, she wanted to meet me twice. My days not only started but also finished with her mawkish questions and sweets trailed by the scent of sweat she could never properly wash away after her morning runs. During these updates, I learned plenty of details about her sports life I would prefer not to know at all: her bike helmet proudly placed in the center of the otherwise empty shelf meant she had bike training; the already familiar blue sportive bag, which she now carefully placed in the lower bookshelf, meant that she would leave the office earlier to have a swimming training. While enlightening me about her sports achievements, Hilde was knocking out my ability to keep track of work: she bombarded me with emails from Carlos, which she marked "FYI[14]" although they required action. And yet she ordered things Carlos never asked for. Isabel and Philipe compassionately

---

[14] For your information

smiled every time I approached them with a new question, so did Karolina. To my surprise, she easily agreed not to be involved in this visit, but amid my frustration, she also started helping me, discreetly though.

The only thing I couldn't understand was why I needed Hilde at all. All my preparations she slowed down and impaired, unwittingly but in a masterly fashion. Besides micro-managing me, she assigned to herself only one thing - the purchase of what she called "the welcome gift." This happened after the Association had informed me they were going to give Carlos a porcelain vase as a greeting present. Since then, Hilde proudly started each update meeting with the words, "The welcome gift is on its way."

The visit was also on its way. After having carefully filtered all the useless emails and questions from Hilde, I finally decided that InSup was well prepared for it. That was a bad shot!

On the day of the visit at six o'clock in the morning, Hilde sent me an email that contained nothing but a subject line: "URGENT. Meet Carlos to discuss China. Best, H." Skipping my breakfast with Ian, I rushed to InSup. Hardly did I switch on the laptop, Cristina entered my office to announce that Carlos was already waiting for me. She sounded friendly, but her offer to proceed together to Carlos made me feel like she was escorting me.

Carlos' office was bathing on a sunny autumn morning. The only dark cloud was Carlos himself. He rolled forward without even offering me a seat.

"We need to talk serjisly. Did you see the agenda of the meeting with the Chinese?" His last words I could hardly understand because he hissed them, but the alarming sound of a rattle I could hear all right.

"The agenda of the meeting with the Association of Chinese traditional medicine was approved by you and afterward shared by Hilde with all the participants," I diligently articulated each word mainly to calm myself down.

His mouth turned into a slit. "Yesterday evening, they sent new questions, and I urgently need a briefing on them. Where is it?"

I had no idea. Luckily, Carlos didn't expect my answer. I took a deep breath and kept silence. He glanced at his wall iconostasis of diplomas as if seeking support.

"Another point – the reciprocal present," he added in a calmer voice. "Frrahnkly it is a disasterr. Do you rehlly think I can give THIS to Chinese?"

"THIS? What is this?" I asked and immediately regretted it.

Even through his glasses, I could see how his eyes opened wide. "It doesn't matter anymore. Take it away and replace it with an appropriate present!"

To my relief, he turned back to me so I could silently slip away. Sweating and feeling a ponderous stone in the middle of my stomach, I ran to Hilde's office. The door was locked. I hit it with all my force. The pain in the toes relieved the stir in my head. Sandra, another InSup colleague, showed her face out of the neighboring office. She shifted her gaze from me to Hilde's door and back to me. "Hilde took a sick leave," Sandra said empathically. "She sent me an email early in the morning and asked to warn everybody who will look for her."

Fighting down a slight nausea, I ran to Isabel. She seemed neither surprised nor worried about Hilde's sudden illness. "We need a crisis manager," she said decisively and, preempting my next question, added, "We need Karolina. Carlos can't keep her away from this visit anymore."

Karolina arrived later than usual, for she had had a headache in the night. Pale, with shadows under the eyes, she calmly listened to my story, glancing from time to time at Isabel, who was standing by me. My tie turned into a garrote around my neck. Karolina watched me swallowing air and repeating the name of Hilde in each sentence. She didn't drop a single sarcastic or ironic question. She just took off her chunky silver earrings (she usually did so when the headache got stronger) and was writing something down. When I finished my saga about Hilde, she only asked, "When are they coming?"

"In one hour."

She stood up. Tall, in high heels, and dressed in a strict black suit, she was like a black queen stepping on the chessboard. On the piece of paper in her hand, I discerned something like a checklist with numbered bullet points. "We have time," she said without taking her eyes off this paper, and I immediately believed her.

"Shall I bring you Ibuprofen?" Isabel asked compassionately.

"I have just taken one," Karolina sighed. "Could you summon Philipe, please?"

Isabel nodded and left.

Karolina turned to me. "Now, may I ask you to share with me the briefing you prepared for Carlos and all the correspondence with the Chinese Association?" I ran to my laptop. "And there is one more person we need to have here," Karolina said aloud, rather to herself than to me. "We need Cristina."

"I am here," Cristina replied, entering our office. She was carrying something big and alarmingly shapeless. Isabel and Philipe followed her. "Hilde brought it to Carlos yesterday evening," Cristina wanted to say something else but changed her mind and just kept gazing at us through her Harry-Potter-glasses.

Philipe came closer, "Let us look at these gifts of the Magi!" He unwrapped an untidy cellophane and took out something that looked like the jacket of a long-term homeless person. Isabel made a noise of stupefaction. The jacket turned out to be a square shoulder bag with a print of Frankfurt's Römer Place on it. Despite being made of natural leather, the bag was badly wrinkled and had a color of wet mud. On the print, I could recognize the timber-frame houses of Römer all right, but the picture appeared blurred. Philipe winced, "Broomy'd better give it to her unloved cousin or a grandfather who scored her out of the will." He glanced at me and added in a comforting tone, "For the Chinese delegation would be acceptable too, but ugly."

"Wait a moment," Cristina said and turned the bag. "What would you say now?"

Isabel hid her face behind her palms. Philipe laughed loudly. The other side of the bag stated with a big font, "MADE IN CHINA."

Karolina remained unperturbable. "What can you suggest as an alternative?" she asked Philipe.

He answered without hesitations. "Frankfurt marzipan, of course, Bethmännchen! Why not? These delights were invented in Frankfurt, look exotic, and taste great. You can get a big box for fifty euros, designed with Frankfurt photos that are of a much better quality than the one from this bag."

Karolina nodded. "I like this idea. Could you get one for each participant as soon as possible?"

"Are you sure InSup will compensate me?" Philipe asked in return.

"Yes," Cristina intervened, "just bring me the invoice, and I will submit the request for reimbursement on your behalf."

"You are so lovely," Philipe told her without irony. He turned to us. "Ok, guys, Cristina and I are going to save you from mesmerizing the Chinese delegation with made-in-China souvenirs."

"Cristina, could you help with another thing?" Karolina asked once Philipe had left. "We need their email with additional questions. The one Carlos received yesterday."

"I saw this email in his inbox. Hilde sent it to him shortly before she brought this disaster to his office. Didn't she share this email with you?"

Karolina ignored her question. "May I ask you to forward this email to Isabel, Maxim, and myself?" Then she turned to Isabel. "I can't give you more than thirty minutes to answer their questions. Get whatever you can and send it to Maxim; he will finalize the briefing."

"Now let me ask you one thing," Karolina said when we stayed alone. "Where are we standing with the meeting room?"

I curdled. "Uh… I don't know."

Karolina slurred it over. "Ok, you have fifteen minutes to prepare everything. Approach Etna, our receptionist, and ask which meeting room we can take. Check microphones and a laptop in the room. Oh, and don't forget to place water on the table. You know these are minor details, but that's what creates the corporate image. After the room is ready, come here and finalize the briefing Isabel will send you." She glanced at me and added in a commiserating tone. "You are doing very well, Maxim. Just stick to our plan, and we'll be good."

"I thought I would resign today," I couldn't help saying.

In the next hour, Karolina wasn't left alone for a single minute. One of us always had a question for her. Even Carlos once appeared in our office. He slipped towards Karolina's desk, trying not to look at me, "Karolina, are we on track with everything? Can I be of assistance?"

Karolina didn't move an eyebrow. "Hi, Carlos," she said without taking her eyes off the monitor, "we are doing well, thanks. I'll be by in 20 minutes, all right?"

Carlos winced, hovered, glanced around, mumbled, "Thank you for the efforts," and slinked away.

Some minutes later, Karolina was standing next to Carlos in the wait for the delegation. With a fresh lip glow and the second Ibuprofen that she swallowed right before the meeting, she radiated self-assurance. She greeted the delegates by perfectly pronouncing each Chinese surname, which caused their approving smiles. Convinced by Karolina, Carlos conveyed only key messages while she gave detailed argumentation. It worked well: Carlos didn't need to look in our briefing note while Karolina knew it by heart and complemented Carlos' words with the passing facts and figures. Having understood that the conversation runs comfortably for him, Carlos was shining like Karolina's lip glow. In the middle, he even deviated from the briefing and started telling jokes and sharing stories about his wife and children. Chinese delegates politely smiled. Karolina skillfully but subtly kept incorporating facts and figures into the discussion. As for my role in this meeting, it was easy. Upon Karolina's request, I took minutes without looking at the people around the table and ignoring the bleary jokes of Carlos.

Finally, holding the Bethmännchen boxes, the Chinese delegation bid us farewell. Exhausted and relieved, Karolina and I returned to our office to find there Isabel, Cristina, and Philipe.

"You, guys, didn't have lunch today, so I brought you sandwiches," Cristina said in a strangely apologetic tone.

"And I came without any pretext," Philipe chuckled. "Just want to see your faces after you read Broomy's email. It looks like she magically recovered from the sudden sickness and is trying to save her iron ass."

Isabel's nose and upper cheeks were peppered with freckles, which I never noticed before. "Now she looks like a hero, and we all – like losers," she said.

I opened my inbox and saw that Hilde had sent her email while the meeting with the Chinese delegation was still going on.

From: Hilde Rosenbohm

To: Carlos de Santos Gomez

Cc: Cristina Tornero, Philipe Fernandez, Isabel Aquilina, Maxim Reut, Karolina Schiller

Subject: Chinese visit – lessons learned

Dear Carlos,

We must improve our business procedures with regard to important visits. After having examined InSup's preparatory process, I would like to point out some lessons learned – to be considered by all colleagues.

1. Our communication with guests should be more efficient, all the questions should be collected promptly.

2. Briefing materials should always be updated and ready for use at any point in time.

3. Each team preparing a visit should be aware of the InSup strategic objectives and should align the meeting agenda with those objectives.

4. Business discipline should be strengthened: deadlines must be set in advance and strictly followed.

5. Last but not least, InSup should have a set of gifts approved by Communication, which can be issued to our visitors.

If we stick to these rules, I am sure next time such visits will be organized and conducted in a much better way.

Best,

H.

"Bravo, our counselor has just won a grand prix at the contest of obvious advice," Philipe snicked.

Reverse of the corporate Fortuna

On a late October day, an email from our HR landed in my inbox. Back then, I couldn't imagine how much agitation these three paragraphs would bring to the entire InSup.

From: Fadila Ribeiro Villescas

To: All_InSup staff

Subject: Appraisal exercise and promotion

Dear colleagues,

On behalf of Carlos, I would like to announce the launch of the annual appraisal exercise.

In the next two months, you are required to fill in the appraisal form, which you can find on the website of the European Commission, together with some useful tips and instructions. Please print the completed form, sign it, and bring it to HR.

HR will decide about those colleagues to be promoted to the next grade with the effect of the next year's start. Happy appraisal time!

Fadila

And minutes later, another email.

From: Fadila Ribeiro Villescas

To: All_InSup staff

Subject: Appraisal exercise and promotion – minor correction

Dear colleagues,

One correction: don't bring your appraisal form to HR! Bring it to your line manager. By the way, you would need to schedule a meeting with your manager to discuss your performance in the year's course, so bring your appraisal form to this meeting.

And one more correction: it's your manager and not HR that will decide about your promotion! HR will only publish the names of those who will be promoted with the effect of the next year's start. Happy appraisal time!

Fadila

And ten minutes later, yet another email.

From: Fadila Ribeiro Villescas

To: All_InSup staff

Subject: Appraisal exercise and promotion - minor correction

Dear colleagues,

And don't forget to discuss with your manager your objectives for the next appraisal period.

Happy appraisal time!

Fadila

"The most useless exercise in the entire year," Philipe said at one lunch that he, Isabel, Cristina, and I started regularly having after what Philipe called the "Chinese tragicomedy". Karolina always was too busy to join us. The waiter has just brought two wheel-sized pizzas with salami and mushrooms.

"Karolina calls it the most important exercise because it reflects on our performance and on what we can do better," I said, accompanied by Cristina's approving nod.

"Our Cinderella of Karolina can draw lessons even from the Chinese visit, although we all know whose performance should be scrutinized," Philipe bent over pizza like an eagle over his kill and distributed to each of us a quarter.

His point was scorching. Since the story with the Chinese delegation, I watched goggle-eyed the corporate Fortuna changing her benevolence towards Karolina. Every time Karolina submitted to Carlos a new assessment, instead of his answer, she received Hilde's – startlingly detailed - comments: the space-saving wheelchair wasn't made from sustainable materials; the software for taking heart sonograms from home violated data protection rules; the electronic pen for detecting dementia at the early stage wasn't a top priority for Europe. Sometimes, Hilde asked Karolina to rationalize her assessment with such facts and figures that jarred even Isabel. "It sounds very much like the German Ministry of Finance," Isabel told me once. "That's where Hilde gets all these questions from, I suspect. Just I have the impression Hilde copied/pasted them from discussions that have nothing to do with our start-ups. I mean, the questions per se are unexpectedly ingenious but off the point."

Carlos, on the contrary, didn't ask for anything but never missed an opportunity to point at the things that Karolina could have done better. He usually did it by email. While dropping just half a sentence that felt like a tiny bite, he venomed it by putting several people on copy: "be more precise", "stay mindful of European priorities", and "Don't lose your 360-degree vision of a project."

And neither of the two ever thanked Karolina for any of the many things she was doing well.

If ever all this made Karolina aggressive, it was only towards her own self. She worked long hours and during weekends. She seemed to have surrounded herself with a fence, which she had no force to vault over anymore. The atmosphere in our office became sullen. Karolina hardly spoke to me. She didn't ask me anymore about my Russian experience, she didn't seek my opinion. I was trying to get her to talk. She reacted with a faded smile and one or two listless sentences, and then our conversation died out. To myself, I started calling her "InSup's Wandering Jew". Miserable, cursed by our mightiest, she couldn't stop typing on the keyboard, her back straight and anthracite eyes sparkling with unshed tears.

"A biblical image, indeed," Isabel agreed when one day we had a coffee break in her office. "And similar to Ahasuerus, Karolina was punished for taunting."

I stared at her. "Are you saying you know why they treat her like this?!"

Isabel looked at me incredulously. "Of course, I do, and everybody does. As soon as I saw the email that Karolina had sent right after the visit of the Chinese delegation, I knew it was a mistake, and Hilde would never forgive it and would try to expose Karolina as incompetent and unreliable. We all know it's not true, but Broomy stands closer to Carlos, and she would win this fight."

I remembered that email very well. Karolina sent it on the same day of the visit but so late in the evening that I saw it only the next morning.

From: Karolina Schiller

To: Cristina Tornero, Philipe Fernandez, Isabel Aquilina, Maxim Reut

Cc: Carlos de Santos Gomez; Hilde Rosenbohm

Subject: Thank you!

Dear all,

I would like to thank you for your great teamwork and prompt efforts related to the visit of the Association of Chinese traditional medicine in Europe.

I have to admit that the preparation for this visit was frail. The briefing was incomplete; the welcome gift was inappropriate; even the meeting room wasn't duly prepared.

We had to take it over just one hour before the visit started and of course, were under enormous time pressure.

But thanks to your devotion, we could correct all the mistakes of the previous coordinator. I admire your team spirit and efficiency. Congratulations!

Best regards,

Karolina

Back then, I didn't take Isabel's explanations seriously. I was more astonished that Isabel for the first time called Hilde by her nickname.

Appraisal

In Russia, I never had an appraisal. Or better to say I had an appraisal twice a month when getting my earnings every 5th and 20th of each month. The Centrobank's paycheck comprised two halves: the salary and the premium. Unlike salary, the premium was changeable, and its size depended only on one person, our director Sergey Vladimirovich Kamarinov.

A heavyset Ukrainian born in Kyiv, Kamarinov passed the Afghan War in the 1980s as a military translator from Pashto, afterward served in the FSB[15] and then was appointed director of external and public relations in the Centrobank. At the beginning of the 2000s, the FSB was placing its people wherever possible, so the "home" institution of Sergey Vladimirovich was neither a secret nor a surprise for anybody. A thick blend of a martinet and a bounder, every morning at 9.00 Kamarinov walked through our offices to check whether we started working on time. Every time he spoke to us, financial analysts, he used swear words (Russian Mat) as if he were a semiliterate Russian provincial who lacked the vocabulary to

---

[15] Federal Security Service (former KGB)

express his thoughts otherwise. In a bad mood, he called us "бараны кастрированные" (castrated male sheep), and in a good mood, we turned into "жопы с ушами" (asses with ears).

In the beginning, I thought FSB intended to damage the Centrobank from the inside by sending such a guy to head external and public relations. Once, I shared my thoughts with Nika, who worked in media monitoring, and her reaction surprised me, "I never heard Sergey Vladimirovich using Mat; what are you talking about?!" Later, I noticed that in the presence of women, Kamarinov spoke a perfectly correct Russian. With a three-man team of financial analysts I belonged to, he didn't bother to censor himself at all.

One day, I observed him at the Centrobank's reception for representatives of foreign banks. He seemed to have a lively talk with a group of bankers. I stopped nearby to listen. He was talking in quite good English with a strong Russian accent though. People around were nodding and smiling. He noticed me and suddenly said in Russian, "Еще вина принеси мне.[16]" I obeyed and couldn't stop thinking that, unlike us, foreign bankers sincerely laughed at his jokes rather than out of politeness.

As a typical Homo Sovieticus[17] Kamarinov was certain that the monthly premium is the best tool for manipulating people. He used

---

[16] Bring me more wine (Russian)
[17] Soviet man (Latin)

it as a reward. Nika, for example, received a 20% increase for having introduced a new format of reporting about the Russian stock exchange. Once, Kamarinov even doubled a premium to Kolja Fedotov, our expert in charge of relations with the State Duma. Kolja managed to stop the central bank's car safely while sitting next to the driver, who died from a heart attack at the steer. But much more often, we heard from Kamarinov, "You'll get your premium cut." It made everybody endlessly lenient.

Only with one person, these threats didn't work — with Nika. One day, she came to the office in fancy jeans with immaculate cuts. Kamarinov got mad. "A central bank employee can't show such disrespect; the clothes must be decent!" he said grimly. Nika replied that as long as she is doing a good job, she should be given the freedom to wear whatever she wants. Admittedly, she had good reasons to be self-assured. For the reports she was putting together, Kamarinov received personal gratitude from the central bank's chairman. But a truly KGB, Kamarinov wasn't driven by common sense but by the wish to suppress resistance. So he told Nika that if he saw her in jeans once again, he would cut her premium by 50%.

The next day, Nika arrived at the bank in the same jeans and in my shirt, which looked like a decent office one, if not an enormous portrait of Che Guevara on the back. The news that "Veronika Makarova came again in a provoking outfit" spread with an astronomical speed. Colleagues, under ridiculous pretexts, were coming to the office of the monitoring team just to glance at her with their own eyes. Everybody was sure that Kamarinov's informants already reported to him, and the entire department was awaiting his appearance. Only Nika kept working without batting an eyelid. When Kamarinov finally entered the monitoring room, the team, including Nika, stood up to greet him. While he was rushing to her desk, she (on purpose) dropped a pen and, to pick it up turned her back to him. For a second, Kamarinov and Che Guevara stared at each other, and then the former burst into laughter. "If I see you in jeans once again, I will cut 50% of the premium from Perevalov," he said and left before Nika could answer. She glanced at Sascha Perevalov, the lead of the monitoring team, who had just got his second child. He looked plaintively back. The battle was lost, and those jeans never saw the Centrobank again.

Personally, I never received an increased premium, but I also never got it cut. Every month when getting my paycheck, I felt I did my work well. This was the Russian style of appraisal.

The European appraisal was new to me. In an online form, I was required to list all my achievements, write whether I fulfilled my objectives, point at my problems, and plan their resolution. Afterward, all InSup appraisals were sent to Brussels, where the HR department of the European Commission had a dossier on each staff member in every decentralized agency.

I felt lucky I had joined InSup in the middle of the year and had twice as little as others to recall. The part related to my objectives and good deeds I could copy from Karolina, but in the second part of the appraisal form, I got stuck. "Why should I write about my problems and criticize myself? If Hilde is our first appraiser, why doesn't she prove I did anything wrong?" I asked Karolina.

"Appraisal is not an instrument to be used against you. It is your opportunity to grow professionally," she replied miserably and stood up. "I'm having my appraisal talk with Hilde now. We'll be back in one hour. Wish me luck."

She came back neither in one nor in two hours. When she finally slipped into the office, I hardly recognized her. The black chess queen was dethroned and crestfallen. Without saying a word, she sat at her laptop and stared at the monitor. Even her chunky hoops stopped sparkling. Her limp face suddenly reminded me she was twenty years older than me. I didn't dare to ask her anything the whole day. Only in the evening, I timidly said, "I am going home. See you tomorrow." Instead of answering, she cried bitterly and desperately and finally told me what happened.

During the appraisal talk, Hilde didn't point out any mistakes. She was murderously abstract: "Karolina lacks strategic thinking to lead M-Unit, which is crucial for the Agency"; "Karolina lacks the management skills necessary to properly organize the work of M-Unit"; "Karolina has serious weaknesses in prioritizing tasks";

"Karolina must gain political and scientific savvy to better position InSup in the innovative world". A glairy and toxic flaw of criticism Hilde hurled during three hours and pinnacled it with a triumphant conclusion: Karolina is not eligible for promotion this year!

"Can Broomy be right about Karolina?" I asked Isabel and Philipe during our next joint pizza lunch. Both of them as well as Cristina and Fadila were the only ones who received their promotion.

As for me, I have just had my own appraisal, at which Hilde announced that I successfully completed my probation period. Otherwise, our talk was surprisingly unspectacular. Besides offering sweets and talking about her Iron Man training, Hilde showed no interest in me and my achievements. While I recited a well-prepared summary of my first months in InSup, she was bored. My problems interested her even less; our talk lasted less than 30 minutes.

"I mean, maybe for team leads, they have additional expectations?" I corrected my question, seeing astonishment on the faces of Isabel and Philipe.

"You have been working with Karolina for almost six months. Why don't you answer yourself whether Broomy is right?" Isabel said scathingly.

Her cold gaze made me ashamed not only of my question but of my thoughts.

Philipe took a big piece of pizza with sardines and green olives. "I forgot to tell you last time," he said, slightly narrowing his eyes. "Appraisal is useless when it's about praising your work. But if they need to smear you in the eyes of others or simply spoil your life, it works very all right. No, seriously: just one useless appraisal talk, and even such a fan of Karolina as you start having doubts."

"What will happen to Karolina now?" I switched the topic.

Philipe shrugged. "What can happen except for lots of bureaucracy? The Commission has clear prescriptions for such cases. They will force her into obligatory training; she will have to write useless quarterly or even monthly reports about her improvement; most probably, they will impose interim appraisal talks on her. But in the end, she will get her satisfactory appraisal."

"Satisfactory?"

Philipe smirked. "In EU institutions, an appraisal can be satisfactory or non-satisfactory. No nuances. And for the latter, you need to do something really bad."

"And if you are very good?"

"All the more reasons to put you down so that you don't annoy others with your excellence."

"In the ECB, one guy got a non-satisfactory one because he watched porno in the office and accidentally downloaded a virus that crashed their entire IT system," Isabel said.

We laughed.

"Karolina will have a bit of circus with the appraisal follow-up, but in the end, nothing will change," Philipe concluded with conviction but turned out to be wrong.

Christmas party

From: Carlos de Santos Gomez

To: All_InSup staff

Subject: Christmas party

Dear colleagues,

It's my pleasure to invite you and your partners to the first Christmas party of InSup.

I am sure you will enjoy delicious food, exciting talks, and a festive mood.

Details on venue will follow soon.

I look forward to spending some quality time with you,

Carlos

In Russia, I never attended a corporate Christmas party. In fact, Centrobank didn't throw any parties at all. Each division celebrated New Year's Eve on its own. In our division, we repositioned our coffee table to the biggest office and piled on it the dishes with finger food bought in our canteen. Men's task was to buy water and alcohol.

Women brought homemade cakes and biscuits. The get-togethers took place strictly on the next-to-last working day of the year, most frequently on 30 December. Celebrating otherwise seemed too much in advance. Therefore, on the very last working day of the year, everybody tried to go home as early as possible. Women came just to mark their presence and, after a couple of hours, disappeared into the preparatory rush for family celebrations. Three or four men from the department stayed until 17.00, pretending to keep the office running. In reality, they did nothing but consume leftovers from yesterday's party and postponed whatever was possible to the next year, which Russian public institutions started on 9 January. Last year it was my turn to run the office on 31 December. I was in the process of choosing a movie to watch when Nika entered my office.

"Stroll on with nonsense; you have a proper job to do," she said morosely.

I jumped on my feet. Only a crisis could make the Centrobank work on 31 December. "Don't tell me another president resigned[18]! What happened? What can I do?"

Nika accurately closed the door. "Fuck me, of course." Before I could say a word, she peeled off her chocolate-brown pullover dress. Under the cozy cashmere, there was nothing but her naked body. She slipped from the high heels and decisively went to me.

---

[18] The first president of Russia, Boris Yeltsin, announced his resignation on 31 December 1999.

"You are crazy; what if somebody enters?" I said, taking her in my arms and forgetting that a second ago I wanted to lock the door.

Nika pulled me to the corner of my team lead, Slava Govorov, behind a small partition wall. Slava rarely came to the office and – I suspected – had a little idea of what his team was busy with. Nobody knew what kind of activity his empty desk benighted. According to the rumors, Slava's only job was to supervise the construction of Kamarinov's summer house, and every day he spent disputing with architects, workers, and suppliers. Nika laid on the polished surface of Slava's desk and grabbed its edge over her head. "Don't undress. If anybody enters, you will simply come out of the partition," she said.

"And you, what will you do?" I teased her.

Her body was incandescent. Under my caresses, she closed her eyes. "I will not move a centimeter from here until you return and finish working on me."

The InSup Christmas party was scheduled for 1 December. "Because Silvia, Carlos' wife, goes to Spain on the second of December to prepare for family celebrations. Carlos doesn't want to have an InSup party without her," Cristina explained after I had wondered why the chosen date was so far away from Christmas.

On the party day, the blissful anticipation was in the air since early morning. Instead of greetings, colleagues were asking each other, "So, going to the party tonight?" In the afternoon, some people, including Isabel and Philipe, left the office "to prepare for the evening and pick up the spouses". As for me, I wasn't in the mood to bring Gayane to the party. Our passion was turning into simulation, and we both felt it. Moreover, demonstrating my private life felt unusual and uncomfortable. In the Centrobank, I always had a feeling that Kamarinov already knew a lot about us. He, too, never introduced us to his family, despite everyone knowing he is married and has two sons. In fact, he never really celebrated with us. Every team invited him to the party, and he dutifully came. It was like a ritual. First, his secretary warned us he was on the way, and one of us rushed to put on a table a crystal wine glass for him (others were drinking from plastic glasses). Kamarinov entered, and all the talks died out. In silence, he wished us a happy new year, sipped his drink, ate one or two bits, jocularly ordered us to behave, and left.

Ian seemed to be immune to the party fever. "Why bother if the party will be in our pizzeria? Couldn't they have found a more interesting place?" he wondered.

My mood wasn't festive either. Karolina's premonitions about her career in InSup transferred to me. In the morning, she sent me an email saying she was sick. The day before, she warned me she would work from home. Yet after lunch, she suddenly appeared in the office, reserved and dressed in black from tip to toe.

"I thought you decided not to party tonight," I said.

She gave me a mortuary glance. "I thought so, too. But I can't miss the first Christmas party of InSup; this is historical, you know." There was a distaste to her voice, which I found historical indeed, but not surprising. Everything that Philipe predicted about the consequences of Karolina's bad appraisal came through. She was requested to report to Hilde daily and weekly about her improvement. Constantly analyzing her own efficiency and strategic thinking took Karolina more time than the work itself. Once, after another "progress interview" with Hilde, Karolina returned in tears.

"What does she want from you?" I asked.

Karolina patted her eyes dry, trying not to smash her make-up. "To be honest, I don't understand anymore. Whatever I do, Hilde says that Carlos expects different things from me."

When it was time to leave for the Christmas party, Karolina pronounced her usual mantra that she still had work to do and would join us a bit later. I knew no suasions would help, so Ian and I left without her.

This time, InSup booked the entire pizzeria: all the tables in the main hall were moved into two rows. This reminded me of a Russian wedding: the groom and the bride's sides and between them – instead of a wedding couple – the third table with food. Isabel and Philipe were already waiving to us. Philipe stood next to a miniature woman with kind black eyes.

"Agustina," he said as soon as we approached, "let me present to you my colleagues Maxim and Ian. By the way, Maxim is the one with an amazing family biography I once told you." His voice softened. "And this is Agustina, the captain of my family ship and the mother of my kids." We shook hands. Agustina seemed shy and quiet, a dove next to this joyful eagle. "What about your boyfriend?" Philipe turned to Isabel. "Where is this handsome guy radiating self-confidence 10 kilometers around himself?"

"He is not coming," Isabel said. "I've got an overdose from his self-confidence."

"I am sorry... for him," Philipe said half-seriously, half-jokingly.

Isabel wore a silk apricot nightgown dress that underlined her long neck and peach-like skin of the shoulders.

"Isabel, you look great in this dress," Ian suddenly said.

Isabel gave him a friendly smile covered with a subtle lip glow, "Very kind of you, thanks."

"What about Karolina?" Philipe asked.

"She must finish something and will immediately join us," I said.

"Can't she, for the sake of Christmas, abstain from her Cinderella pattern?!" Philipe asked mischievously, without expecting me to answer.

I looked around. Colleagues were eyeing with curiosity each other's festive clothes and were proudly presenting their partners.

"Hello, hello, one, two, three." Carlos, in a scarlet tie and a handkerchief of the same shade, was checking the microphone together with a restaurant worker and we all automatically made one step towards him. "Does everybody have a drink?" Carlos asked, and people started hastily grabbing wine glasses.

"Dear colleagues, dear friends," Carlos continued, "the fehrst full year of InSup is coming to an end. Many of you joined us in the kehrse of the last twelve months, but four of you - Fadila, Cristina, Isabel, and Philipe - have been with me since day numbehr one. I would like to thank them and all of you, of course, for your commitment and wehrk. You all are great professionals and amazing people."

As usual, Carlos was failing to take enough air in his lungs, and the last words of each sentence were dying in his throat. "It is a great honor to wehrk together with you!"

We applauded.

"And let me thank my wife Silvia", Carlos continued, "for her patience with me and with our kids and for the inspiration I receive from her every single day! I would be lost without you!" He turned to somebody and started applauding.

"This lady in red is his wife?" I asked Philipe.

"Yes, and the mother of two pairs of twins, in case you still don't know."

80

By then, I already heard several times about it both from Carlos himself and many other colleagues. The whole InSup mentioned those pairs of twins with such an aspiration, as if being secretly proud of this kind of productivity.

Carlos' wife looked splendid in her scarlet dress that was of the same shade as Carlos' tie and handkerchief. She stood behind Carlos, but since she was slightly taller than him, I could see well her complicated hairstyle, shiny make-up, and a chunky golden collier. She smiled queenly while Carlos and we were applauding her.

"And of course, I would like to thank again Cristina, my right hand," Carlos continued, and we applauded Cristina, who turned as red as the dress of Carlos' wife.

"I wish all of you a Merry Christmas and look forward to our joint wehrk next year. And now I would like to pass the floor to Fadila."

In her dark blue velvet dress, Fadila smiled with four rows of pearls - two in her mouth and two on her neckline.

"Thank you, Carlos," she said. "We are not just an agency; we are a family. And like all the families we have our common song, which we are going to sing now. Please distribute the lyrics." People started passing to each other the paper sheets. By the time I received the lyrics, somebody switched on loud the Queens's "We Are the Champions". The paper sheet contained only the refrain of the song, which we started singing upon Fadila's signal: *We are the champions, my friends… we are the champions… no time for losers…"*

"Our Fadila didn't challenge herself with tailoring the lyrics," said Philipe between two refrains. "I told her three times the song should refer to InSup and proposed to change the lyrics of 'Satisfaction' into 'Innovation', but it was an impossible stretch for her imagination."

"I like it nevertheless, " I objected. "In the Centrobank, we didn't sing at all."

"And I once worked in an EU agency that had an anthem with originally composed music!" Philipe sniggered.

After the song, Fadila invited us to sit. Karolina was still missing.

We chose the place at the far end of the table and occupied an additional seat for Karolina. "I thought Karolina also joined the Agency as of the first day. I remember her saying she has been here since January; that's when InSup started, isn't it?" I asked Isabel, who sat next to me.

"Right, InSup started on 1 January, and by then, only people from EU institutions could join it because beforehand, InSup couldn't start with recruitment campaigns." She leaned forward, and I deeply inhaled the wet grass scent of her perfume. The white skin on her neckline was covered with freckles and made me think of a warm sun. "So, Philipe and myself came from Brussels on the internal mobility basis, Cristina was in the European Commission representation in Berlin and Fadila moved from the European Central Bank."

"And Karolina?"

"Karolina came from the ECB too, but she had to finish something important there and could join only two weeks later, on 15 January. Carlos took it personally. He wanted her to join together with us, but she insisted on the two-week delay. That's why he didn't mention her."

"Then I am glad she didn't hear his speech."

"I think Karolina doesn't have illusions about Carlos' attitude now when Hilde moved her out of M-Unit," Isabel sighed.

I jumped on my chair "Moved her out?!"

"Shhh... not so loud," she interrupted me and simultaneously smiled at Philipe and Agustina, who were heading towards the buffet. "Hilde announced it yesterday at the meeting with team leads. Right afterward Karolina went to Carlos, asking to keep her in M-Unit, but he refused. There she is, by the way."

Both Isabel and I waved to Karolina, who just entered the hall. She looked like a black thundercloud. She approached us without looking at anybody around, threw herself in the chair next to me, and immediately immersed herself in her smartphone.

"Can I bring you anything, Isabel?" asked Ian.

"Let's look together at what they are offering today," Isabel suggested, standing up.

My shock from Isabel's news mixed up with amazement from the party. Neither job titles nor seniority mattered. One head of the unit organized for us a quiz: he enjoyed walking along the tables with a microphone and challenging us with dozens of questions he composed himself. I thought that in the Centrobank never would a manager entertain his employees. Then Fadila invited us to dance, and everybody went on an improvised dance floor without paying attention to the corporate hierarchy. And to my surprise, nobody was drunken like it often happened with male colleagues in the Centrobank.

Only Karolina sat next to us, listless and sullen. Isabel sympathetically smiled at her, "My dear, as a mentor of Maxim, you should show him how to disconnect, at least during the Christmas party."

Karolina looked at her absently as if not knowing where she was. "But I can't disconnect from my own life," she said abruptly and jumped out of her seat. I thought she wanted to leave, but she went to the buffet instead.

"Usually, she doesn't find consolation in food, but maybe today she'll make an exception," Isabel commented, watching Karolina go.

Carlos walked around chatting with people. "Interesting," I said, "he behaves like a party host who entertains his guests."

"This is how it should be," Isabel echoed.

"Not in Russia. My former boss was treated at our get-togethers as a dear guest. When he came, everybody turned silent to listen to his stupid jokes, trying to laugh at the right moment. And when he left, everybody felt so relieved. Here, it's different. Carlos pays attention to each of us, even to the spouses. By the way, I heard him speaking Spanish with Philipe's wife, so nice of him."

"I don't want to spoil your enthusiasm, but Carlos knows Agustina personally. She is befriended by his wife Silvia," Isabel said. Suddenly, her eyes widened. I traced her glance and saw Karolina and Silvia facing each other. Both looked scared. Karolina grabbed Carlos' wife by the shoulder; both jerked, couldn't keep their balance, and fell on the floor. The plate with a chocolate pudding, which Silvia held in her hand, flew up in the air, dripping a sweet mass. I jumped from my seat, and people around us screamed and rushed to both of them. Karolina was already getting on her feet. Silvia was helped as well. Karolina started helping somebody else. I froze: it was Carlos, one eyebrow bleeding, the round glasses not broken but distorted, and the pudding in the hair. Silvia's scarlet dress was desperately spoiled with the chocolate mass, which some female colleagues were trying to wipe with napkins, making it worse with every move. Silvia didn't notice it. She kept staring at Karolina as if nothing else around her existed. Carlos looked like after a fight. He was telling Silvia something, but she didn't pay attention to him either. Finally, a waiter brought Carlos and his wife away, probably to the toilet.

I helped dumbstruck Karolina to her seat.

"What happened?" Isabel and I asked simultaneously.

"I am not sure," she said. "Silvia asked me something, and then we both fell."

Soon afterward, Carlos appeared again at the standing microphone. "Guys, unfortunately, I have to leave. Enjoy the evening, and Merry Christmas," he mumbled.

"I am sorry, Carlos," Karolina told him when he passed by our seats.

"That's ok," he answered without looking at her and went on saying goodbye to the others.

Once Carlos and his wife left, nobody felt as relieved as it would have been in the Centrobank. On the contrary, the joyful atmosphere dwindled, and people started leaving. Without Carlos, the party seemed to have lost its attractiveness.

"Karolina, you managed to make the first InSup Christmas party memorable," Philipe laughed returning to his place with a sizeable piece of chocolate pudding, the same as what Silvia dropped. "But smearing a 500-euro Adolfo Dominguez dress was a bit too much!"

Isabel looked at him reprovingly.

"We all understand that it was an accident," Philipe immediately added, catching her gaze.

He turned out to be wrong again. In the next few days, I heard many colleagues saying that Karolina pushed Silvia to revenge her removal from M-Unit. In response, I shamed them for spreading silly rumors. But deep inside, I had to admit that what I saw that evening looked pretty much like a successful attempt to spoil Carlos' party.

European fairness

In the next December weeks, I found it hard to share the office with Karolina. She greeted me and answered my questions but otherwise behaved as if I was not there. The silence between us was full of unspoken questions that swarmed in my head: will she resign? Will she try to defend herself? What shall I do without her?

Finally, she broke the ice. One hollow winter morning, she didn't drop her "hello, hello" without taking her eyes off the monitor as usual. Instead, she said, "Oh, hi, Maxim. Isabel told me you frequently go to an amazing bar. I am curious to see it. Shall we have an after-work drink there?"

The whole week Barenik hosted a photo exhibition entitled "Populous". Its author, a Dutch photographer who studied together with Kirill at the university, pictured street crowds in busy places around the world. The photos that covered the walls of Barenik showcased the same artistic style: in each picture, the photographer slightly blurred all the people except for one. This single sharp figure was caught by the camera in what probably was an important moment of their life. The photo that hypnotized me was taken according to the caption in Rome on Via del Corso. Battered by the summer sun, the crowd stepped on the pedestrian crossing. The main character of this photo was a girl in jeans and a white spaghetti top contrasting with her long, black curly hair. At first glance, it was just a beautiful girl. But when watching it longer, one could notice that her face is aghast, and she looks at something or somebody beyond the camera cover. I spent long minutes thinking of whom or what is she seeing at that moment.

Probably other guests were taken by the same thoughts when watching the exhibition, that's why Barenik was unusually quiet. I explained the concept to Karolina. She listened and nodded, but I could feel that she was distracted by her own thoughts.

"I think we must talk," I suddenly said to shift her focus on me.

She seemed to wait for me to say something like this.

"I am moving out of M-Unit," she immediately responded and burst into tears.

Not to embarrass her, I ran to the bar to get us two cups of tea, in which I asked Kirill to pour a shot of rum. When I returned, Karolina already gathered herself. She said Hilde was moving her to the unit "Corporate Affairs." Philipe called this unit "Corporate Who-Can-Take-Cares" because they constantly looked for "volunteers to take care" of different tasks they weren't able to fulfill themselves.

"But at least Broomy won't fire you. Isn't it good news?" I cautiously asked.

Karolina's anthracite eyes moistened. She took a deep breath before answering me. "I am so bitterly sorry that I can't be in M-Unit anymore. I love assessing start-up applications. I thought I finally found a job that would add value to Europe."

I smiled wryly. My parents and Moscow friends often heard me saying the same when I was explaining to them what InSup is and what I am doing there. But now, hearing Karolina talking about value for you, Europe, I felt nothing but revulsion.

"What are you going to do in Corporate Affairs?" I asked in an attempt to distract her.

"Transparency register."

"What is that?"

That was the right question! She looked at me surprised and then turned into the old Karolina, who enjoyed explaining things to a newcomer. "This is a kind of database. It shows European citizens whom and when the Agency met, and most importantly, whose interests were represented during those meetings. The European Commission requires all decentralized EU agencies to have such a transparency register and to share it with the public. Remember the Chinese delegation we had earlier this year? That meeting should definitely be included in the register with the names of all the staff from our side who attended it, the name of the head of the Chinese delegation and preferably all the delegation members plus the questions or at least the topics that were discussed."

It sounded like a hell of a job because everybody in InSup had plenty of such meetings.

"Teleconferences and bilateral phone calls should be registered too. And I would need to register everything that had happened this year," Karolina added.

I gasped. "Nobody kept track of those meetings during the whole year?!"

Karolina energetically nodded. The more she explained her new assignment to me, the more she sounded inspired. "Indeed, it's bad governance; we should have started earlier. But we are a very young agency, no wonder certain obligations were out of our radar. But not anymore. I plan to implement the register as soon as possible. Accountability to European citizens is a very serious thing!"

"Sounds like an important task," I agreed to maintain her improved mood.

Karolina winced as if remembering something unpleasant. "Actually, I asked Carlos why he had chosen me. He said Corporate Affairs collected an enormous backlog of unregistered meetings and didn't have the energy to process it. He said he doesn't see a more suitable person than me for doing so."

"No energy?! This is a valid argument?" I couldn't help saying. "My Centrobank's boss Kamarinov wouldn't pay them their monthly premium, and then they would quickly get enough energy to clean their shit."

Karolina rolled her eyes, "That's not a legitimate way to manage people. EU institutions tick differently." She looked somewhere past me and, after a long pause, added, "If you failed, it simply means that those who had given you this task made a wrong choice. They should correct their mistake and pass your work to somebody capable of accomplishing it."

"And rewarding Corporate Affairs by giving their task to you is very legitimate," I snorted.

Karolina's face darkened again. "It's ok if it's for the sake of the Agency. But it feels so hard to sacrifice my preferences..." She sipped more rum tea and suddenly gave me a level stare. "Look, Maxim, I think I found a start-up that could change a lot in the European medical market. If I were not bound by our ethical rules, I would have invested in them myself. The assessment is almost ready, and I wish I could finalize it and, like this, be part of their future success. But no chances..." She gulped the rest of her tea and said, holding the cup in both hands as if it were a lifebuoy, "Maxim, please complete this assessment instead of me!"

We stayed in Barenik until midnight and had Azerbaijan kutabi with salted cheese and parsley and another round of rum tea. Despite the late hour, Karolina turned into her usual self, curious about everything around her and energetic. She asked about my friendship with Kirill. We even went around to see the exhibition. Karolina liked the most the snapshot taken in Oslo on the Acrobat pedestrian bridge. The crowd on the bridge with tense faces was obviously suffering from cold. However, one girl in a woolen hat looked up with a happy smile.

"This picture is very much like me," Karolina said breezily. "I also see the sun everywhere. And I am so thankful for this wonderful evening," she added. "Isabel was right. We should have come here much earlier!"

"Do you think it was Broomy's revenge for her defeat with the Chinese delegation?" I said in response, risking to spoil this evening irrevocably. "Sorry for asking but it has been bothering me for many weeks. Revenge for good performance – how is it possible if you are working for Europe?"

She lowered her eyes. "Everything is possible in an EU institution." She shook her head as if shaking this thought out and added, "But I have more important things to do than cherish my insulted feelings. I prefer to forget about the past and focus on the new."

Chapter 3 The Diadem Project

New year begins

From: Valeria Coletta

To: All_InSup staff

Subject: Help yourselves with Panettone!

...Brought from Italy and left in the kitchen on the 24th floor.

Happy New Year!

From: Rafael Mautinho

To: All_InSup staff

Subject: RE: Help yourselves with Panettone!

...and in the fridge of the 25th-floor kitchen I left for you the Portuguese pastel de nata.

From: Lukasz Walecki

To: All_InSup staff

Subject: RE: RE: Help yourselves with Panettone!

...and the Polish pomadka that I brought from my home country can be found in all the kitchens. Enjoy!

My first working morning in the New Year on 2 January was sweet both literally and figuratively. I was running to different floors, tasting delights brought by colleagues who wanted to share with everybody little bits from their homelands. While I was considering taking Dutch waffles, I got an Outlook invitation from Hilde in her usual telegraphic style: 'Happy NY, could we meet right now? Need to discuss your working plans. Best, H.'

The New Year seemed to have bypassed Hilde's dreary office. The acid-green biscuits she offered me, were suspiciously dry. Her wrinkled, off-white shirt, on the contrary, looked as if taken directly from the washing machine.

"Did you visit your family during the season break?" Hilde asked. After I said "no," she mumbled something about admiring me and other non-German colleagues for being so far away from their home countries. She couldn't imagine herself without her loved ones, not speaking her mother tongue, not living the accustomed life. The more she spoke, the more disinterested we both were getting. Finally, she rippled her long nose and shot out, "You are probably aware that Karolina no longer works in M-Unit?"

I nodded.

"I will be your new team lead!" she declared and triumphantly paused.

I squeezed a smile on my face. "I am glad not to be alone," I said rather to comfort myself than to show my enthusiasm. "We have a big backlog, nice that we can split it between the two of us."

Hilde's smile faded. "How big is the backlog?"

I shrugged. "Thirty or forty applications. Shall I bring you half?"

She stared at me steadily. Behind these colorless eyes, a certain thinking process was ongoing, I could feel it. "Why so many?" she bleated.

"Because in the last months, Karolina was busy with improving her strategic thinking and writing reports about it."

"Didn't she make a proper hand-over with you?" Hilde asked ignoring my acid tone.

"She did. She handed all these applications over to me."

Hilde masterfully ignored again my inflection. "Then I prefer you process what you received from Karolina during the official handover. If you need my guidance, you know where to find me."

I gasped, not believing that she had just refused to help me anyhow. She started twisting her seal-ring on the left little finger. "Carlos asked me to take M-Unit temporarily, in addition to my core tasks." (I thought I heard apologies in her voice). "He reassured me he will soon reinforce you with another experienced and motivated colleague. But for now, you have to pull it through." Before I could answer anything, she fired off, "When can I expect the first assessment from you?"

I didn't know when. Karolina left me her drafts and remarks, but I hadn't decided what to start with.

Hilde constructed her facial muscles into an expression of engagement. My brokenness seemed to have delighted her. "I am really sorry to hear that Karolina wasn't in control of the workload. Let's start with good planning. Please send me your activity plan for those thirty or forty applications in three Excel columns: name of a start-up, when InSup received it, and by when you plan to assess it." She stood up. I followed her. "Please do so by lunchtime, this afternoon I want to report to Carlos."

Isabel entered my office right after I had returned from Hilde. In a skirt suit of a color she called "dusty lavender," she looked fresh and energetic. "Happy New Year, Maxim!" She hugged me with one arm because, in the second one, she held a big package. "Wanna taste 'honey rings', these are the traditional Maltese Christmas cookies? Take more than just one! The rest I'll leave in the staff kitchen and will add another line to that lovely long email." She put one honey ring in her mouth and winced. "Could be better, my bad. It's only in the airport that I realized I hadn't bought anything for the Agency." She gave me another look and her joyful smile melted. "Hey, you don't look like the new year has just begun."

She pensively listened to my report about the first New Year meeting with Hilde. After I exclaimed, "How can I know in advance how many start-ups I will assess per month?!" she interrupted me with a placating gesture.

"Do you know what it means when somebody in a European agency gives you a task that should be completed by lunchtime?" she asked and went on without waiting for my answer. "It means that you shouldn't take it seriously and do it properly. I'd say it's a 20-minute job. First, think of what you can do quickly. Collect the low-hanging fruits, understand? Pick up two or three projects for January, preferably those you and Karolina have already started working on. Spread the rest of the applications across other months randomly. Nobody is going to check. In two weeks, Hilde and Carlos will forget about this plan." She gave me a piercing glance and then suddenly winked. "Oh, and another piece of advice, if I may: don't rush! Send Hilde your plan not before but after lunch and apologize that it took much longer than expected. In EU agencies, delayed replies always look more credible."

Maxim to Veronika. Cosmopolitan Christmas

Nika, privet,

I see you had an amazing Christmas time, happy for you. Making love on the floor at the bottom of the Ngong Ping cable car is a cool idea, especially in a cowgirl position. I could easily imagine you on the glass floor with the water below and the wooded mountains of Lantau Island coming closer every second. I couldn't help googling how long a cable car trip from Hong Kong to Lantau takes: 25 minutes! You are getting better in the sprint, I see. Also given that you found time to make that great picture of your naked breast and the Giant Buddha among the mountains in the background. I am moved that you shared this moment with me. Keep doing so.

As for me, I on purpose decided not to return to Moscow for Christmas or travel anywhere else. I was curious to experience the Christmas holidays in Frankfurt. Apparently, European institutions have the same 9 days off as Russia, just in Europe they start earlier. We stop working on 24 December and return to office on 2 January. It was hard to bestir myself over working on 2 January while for all the Russians fun has just started and will last until 9 January!

Ian went on holiday to Ireland, so I decided to celebrate in the city and with the city. I wanted to spend 24 December on the Römer Platz where a big Christmas market opened in end-November. My plan was first to have dinner with gray bread, tomatoes, and mushrooms covered with melted Swiss Raclette cheese. Then have a crêpe with apple mousse. I wanted to ramble among kiosks with wooden decorations and candied almonds; to watch a sugarloaf soaked with rum slowly burning blue in the kiosk selling Feuerzangenbowle[19]; to absorb all the fragrances and sounds of Christmas.

---

[19] Traditional German alcoholic drink sold on Christmas market

I arrived at Römer at around 20.00 and guess what I saw? The Christmas market was gone! All the picturesque kiosks were being dismantled. Only the 30-meter Christmas tree was still there, mourning over the market residue.

I noticed the glühwein shop owner from whom I bought my after-work drink in the course of the last month. "Why are you going away, Christmas has just started?" I asked.

For the first time, he didn't carry his usual welcoming smile and his tone sounded rather discontented. "Genau deswegen, wir alle möchten auch zu unseren Familien!"[20]

Bemused and disoriented I ended up in the only place that came to my mind – Barenik. "This is Germany, my friend," Kirill explained. "The national idea of this country is that holidays must be holidays for everybody. No matter if you are missing the most profitable days of the year, important is to have your Ruhe[21]. Personally, I find it nice, they are not greedy and allow Barenik to profit from Christmas."

Indeed, Barenik was open all Christmas night long. Kirill decorated it with the Christmas tree attached to the ceiling upside down. The place was filled with the anticipation of the party. "Cheer up, bro, tonight we are going to celebrate like hell!" Kirill declared. He was right. So many people who like me were far away from their

---

[20] Exactly for this reason, we also want to be with our families (German).

[21] Rest (German)

relatives, came here and formed a new, big family just for this night. I think on that night I tried everything possible: quizzes, games, live guitar songs, and a rich selection of exotic cocktails. So instead of a traditional German Christmas, I have got a cosmopolitan party like I never had before.

I left Barenik early in the morning together with Rita, a splendid Brazilian girl who won me twice in a dance lottery. We both took it as a sign although Rita came to the party with another man who, in turn also won somebody and was happy with his prize. The whole of 25 December I spent in bed, I don't have pictures, so leaving them to your fantasy. However, on 26 December, I suddenly felt that the Christmas spirit left Germany completely. The days between Christmas and New Year are usually working days and despite Christmas decorations, the city was gray and lethargic. Rita took a shower, washed away the glitter makeup, and turned out to be pale and boring. We spent a day together and in the evening she left home with the words 'See you in Barenik again' (without specifying the day and the time).

Apparently, for Germans, New Year's Eve is a much less important day than Christmas. In fact, you can hardly distinguish it from any other day of the year. Except for its very first hour. On 31 December I stayed at home, chatting with my parents and Moscow friends on WhatsApp. Thanks to the time difference, I could congratulate everybody two hours before my midnight. Short before twelve o'clock, I raised a champagne glass and closed my eyes to speak out a wish.

Initially, I wanted to wish myself not to get lost in InSup without Karolina. When I thought of it twenty seconds before midnight, I smiled. This wish seemed ridiculous and insignificant compared to my loneliness. Nika, I thought of how much I wish to be with you again. Buy the first ticket to Hong Kong, get you in my arms for a single day. That was the wish I was about to speak out. Suddenly I heard puffs and whooshes. I ran to the balcony thinking that the third world war started because the shots were heard from everywhere. From time to time, I could see skyrockets and only after I had seen flamy florescences here and there, I understood that these were... fireworks! Many of them I could only hear, and those that I saw were neither rich nor sophisticated. But the variety of noises was remarkable!

For more than one hour, the space around me was bursting, crackling, and exploding with different intensities. In the end, it became so monotonous that I stopped paying attention and fell asleep. Later, Kirill explained to me that every supermarket sells lots of those fireworks before Christmas Eve because Germans like to launch them right after midnight. So now I know: no way the first hour of the New Year in Germany can be missed! Maybe next time we will experience it together?

101

Trip to Heidelberg

In Moscow, I used to spend one hour on average to reach any destination. Wherever I went, be it work or fun, every journey required plenty of monotonous time in the metro or on the bus. But when you live in a megapolis all your life, you don't notice how much time traveling takes up in your daily routine. The way to Heidelberg by train took 51 minutes. How could I refuse to travel there if in Moscow this would be shorter than getting to my parents, whom I tried to visit every Friday?

Compared to the buzzing and dirty Main Train Station area in Frankfurt, Heidelberg's train station was neat and deserted. Ten minutes later, the untalkative taxi driver brought me to a little colorful building with the signboard "VorschungsLab[22]". I pushed the entrance door and found myself in a big open space. Everywhere young people either stared at the screens or chatted. Nobody paid attention to my arrival. A visitors' desk seemed to be non-existent. I noticed two young men wearing similar blue T-shirts with the word "BrainPower" printed on their chests. *This could be a start-up uniform*, I thought, and went straight to them.

"Entschuldigung[23], I am looking for Alice Kern."

---

[22] Research laboratory (German)
[23] Excuse me (German)

"I will show you her desk," immediately reacted one guy and rushed away. I ran after him. "Ein Besucher für dich, Alice[24]," he said in a loud, disinterested tone and disappeared before I could thank him.

"Danke dir[25]," a girl shouted in his direction. She was talking on the phone and showed me a victory sign, which I interpreted as a kind request to wait for two minutes. I nodded and kept standing at a distance to let her finish the conversation. While waiting, I asked myself whether Karolina had made a wrong assumption. She was convinced that this start-up had the potential to change the medical market in Europe. "A gadget that can cure migraine without medications, just imagine how cool it is!" she said and after observing my reaction added, "Oh, I see you belong to those lucky people who don't know what a migraine is."

Indeed, when in Barenik Karolina with sparkling eyes explained to me this innovation, it didn't impress me more than, for example, a polymeric gel that stops strong bleeding or a patch that speeds up the regeneration of burned skin. Alice's application was called "The Diadem Project". She claimed that the device she invented together with her peers could cure migraines with a sort of electronic compress for the upper part of the head. The compress changed its temperature depending on the migraine intensity. The only

---

[24] A visitor for you, Alice (German)
[25] Thank you (German)

advantage I saw in this start-up was that Karolina had already completed its assessment and even sent it to Carlos. But the latter noticed that the start-up was located in Heidelberg, he suggested Karolina look at it with her own eyes. Karolina found it a good idea, but soon after the talk with Carlos, Hilde removed her from M-Unit. "I wish I could go together with you," Karolina told me. "It's so exciting to see the beginning of a big story."

Well, my plan was less emotional. I just wanted to glance at this start-up with my own eyes and resubmit it to Carlos without touching it. Now, when I was observing Alice Kern, the co-founder of the Diadem, I felt dismayed. At first glance, she was younger than me, 22 or 25 years old; dressed in jeans and a gray tatty pullover, she looked powerless and brittle. *An insecure student rather than a big story*, I thought. *Maybe Karolina's intuition let her down and instead of wasting time in Heidelberg, I should have rushed back to the office and started assessing another project?*

"Good morning, Mr. Reut. I was expecting you a bit later, sorry," Alice interrupted my thoughts. She had an energetic grasp, but the most striking was to meet the attentive glare of her dark eyes. I felt like she had just read my mind, and it made her sad. It embarrassed me somehow.

"No need to apologize. I've never been to Heidelberg, and I came much too early," I comforted her. "It's my first assessment interview, you know," I suddenly added. I cursed myself for the unexpected openness, but she peered at me so encouragingly that I felt rewarded.

"I know how you feel. It's my first assessment interview too," she said. "Let's help each other then!"

We laughed, which I immediately regretted. Going beyond the roles of "assessor versus applicant" didn't feel professional. Alice seemed to have read my mind once again. She became serious and politely asked whether I would like to have a coffee beforehand. The staff kitchen was crowded, and it took us a while to make two espressos. I was standing behind Alice and had plenty of time to examine her thin body and unglossy black hair pulled in a high ponytail. *No wonder her employees don't let her take coffee first, she doesn't look like their boss*, I kept thinking. Finally, equipped with two tiny cups, we landed in a little meeting room.

"For a start-up, you have a very big team," I said.

"Team?" Alice asked and drank her espresso in one gulp.

"All these people here, aren't they in your team?"

"Oh God, I hardly know most of them," she laughed. "VorschungsLab supports the projects of students and junior researchers. We can use computers, printers, and meeting rooms, but we don't necessarily know each other."

"Sort of co-working?"

"Exactly. VorschungsLab has such spaces almost in all the cities with University hospitals. And we move from city to city depending on where we get the offer to test our projects."

"Why University hospitals?"

"Because in Germany they have the biggest budgets and, thanks to that, can drive most medical research projects."

"Uh… interesting information, I didn't know that," I admitted.

"I am not sure it's well known," Alice tactfully said.

I took out of my rucksack a folder - her funding application. "Since you submitted it to us several months ago, I just want to check whether the information you provided is still valid," I explained.

"May I?" She opened the folder. Her long fingers were quickly moving from the top to the bottom of each page. Her hands were those of a doctor. The shortly cut nails visually increased finger-pads; the upper phalangeal bones of her fingers were bending down as if in constant tension. I got almost a physical wish to cover her hand with my palm, but fretfully chased it away.

"We increased the number of people that are testing the Diadem and the number of reactions increased too," Alice interrupted my thoughts. "These new numbers only confirmed we are on the right track, so no need to change the overall description. Everything is still correct. The updated figures I will send you."

She smiled, but her face looked sad, probably because of her gray skin and the black circles around her eyes. I recalled that 20 minutes ago I wasn't sure at all I wanted to deal with her application. There was only one way for me to make a final decision. "Could you show me your invention?" I asked.

Her face didn't change. "Of course. I thought that was the reason for your visit and already warned my colleague. She is waiting for us, let's go."

"Where to?"

"To the University Hospital."

Unicorn hunt

The January sun was neither bright nor warm. The air wasn't cold, but unpleasantly humid.

"My car is parked a couple of quarters from here," Alice explained turning her face to indifferent sun rays and obviously enjoying the walk. In the morning light, she looked deadbeat.

"Nice city." I glanced at the accurate rows of yellow, creamy, and beige houses. "Very...," I was about to say "small" but quickly corrected myself, "very cozy."

"I also found it small after my own city," she replied as if talking to my mind rather than listening to my voice. "But I don't see much of it anyway: the University Hospital – VorschungsLab – shopping

- home, I hardly notice what happens outside these destination points."

"Which city are you from?"

"My family used to live in Hamburg. When I was a child, we moved to Tel Aviv and five years ago, I returned to Germany to study in Berlin."

Her complicated answer resonated in me and I automatically quoted aloud the verse, which often came to my mind since I left Moscow. "Wherever bitter fate would send us trailing; Or blissful hope accompany to roam; We're still the same and deem the whole world alien; Tsar's Village is our country and our home,[26.]"

Alice looked at me curiously. "Tsar's Village, where is it?"

"It's a suburb of Saint-Petersburg where the Russian poet Alexander Pushkin graduated from high school. He considered those years the happiest in his life."

Alice nodded pensively. "And where is your own Tsar's Village?" she finally asked.

I glanced at her face. Serious, full of sympathy, and without any sign of flirt. It was the face of a doctor who cared about her patients.

"I always thought it was Moscow," I said simply. "I used to be a spoiled Muscovite, that's how many of my university mates thought of me. Spoiled because, unlike them, I didn't need to conquer the

---

[26] Quote from the poem "19 October" by Alexander Pushkin

capital of Russia. I was part of the capital from birth and comfortably lived with my parents during the whole university time. But now I am in Frankfurt, I thought this would be my new home. But somehow it doesn't feel like it and Moscow doesn't feel like home either, not anymore..."

We approached Alice's car, an old Audi. "I think I know how you feel," Alice said programming the way in GoogleMaps (as she explained, she rarely used the car within Heidelberg, the bike was much more convenient). "I only can advise you to give yourself time. Your home will find you."

Her words cooled my irritated homesickness like a compress. Maybe Alice Kern wasn't a naturally born start-upper, but she had certain potential. We got out of the car and entered the territory of the University Hospital. This giant place living according to its own laws and rules made me feel helpless. With every step, I was turning from a respectable InSup inspector into an intimidated and ignorant patient. All my life, hospitals belittled me. Next to me, Alice was undergoing a contrary transformation: she was exchanging greetings here and there; some people, obviously patients, looked at her with respect. I couldn't put a finger on what exactly had changed. Only one thing I noticed for sure: she didn't look like a student anymore.

The last time I landed in a hospital was when my father had a hernia operation. The waiting room was full of people, tired and sullen. The guard didn't let me in because my name wasn't on the list of visitors. Mum was already there, but I couldn't reach her. While waiting, I noticed that my despair matched the mood of others. A mother with a son of my age next to her in a crying voice was telling how they had traveled several days by bus from Kazan[27] and that for one week they still couldn't speak to a doctor. An old unaccompanied man was swaying from side to side and moaning from pain. I felt an almost physical relief when Mum finally came to pick me up and we went to Dad's sick room.

The waiting room in the University Hospital of Heidelberg didn't radiate suffering or despair. A couple of people immersed themselves in their smartphones or talked over the phone. A businesslike waiting, like in a bank.

"I always thought University Hospitals are full," I couldn't help saying after we passed the waiting room and marched through a long corridor.

"This is usually the case in the Emergency, especially over the weekend. But in the House of Neurology, people mostly come by appointment," Alice replied. In the middle of the corridor, she stopped in front of a door and pulled it. "This is our working room. Please come in."

---

[27] Kazan is located 720 km from Moscow

I entered and froze. In front of me stood a white lab coat with a pile of silver-pinkish-blueish long hair above it. The pile turned and showed a lively face with Asiatic eyes.

"Hallo, Yinzi, da sind wir,[28]" Alice entered the room after me. "This is Maxim Reut from the Agency of Innovation Support," she switched to English. "Yinzi Vu, my friend, start-up co-founder, and a member of the research team."

Yinzi was small, quick, and elfin looking thanks to her silver hair. The only thing that didn't fit this look was her lab coat. Yinzi turned out to be a German in the first generation. Her parents, both students of Humboldt University, applied for political asylum after the crackdown of the Tiananmen Square protests in 1989. Yinzi was born and raised in Berlin. She and Alice studied together at Charité – Universitätsmedizin and then moved to Heidelberg.

"Where are the two other co-founders? According to the papers, you are four." I looked around with mistrust. Narrow, with one window, one desk, one armchair, a couple of chairs, and a shabby cupboard, the room hardly looked like an office for four.

"Here in Heidelberg there are only Alice and myself," Yinzi said with a sad smile. Expressions on her face changed with every new emotion she had.

---

[28] Here we are (German)

"The other two team members work in Berlin, but we constantly exchange observations and test results," Alice added appearing from behind the wardrobe. I stared at her. She put on the lab coat, the same as Yinzi's, and it changed everything. A student disappeared. Now Alice looked older than me and self-confident. I recalled my father's saying that there are two types of clothes that make you look better than you are: a military uniform and a white lab coat.

"Wouldn't it be more convenient for you to stay together?"

Yinzi sent me a pert glance. "Oh yes, it would be great. But we didn't get this chance." Suddenly she rolled her eyes in an artificial horror. "Actually why am I saying so? We can consider ourselves very lucky: none of us is alone! Isn't it?"

"Indeed. And in two different places we can get double more volunteers to test the Diadem," Alice agreed. Suddenly she has got the look of a conferencier announcing a prime spot. "Mr. Reut, I think that the best way to inspect our innovation is to test it on yourself. Would you be ready to do it?"

Yinzi clapped her hands. I cautiously smiled. "I am afraid you want to cure something that I never had. Does it make sense?"

Alice nodded. "The Diadem contains the relaxation regime, which we designed for prophylactic reasons, so to say. We still don't know what exactly causes migraine, but we believe that relaxation is good for everybody. Users can opt for this regime in case they have insomnia or need to calm down after a stressful day." I had a feeling that she is used to answering this question and has a ready wording at hand.

"Does it last long?" I asked.

"A couple of hours. As soon as a patient falls asleep, the Diadem switches to the sleeping mode." She paused a moment to see my reaction. I tried to look unflappable. I risked losing the entire working day just for one start-up, but I reminded myself that it was a rare chance to test the innovation, that InSup would fund and, as a responsible analyst, I couldn't miss it. Alice seemed to be satisfied with my reaction. "I am impressed by your readiness, but allow me to comfort you. You are going to test the shortest and lightest regime, it won't take longer than 20 minutes."

"I am ready for whatever you will offer," I said enthusiastically. Somehow, it felt good that I could impress her.

Yinzi's face brightened and then became preoccupied. "Alice, shall I conduct the test? You have just had a night shift, a terrible one. Maybe you'd better go home?"

Alice shook her head. "I program and you record the indicators and results, would it do?"

"Of course!"

Then she turned to me and pointed at the armchair, "Make yourself comfortable." She opened the laptop and sat next to me on a chair.

"Why didn't you ask me to postpone my visit to a day when you wouldn't have a night shift?" I asked. I felt sorry for her and embarrassed of my critical thoughts and doubts.

She shrugged. "Tonight's shift was unexpected. My supervisor just put me on it without asking. Happens sometimes."

"Ms. Vu said it was terrible, why?"

Alice pursed the lips. "A couple of difficult patients in the station I was assigned to. But now everything is ok." She continued in a more businesslike tone. "The Diadem develops an individual temperature regime for every patient. Changes between hot and cold impact the trigeminal nerve the way that it stops transmitting pain to your brain. In the light regime, your trigeminal nerve will just relax. You won't need to focus your thoughts on your breath, but the result will be like after a short meditation. Now, to tailor it to you, I need to insert your data: age, weight, height."

While telling Alice how much water I drink per day, how physically active I am, and many other things, I wondered whether testing the Diadem would indeed be in line with InSup's working ethics. When Carlos insisted Karolina go to Heidelberg, maybe he meant we should meet the start-uppers rather than contribute to their work. Then I forced myself not to think of it, for doubts it was too late.

Alice ran through all her questions and left to pick up the device. She returned with something that looked like a motorcycle helmet with an open top. "It should set tight but not painfully on your forearm, temporal fossa, and back of the neck. Inside we put one-off polyurethane plates that very well transmit temperature. These plates can be recycled." She turned the helmet from side to side as if she was going to sell it to me.

"Can one really sleep in such a helmet?" I suspected. It looked unprepossessing and lacked what I would call a "start-up appeal."

It seemed like Alice was well-prepared for this question. "It only looks like a helmet, but it's elastic and soft enough to sleep. And we are already working on a new design." She looked straight at me. "I need to touch you now, is it ok?"

"Feel free," I said, trying to sound flat.

And then something happened.

Alice took my head in her palms and I shuddered from the hit on both sides of my head. I closed my eyes and wished it lasted.

"Are you all right?" Alice's voice sounded emphatic.

"It's unexpectedly warm," I said forcing myself to open my eyes.

Alice looked at me doubtfully and immediately took off the Diadem from my head. "Are you sure?" she asked touching its inner side. "It's not warm because it's still off."

I touched the device too, indeed it felt like room temperature.

"Maybe it's your hands?" I asked and put my palm on hers. Her hands were of a normal temperature, nothing remarkable but something inside me responded to this touch. Not without an effort, I took my hands away. "Apologies, let's just go on."

Alice nodded. "I was concerned that it's not functioning, but it all looks all right."

It did. The Diadem felt almost unnoted. Alice moved it and then fixed it with a click. "The size can be regulated," she explained. "By migraine, it's important that patients are by maximum isolated from sounds and light." She put down the plates on my eyes and ears and it became pleasantly dark and quiet. "Yinzi, bist du bereit zu starten?[29]" she asked.

"Jawohl[30]." Yinzi's voice sounded lower, the sound isolation of the Diadem seemed to work well.

"Get started," Alice said firmly.

In the first seconds, I had the impression that the Diadem became tighter on my head, but then I understood that it simply got warmer. My body jerked because somebody sat on my knees. Somebody light, a child, or maybe Yinzi. "A unicorn among start-ups is hard to find. What if you found one?" said a voice that sounded like Veronika. I wanted to ask how she found me, but couldn't pronounce a word. "Hunt it," Nika whispered in my ear. But I didn't care

---

[29] Yinzi, are you ready to start? (German)
[30] Sure (German)

anymore about the Diadem. "Nika, will you stay with me?" I asked thickly. In response, she slapped me in the face.

"Mr. Reut, we are done," I heard Alice's voice. I understood that it wasn't a slap. Alice removed the plates from my eyes and it felt painful to have all the light and sounds back. "How do you feel?"

I felt confused but good. My head was pleasantly cold (obviously at a certain point the Diadem cooled down).

"Interesting. For a moment I fell asleep, but now I am energized somehow." I stood up, feeling a bit estranged from my own body. "You know, I think the tension in my shoulders and upper neck has loosened," I said and suddenly added, "oh, and it's very pleasant to look again at Ms.Vu's hair, they are amazing!"

Yinzi giggled, covering her mouth with her fingers like a schoolgirl. "This hair color is called 'unicorn', I enjoy experimenting, you know."

Alice kept a serious face, but I could feel her joy. "Nice that we could not only show you the device, but also enrich our studies. That's what I call efficiency!" she said.

"Efficiency is something we always welcome," barked a tall blond man entering the room.

By the manner Yinzi jumped out of her seat, I understood it was a boss or something like that.

"Guten Tag," he said shifting his gaze from Yinzi to myself. His disdainful face with straight features seemed to be cut out of stone.

A face of a cruel German doctor from World War II movies, I thought.

"Hallo, Herr Doctor Roth," Yinzi said timidly, looking at the floor.

"Hallo," I said but Doctor Roth already turned to Alice. "Darf ich Sie kurz sprechen?[31]"

Alice nodded and turned to Yinzi. "Please keep recording Mr. Reut's feedback. See you." And without waiting for our reaction, she followed Doctor Roth.

"Scheiße[32]," Yinzi said when the door after both had closed. "Doctor Roth never brings good news, at least not to us."

"Are you working for him?"

"Yes, he is our supervisor, responsible for all the junior researchers in Uniklinikum[33]." She suddenly looked at me confidently and lowered her voice. "I have the impression he is looking for a pretext to kick us out."

"Why would he do so?"

Yinzi made a large sway with her fantasy hair. "I don't know. In the beginning, everything was ok but then he suddenly changed.

---

[31] May I talk to you quickly? (German)
[32] Shit (German)
[33] The University hospital (German)

Probably he doesn't like Alice and myself, but maybe he simply doesn't believe in the Diadem."

Alice came back right when we were about to finish recording my feedback. She looked even more weary and miserable.

"Also was[34]?" Yinzi asked.

Alice sighted. "Our presentation to the Scientific Council is postponed."

Yinzi's mouth turned into a letter "o". "Again?!"

Alice looked at me gingerly, as if deciding whether or not to keep talking. "Doctor Roth thinks we need to test the Diadem on many more patients before drawing any conclusions. I disagreed, but he said it's not disputable," she finally said. Yinzi winced like from something sour she had to swallow. Alice looked like a bulb that was going to fade away. Both kept their gaze on me. I felt they were expecting me to say something.

At this very moment, I made up my mind. I had to tell them the truth. I cleared my throat. "In InSup we must assess the submitted applications," I started. "Meeting you and testing the Diadem was an add-on my Agency could allow because we are located close to each other. It was nice to have, but not a must. To draw my conclusions, I will only use what I saw with my own eyes. The opinion of Doctor Roth cannot and will not count."

---

[34] So what? (German)

Brain twister

From: Maxim Reut

To: Hilde Rosenbohm

Subject: For approval: Assessment of the start-up "The Diadem Project"

Dear Hilde,

Please find the <u>link</u> to the above-mentioned file - for your approval.

The assessment was done by Karolina last year. I only ensured that all the information is up to date. Following Carlos' suggestion, I recently met the start-up founders in Heidelberg. My impression was positive and allowed me to confirm the conclusion of Karolina that the Diadem is worth the European funding.

Should you have questions, please let me know.

Kind regards,

Maxim

From: Hilde Rosenbohm

To: Carlos de Santos Gomez

CC: Maxim Reut

Dear Carlos, see below.

Best,

H.

From: Carlos de Santos Gomez

To: Hilde Rosenbohm; Maxim Reut

Subject: RE: FW: For approval: Assessment of the start-up "The Diadem"

Dear both,

Thank you for the file, which I carefully examined and saw that its quality leaves room for improvement.

At this stage, approval would be premature.

Kind regards,

Carlos

The flow of energy in Isabel's office was almost tactile. Was it in the big carafe of water where she added the slices of lemon? Or in her silk blouse of a refreshing color, which Isabel mysteriously called "coconut cream"?

She was on the phone, one of her pencils in her hand, with a faint smile on her thin lips. "By what time do you need it? I'd say tough, but not impossible. You will hear from me, bye." She put down the phone. "Ecology Unit is behind deadline as usual. This time they are rushing to save the world with plastic bags that dissolve in water," she explained pouring me a glass of lemon water.

"That's what I love InSup for. We can make the world a better place in many diverse ways."

Isabel raised an eyebrow. "That's what I love my job for. Every time somebody wants to save the world, it's me who should wrack my brain. Just look at this. For their impact assessment, the E-Unit guys asked me to find out how many plastic bags end up in European lakes and rivers. To get these data, I will have to approach my contact in Greenpeace Europe. And he is not easy to handle: he gives nothing unless I offer something attractive in exchange."

"Like what?"

She started with her usual exercises for relaxing the neck and shoulders. "I don't know yet, would need to think. For example, I could introduce him to the new adviser in the Commission's environmental directorate who is in charge of all the ecology-related projects. It's a former colleague of mine who has been promoted recently and would like to meet somebody from Greenpeace." Her face brightened. "Actually this could work if I sell it well to both sides. Time for me to go back to Brussels for some networking."

Isabel came close to the window. Under the dim February sun, her coconut blouse shined softly. "If I were ecologists, I would have requested from Research a totally different information," she said pensively. "For example, how many European producers of plastic bags might switch to the production of dissolvable bags? I think I know where to get the answer."

"Why don't you offer it to E-Unit?"

122

Isabel went back to her desk and poured herself a glass of water. "Bear in mind: this is a European institution. Here you must give your advice only at the right moment, otherwise, it will play against you."

This remark returned me to my anxious thoughts. "Well, for advice to me it's the right time," I sighed.

Isabel could be a good psychoanalyst. She didn't say a word while I was telling her how during two weeks Hilde had made me triple-check every conclusion in the Diadem assessment and how she insisted that everything I do I show first to Karolina. An extensive quality check didn't seem to reassure her, so she ordered me to show the entire assessment to "somebody in research". Isabel pierced me; her lively eyes and expressively moving eyebrows encouraged me to get more emotional. "I reminded Broomy you already contributed to this assessment last year when Karolina started it, but she insists. I am wracking my brain too. Sometimes I think Hilde asks for everybody's opinion because she doesn't have her own," I said bitterly.

"I know what you need. Sit down," Isabel said imperatively when I finally stopped complaining. I obeyed. She started massaging - surprisingly strong - my shoulders. "Listen, Maxim, you must make a pause with this assessment," Isabel went on without stopping the massage. I opened my mouth to object, but she didn't let me. "Hilde – exactly like you – has no clue why Carlos didn't approve the assessment and what he wants. But unlike you, she has no appetite to show this assessment to Carlos once again. You asked me for advice, so here it is. Focus on other start-up applications and in the meantime send me The Diadem Project. I'll see what else we can do." She pressed something on my back so that I screamed in pain. "You stress yourself much too much," Isabel echoed in the tone of a researcher who observes monkeys in a zoo.

"How do you manage to stay so calm?" I couldn't help asking.

She let out a wan laugh. "Ten years in different EU institutions, I saw it all." She jokingly kicked my back with the palm. "One substantial explanation I can give you though: don't be enthusiastic and hard-working. It disturbs all those who for years have been doing their job in a tempo comodo[35]. They don't appreciate being disturbed by quick-firing newcomers."

I turned to her so abruptly that she jerked from surprise. "You tell me this?! You, the most enthusiastic person in InSup, who is so efficient and keen on doing their job well?!"

Isabel looked through the glass wall and shook her head. "It's not enthusiasm, mind you, but engagement. A very controlled engagement. Do you see the difference?"

---

[35] At a moderate pace (Italian)

Dancing with Alice

From the back, her modest, unprotected posture looked familiar. It was certainly Alice Kern.

"Hi, Ms. Kern, thank you for coming," I said. She turned, and I thought I was mistaken. The girl at the table looked alien. I was about to apologize but she said, "Hello, Mr. Reut." Her energetic handshake eliminated all my doubts.

"I didn't recognize you," I admitted, desperately trying to spot the difference with the Alice I had met in Heidelberg, "somehow you look... more mature."

Alice beamed. "I always look the way I feel. Last time we met right after my night shift in the hospital, I felt like a student who wants to go to bed after a sleepless night of preparing for an exam."

"And how do you feel today?" I asked seizing her shiny hair of a dark chocolate tone and the bronze smoky make-up underlining her attentive brown eyes.

Alice thought for a moment. "I feel official," she finally said.

I knew why. She took part in the conference organized by Frankfurt's University Hospital. According to the program, she even made a presentation about innovations in medicine.

"Being official suits you very well!" I said with aspiration. In her dark-blue skirted suit, refreshed with an ivory blouse, she radiated confidence and strictness. This time, I could have immediately believed she was a start-up founder.

Alice shyly smiled back and looked around. "I've never been here, an unusual place."

I invited her to Barenik of course. After Isabel (quicker than she promised initially) proposed to enrich the Diadem assessment with some additional aspects, I called Alice to gather more data. Since she happened to be in Frankfurt, we agreed to meet. I could have invited her to InSup and labeled her visit as "an interview with the applicant". But somehow, it didn't feel right. I didn't consider myself unbiased, and Alice wasn't just "an applicant" anymore.

Barenik wasn't crowded yet. These days Kirill hosted a video installation named "Horizons". On a screen, the viewers first saw the world atlas painted in the stylistics of medieval mapmakers. Then the whimsical outlines of countries and continents started changing, getting increasingly precise based on the Ptolemy Geography, on the gained by the humankind knowledge that our planet is not flat, and finally on the geographical discoveries made by Vasco da Gama, Ferdinand Magellan, and others. The video offered more and more details and finally wrapped up with a picture that reminded of a snapshot from Google Earth. "It's hypnotizing," Alice said, watching the video from our table. "Is it part of the interior design?"

"Unfortunately not. In a couple of days, this installation will reach its destination – the Festival of Digital Art in Utrecht. Nicos, the author of the installation, wanted to show it to somebody in Frankfurt. So, he agreed with Kirill, the restaurant owner, to keep it here for a week. Many artists use Barenik for this, especially if they are Kirill's friends."

Alice looked at me curiously. "Do you know this artist personally?"

I steered. "I saw him when Kirill presented to us his installation. As far as I remember, they got to know each other when Kirill went on a business trip to Greece. Nicos is well known in Greece, but I can't even repeat his surname, it's long and ends up with 'tis'."

I took out the list of my questions and tried to sound more business-like. "Now let me explain why I asked you to meet me. In European institutions we pay a big deal to diversity," I went on in a teacher's tone. "I would need to cover it in my analysis of The Diadem Project. I thought we could talk and maybe find together how to better present the project from a perspective of diversity. For example, Ms. Vu is a German with a Chinese background. This is very good. Are there any useful details about other co-founders?"

It was an easy talk. Alice didn't show any surprise or discontent with my questions. She readily told me that three co-founders, including Yinzi, are Germans, of which one also has a Hungarian background. As for Alice, she was an Israeli citizen. Her paternal grandmother survived the Nazi camps in Lodz and Auschwitz. After the deliberation, she lived in the Zeilsheim camp for displaced persons under the protection of American militaries, but felt that even after Hitler's defeat, antisemitism in Germany didn't disappear. She decided she couldn't stay in the country, which had little regret for having killed her parents and two sisters and immigrated to Israel. Some years later, she returned to Germany where she married a Jew whose family survived because right after Hitler came to power, they smelled what was afoot and moved to Switzerland. Alice's parents, in their turn, became disappointed in Germany and moved to Israel. Her school years Alice spent in Tel Aviv, but when it was time to enter the University, she went to Berlin. "We speak German at home; as a child, I often went to Germany. Somehow, I always knew I would come back," Alice sighed. "It looks like every generation in our restless family is struggling to decide where our homeland is."

Her family story opened me up. I told her about how my grandparents had met. I could see that it impressed her, and I liked it. Alice already answered all my questions about the selection of volunteers and the sustainability of materials the Diadem was made of. In principle we were good, but I went on with another question, which Isabel marked as optional. "Are any co-founders LGBT? It's not a curiosity, I am asking because it could be an asset," I said trying to sound disinterested.

Alice shrugged. "We are heterosexual, but none of us ever showed disrespect or discriminative attitude towards LGBT."

"Are you married? Have kids?" I bent over my notes, trying not to look at her.

Again, she answered my inner question rather than the one on my tongue. "I was together with a doctor from Charité, but we split after I moved to Heidelberg."

"Do you mind if I invite you for dinner?" I shot out unexpectedly for myself and then, to cover up my too-obvious joy, I added apologetically, "I used up so much of your evening."

Alice didn't object. I ordered for both of us the Russian pelmeni filled with chicken and green tea with thyme and honey. She allowed me to have fun watching her joyfully fearful facial expression when she tested pelmeni for the first time in her life.

I was about to order us a dessert when Kirill suddenly announced the evening of медляки[36]. This meant live music and quoting Kirill "a chance to hold each other in the arms under the pretext that it's a dance". I rushed to tell Alice that I had no idea about tonight's program, which was the truth. She slightly flushed and said she believed me. Barenik filled in with stir and excitement. The tables in front of the stage were moved to free the space for dancers. I knew the musicians that came on stage, but they brought a new singer,

---

[36] Grave dances (Russian slang)

who turned the evening into a phantasmagoria. Miniature, faceless, with long colorless hair she looked like an uncomplicated pop performer. But when she started "Walk Away" by Christina Aguilera the entire Barenik froze dumbfounded. Strong and moving, her voice covered us like a waterfall. Nobody dared to dance. Caught in the bluesy slavery of her voice, I recalled the hit of Alice's hands when she touched my head in Heidelberg. I suddenly felt the need to test whether the hit would return if she touched me again. I longed for it. Barenik guests started dancing. It would be so easy to invite Alice for a dance, but earlier I assured her that медляки were completely out of my plans for tonight. I could only smile at her amid the increasingly erotic dance moves and music. Alice was smiling back.

When the singer announced the next song, "Stop" by Sam Brown, Alice drew a deep breath. "It has been my favorite song for many years." She looked straight into my eyes. "Thank you so much, Mr. Reut, for bringing me here."

Looking at her shiny eyes, I couldn't help saying, "You can call me Maxim."

"Maxim, wenn du dein Date nicht zum Tanzen aufforderst, würde ich es gerne für dich tun[37]," another Kirill's friend whose

---

[37] If you don't invite your partner to dance, I'll be happy to do it for you (German)

name I forgot popped up at our table. "Erlauben Sie?[38]" he tended his hand to Alice. The gesture was self-explanatory and since I didn't understand anything except for the word "Date" I let Alice decide.

"Warum nicht[39]," she answered and went on.

While I was watching Alice approaching the dance area, somebody put hands on my shoulders. "Shall we dance too?" a familiar voice said.

It was Katja. A month ago, I met her in Barenik, which put a painless end to our cooling down relations with Gayane. I thought in Katja I found another Veronika. Direct and defiant, she knew well her beauty and smartly used it for anybody to resist. The latter was professional, though, because Katja was a model. After our first night together, I was about to proudly report to Veronika that I finally had her perfect substitute. To reinforce my news, I wanted to attach our joint picture from Barenik but I didn't have one. The email to Nika was postponed and soon I understood I'd never send it out. Katja had zero interest in the part of my life, that I didn't spend with her. She could hardly fight boredom every time I started talking about InSup. It was so different from the way Nika listened about my Centrobank's stories while making mercilessly precise comments. I couldn't stand this difference.

---

[38] Would you allow me? (German)
[39] Why not? (German)

Suddenly, I remembered the name of the guy who invited Alice to dance. He was a photographer and belonged to Katja's network.

"Was it your idea to send Martin to us?" I stood up, trying to sound calm and strict.

Katja tossed her freshly curled, wheatish hair and leaned forward, besotting me with the scents of almond and vanilla perfume, red wine and God knows what else. "Simmer down. While Martin is busy with your companion, you won't have a bad conscious when dancing with me." She took my hand. "Let's go. Just one dance."

It was hard not to obey her. Katja looked and smelled like a ripe apple, endlessly sweet and seductive. There was no bra under her silk green turtleneck and another day I would have simply put my hand under the tissue to feel her skin. But unfortunately for Katja, two meters away from us, Alice and Martin were dancing, and I was focused on them.

All that I have is all that you've given me[40]

The singer filled the whole space of Barenik with her powerful voice.

Katja couched her glamourous head on my shoulder, I didn't react. So she changed her tactics and started whispering how she missed me during her recent trip to London. Another day I would

---

[40] "Stop!" by Sam Brown, Gregg Sutton, Bruce Brody.

have let myself believe her, but not tonight. Even when Katja put my hand on her bottom, packed in ultra-narrow jeans, I kept looking at Alice. I couldn't get rid of the feeling that Martin was touching something that belonged to me. Suddenly I felt a strong desire that her fingers with bent upper phalangeal bones lay on my shoulders, not on Martin's. Alice caught my glance and smiled. I jerked my gaze away, fearing that she would read my mind again.

"Don't be shy," Katja said. She ran her fingers through my hair and, before I could react, gave me a long ecstatic kiss. Her lips, the singer's voice, and my desire to touch Alice were too luscious, and I responded.

Oh, you'd better stop… babe stop…you'd better stop, stop, stop…

When I returned to the table Alice was already there, avoiding looking at me. I was observing her for a moment. She looked sad and lost. *Maybe she likes me too?* flashed in my head.

"Ms. Kern," I called and leaned forward, "would you look at me, please." She obeyed and her gaze filled me with joyful hope. "I know you are not interested, but I would like to explain it," I went on. "This girl's name is Katja. We are not together, uhm…not anymore. But when we tumble upon each other, she shows a certain nostalgia. And I sometimes can't help flirting back." Alice nodded, but still looked lost and sad.

The evening of медляки went on, but something between us cooled down and was business-like again. We both seemed to be relieved to just listen to music and watch the dancers without talking to each other. Later, while we walked together to her car, Alice said, "Thanks for showing me a new place. I hope I can come here again and will definitely recommend it to others."

"I will tell it to Kirill, he'll be pleased."

She was about to sit in the car when I suddenly added, "Thank you for your help... Alice." I enjoyed calling her by name and watching her reaction. Since it wasn't clear whether she liked it, I quickly added, "I appreciate you found time to answer my multiple questions."

We said goodbye in the most courteous manner. I concluded that Alice would prefer to keep her distance, but before driving away, she peered out of the car window, said, "Good night, Maxim," and took off without waiting for my answer. It made me long for her. I wanted to send her an SMS, just to wish her a safe journey to Heidelberg but stopped myself because it didn't look like a dry business ethics. On the contrary, what I was about to do was unethical. The thought that Karolina or Isabel might find out that I have any relations with an InSup applicant besides the submission-related ones, spooked me. I even felt a sort of gratitude towards Katja: although unceremoniously, but she prevented a big mistake of mine. *You must not have any relations with Alice. Not now.*

Maybe later. When she gets the EU funding, the ethical rules won't apply to you anymore, I ordered to myself.

New mission of Karolina

Every time I reminded Hilde that the improved assessment of the Diadem awaited a new approval, she switched on her syrupy smile and got me stuck in it. "If I am not mistaken, there is another assessment Carlos wasn't happy with," she answered, and I had nothing to say in response.

Indeed, without Karolina, things in M-Unit went increasingly wrong. Carlos returned every second assessment with the comment "insufficient grounds for conclusions" or "not sure we can live with it."

"Not sure I understand what's going on," Isabel said, thumbing one of my unpassed works in disbelief. "It's a good one. If Carlos is missing anything, why doesn't he simply say what?"

"Carlos can't meet us." Hilde shook her head after I had suggested we speak to him. "He is preparing for his first yearly hearing in the Parliament's committee on industry, research and energy."

Indeed, Philipe told me about this hearing. To be more precise, Philipe laughed about it. Each director of a decentralized EU agency had to present to the European parliamentarians in Strasbourg the agency's annual report and withstand a subsequent questions-and-answers session. I thought Carlos was looking forward to this hearing since he constantly spoke about serving Europe and being accountable to EU citizens. But the perspective of being grilled by MEPs[41] "made Carlos' bottom burn without fire" as Philipe expressed himself. So, Philipe had to coach him. They met at the office on Sunday and for several hours Philipe first invented nasty questions and then found the suitable answers to his own questions. "Carlos would love to delegate this hearing to me, but he can't, it's his legal obligation to report to the Parliament," Philipe smirked.

"Philipe is certain that Carlos is well prepared for the hearing. I need him to answer only one very concrete question. Can't he really find time to answer it?" I asked Hilde.

Her face suddenly brightened. "Philipe told you about the hearing? Why don't you ask Philipe for advice about the Diadem? He is very good. Maybe he will even be in a position to answer your question, or at least share some fresh ideas?"

I never saw Philipe sitting at the computer and working. I met him in the staff kitchenette or at the desks of other colleagues. Every time I entered his office, he was on the phone or chatting with his office mate Lukasz, head of the Sport Unit. When I came to see him this time, he was already at the doorway, going downstairs for a

---

[41] Abbreviation of "Member of the European Parliament"

cigarette. I followed him. We arrived at an emergency exit with a big glass penthouse protecting smokers from the wind.

"I need to have a rest from the office, you know," Philipe sneered, lighting up the cigarette.

He offered me another one. I couldn't resist although the last time I smoked was when I was a student. A few puffs did me good. "Nice place," I said, watching the dark mirror of the River Main under the lukewarm February sun.

Philip nodded. With eyes half closed, he looked like a tired eagle after the successful hunt. "So what can I do for you?" he suddenly turned to me.

To start with, I told him how my Centrobank boss Sergey Vladimirovich Kamarinov asked Veronika's team lead Sascha Perevalov to improve the media monitoring report. It was one of those moments when Sergey Vladimirovich was in a bad mood and was expressing himself mainly with unpronounceable swear words. Poor Sascha ran back to the monitoring team. Having no clue how to proceed, he opted to do everything possible. He requested Nika and others to add more articles, make each summary longer, and purchase more subscriptions. Late at night Sascha, sweating from tension and fatigue, presented to Kamarinov the new media monitoring report. By then, Sergey Vladimirovich's mood improved, and he explained that he only wanted the first sentence in each item to be highlighted in bold.

I sighed. "Philipe, I think I am in the same trap as Sascha Perevalov. Carlos wants me to do better, but I am sure he has in mind something specific. Unfortunately, I can't read his mind, but Hilde believes you might help me."

Philipe constructed a crooked smile on his lips. "Broomy sends you to me? What's the point?!" After I told him about all my misadventures with the Diadem assessment, he grinned. "I understand it better now. I feel for you and I am happy to help you right away." He crisscrossed me with the edge of his hand still holding a cigarette and said in a bass voice imitating a priest, "I empower you thereupon to tell Broomy that me, Philipe Fernandez, said your assessment is good."

"And you won't even look at it?"

Philipe waved me off. "Why should I? Broomy simply wants to cover her ass with my name. Let it be."

"Why would she need it?" I asked.

Philipe looked at me with a playful horror and let out a long stream of smoke. "Because our dear Broomy hasn't the faintest idea what Carlos wants and even less does she know what to do. So, she found a smart way out: she hopes Carlos will not dare to reject your assessment if she tells him I found it good." He butted out his cigarette, threw it in the ash bin, and added, "Now when I am telling you this, let me be more cautious and glance at it."

Philipe went the extra mile with my assessment: he tweaked the text here and there, and only afterwards sent me an email with a two-paragraph positive feedback. This didn't work. Seeing no revolutionary suggestions from Philipe, Hilde didn't dare to resubmit the Diadem to Carlos. After my persistent reminders, she came up with a new idea. "Let us improve all the assessments that he criticized and send them to Carlos in one go," she told me in an oily voice.

I was underwater. The thoughts about backlog from last year, badly done assessments, and new applications that arrived every week were tail lamping in my head and didn't allow me to concentrate. I started skipping our joint breakfasts with Ian. I simply couldn't sit and chat when so much work was waiting for me. I found it irritating when colleagues in the staff kitchenette tried to make small talk with me. It felt like they were stealing my time. Every morning I bought in a supermarket two packs of sandwiches and ate one for breakfast and another one for lunch. In a couple of weeks, I couldn't look anymore at those triangle bread pieces cemented with creamy cheese and unidentifiable chunks of meat. But I kept buying those sandwiches to punish myself. *When you perform better, you can start having normal breakfasts and lunches again, but now you deserve only this*, I said to myself. One Sunday morning I woke up so terrified that I couldn't stay at home anymore and ran to the office. Hardly did I switch on my laptop, I saw Karolina with two carton cups of coffee.

"I saw you entering the building and decided to wish you a good morning," she said joyfully, holding out a coffee. "Do I remember right, you drink Americano?"

It came to my mind that I forgot to eat at home. I couldn't even recall whether I had brushed my teeth. "Do you work on weekends because of the transparency register?" I asked, taking a coffee cup and secretly checking whether my jeans and hoody looked clean. Karolina, dressed casually in jeans and a black pullover, looked much more business-like compared to me. She was full of joyful energy and keen on sharing it.

In the beginning, the transparency register was hell. Nobody in the Agency knew InSup should keep count of meetings with externals. Nobody recorded or worse, remembered anything. In December last year, the request of the European Commission to submit the transparency register came like a thunderbolt from the blue. Carlos became nervous and begged Karolina to step in. (I was about to remind her that Carlos didn't leave her the choice, but she seemed to have accepted the new version of December events, and I shut my mouth up). Karolina approached her new task with the usual thoroughness. She started by asking the Commission to postpone the deadline. Then she checked the outlook calendars of Carlos and all heads of units, analyzed the Agency's visitor notifications; talked to the financial unit in charge of compensating the staff travel expenses, and finally brought all these bits into a single database. It was still not ideal, but good enough to be shared.

At least Karolina didn't receive any complaints from the Commission's Directorate General for Internal Market and Entrepreneurship, to which InSup must report. She gazed at me, not without pride: but there is no time to rest on the laurels. Now Karolina was busy with developing a better tool for recording our future meetings.

The way she explained the details about our new transparency register reminded me of the day we met. The day I decided I wanted to be like her. Karolina had a manner of approaching problems not as tragedies but as challenges that she could successfully solve. Now she seemed to have found a new mission, which made her enthusiastic again.

I also understood why she looked more business-like than me: on Sunday morning she wore her usual black kajal make-up and a chunky silver neckless. *All her despair and offence she left in M-Unit, with me*, I thought sadly.

"What about yourself?" Karolina finally asked.

I don't think she meant to pose a psychoanalytical question, but she did. I couldn't help telling her that Carlos rejected The Diadem Project. My words ran ahead of my thoughts when I was telling how Isabel and I enriched the assessment; and how Isabel got from her European Commission counterpart the breakdown of migraine complaints by age group. Thanks to these statistics, I could significantly change the narrative of the assessment. I presented the Diadem as an improvement for the "senior European generation," "the working EU generation" and "the European youth." Isabel incorporated all possible "favorite topics of EU institutions": strategic thinking, encouragement of diversity, bringing added value to Europe, and ensuring the quality of life of EU citizens.

Yet, the Diadem still wasn't approved and M-Unit was sinking under the applications that Carlos kept returning to me and those I had no time to assess. "I was wrong when I thought I could work in an EU institution," I said bitterly to Karolina. "I can't, I don't understand what they all want from me."

I talked non-stop for quite some time. Only when paused, did I notice I pronounced my monologue in unison with the wind, which in stormy weather got loud on the 25th floor of our skyscraper. I went silent, but the wind kept moaning. Karolina looked at me empathically.

"You know, working for Europe is a big responsibility and a big challenge," she started in an emollient voice. "We all need to reformat ourselves and constantly improve. Sometimes it's hard, but I am sure you will manage."

"What makes you think so?" I grumbled.

"UUUH," howled the wind, confirming my doubts.

Karolina came closer and touched my shoulder lightly. I felt like hugging her but didn't dare. "People like you are very much needed here because you want to change the world for the better," she raised her voice to thunder down the screaming wind. "Please don't give up. Learn from Carlos and Hilde, keep working, keep improving. This is what an EU institution is about!"

Chapter 4 U-Turn

On the Philosopher's Walk

I can feel it coming in the air...[42].

The song of Phil Collins ear-wormed in my head the entire way to Heidelberg. Tonight I had no questions about The Diadem Project. After the evening of медляки in Barenik, we spoke on the phone twice. Both times I ordered myself to be disinterested and official but slipped into being myself. I don't remember why we started talking about Heidelberg and Alice suddenly said, "You never actually saw it. Why don't you come over this Friday and I'll show you the city?"

I took a breath to pronounce a dry "sorry-maybe-next-time" but instead I heard myself saying, "Thank you, I'd love to." Now the notion that I am meeting an InSup applicant for no reason, planted the stirrings of dismay in me.

Alice was waiting on the platform. As soon as she noticed me, she waved and went forward. "After that lovely evening in Frankfurt, it's my turn to offer you a pleasant afternoon in Heidelberg," she said joyfully.

In the spring light, her brown eyes got a ripe-cherry touch. She was dressed simply but carefully, wearing dark blue jeans, and a

---

[42] "In the air tonight" by Phil Collins

light-beige woolen jacket over a thin burgundy pullover. She looked subtly seductive.

"You found that evening lovely? After everything you saw?" I asked, observing her face.

Alice pressed her lips together. *She put on lipstick*, I realized. A bit of peachy lip gloss underscored the beautiful line of her mouth.

"I didn't see anything that would make me feel bad," she slightly blushed. "And after all, I am sure you didn't want it that way." She regarded me levelly.

Her blushing warmed up my heart. Suppressing a smile, I returned her gaze, "You are very sharp-sighted, as usual."

We drove a couple of stations by tram and afterward marched through the historical Heidelberg. Its colorful streets offered a view of the mountain Odenwald covered with the light green fog. The weather was ideal: sunny and cool.

"I hardly remember the beginning of March being so beautiful," I couldn't help saying when we turned and went out to a large quay.

"Heidelberg is one of the few cities in the Rhein-Main area that was not destroyed during World War II," Alice replied in a tone of a tour guide. "I guess you know that the city center in Frankfurt was rebuilt in the 20th century. But here, in Heidelberg, everything you see is authentic." We went to a bridge. "This is the most famous bridge, the Alte Brücke." The wind disheveled her dark chocolate hair, making me wish to touch it. "From here you can see the Heidelberg Castle and opposite is a fancy area of Neuenheim."

Neuenheim looked like an overturned glass of matcha tea: a light-green mountain on top and the whitish foam of almond trees at the bottom. The quay was covered with little café tables. We walked through the sounds of conversations and fountain waters. Alice was telling about the tragic destruction of the Heidelberg Castle by the Sun King. I liked her voice and her long fingers with bent-down phalangeal bones that were pointing at the things around us. Somehow, I knew her fingers were warm and if I pressed them between my palms, I would be warm too. But every time I was about to succumb to this temptation, I stopped myself. I knew I didn't deserve it.

We bought crêpes with cheese, ham, and herbs, and kept walking. "I hope you are not against going up the hill," Alice said. "I am bringing you to the Philosophers' Walk. It offers a delightful view of the city."

"Who were those philosophers?"

"The city's legend says they were university professors and students. For locals, they all were 'philosophers'. They liked this area a lot."

We approached a narrow street flanked by stone walls. It ran up and to the side. "I won't be surprised at all if a crusader on a horse or one of Robin Hood's bowmen pops up on this street." I touched the wall fleeced with moss. It was soft.

"This is our Snake Path," Alice said. She put her hand next to mine on the wall, which made me shiver. "In summer these dry-stone walls are getting warm, so lizards and little snakes come here to sunbathe. That's where the name comes from. According to another legend, the Snake Path was called like this because of the many twists of its course. Shall we?"

The Snake Path turned out to be quite steep. For fifteen minutes, we marched in silence. But then it paid off: we ended up in a romantic landscape. Surrounded by the tender green of spring trees, we looked at Heidelberg below and far over under the darkening sky.

"I think I saw this place in fine art museums. The only difference is that on paintings there are mythological or biblical characters around and here there is nobody," I said.

Alice laughed. "Well spotted. The city is located in a warm valley. There are cypresses, lemon trees, rhododendrons, and other plants that grow in Italy, for example. So Heidelberg's inhabitants enjoy the same landscape as Renaissance painters did."

We sat down on a bench, Alice took out of her small rucksack two little bottles of water and held out one to me. "I always prepare a lot of water for the Philosphers' Walk." She made a big sip and gave a long look at the horizon while smiling to herself. In front lay the river Neckar and the orange-red scattering of roofs. Quietness surrounded us like a cloud and the city sounds seemed to come from far away. I was sure if I tended my hand and embraced her shoulders, she would move closer to me. But I prohibited myself to think of it.

"It feels like being somehow above the daily routine, like watching life from the Garden of Eden," I said after a long inner fight with my instinct.

Alice nodded. "A perfect place to disconnect and clear your mind, especially before a long shift in hospital."

"Before, not after?"

"After the shift, I only need a long sleep. But before work, I must not be preoccupied with my problems. Otherwise, it's difficult to talk to patients."

I was glad I could redirect my longing into questions about her attitude toward the people she had to cure. She said she often wondered why medical schools didn't teach students how to talk to patients: how not to scare them, how not to raise false expectations, and how to foster a collaborative relationship with a patient and their family. Everybody thought that such mastery came automatically as long as a doctor had good medical knowledge. But this was so wrong. She, Alice, spent quite some time teaching herself to be a sympathetic doctor while protecting herself from an emotional burn-out.

She sighed, took another sip, and stretched her long legs in jeans and white sneakers. It was another suitable moment to hug her and keep sitting on the bench like this, but I couldn't do it. The only thing I had the guts to do was be honest with her.

"Alice, maybe the Diadem won't receive the EU funding from InSup. And the reason for it is me," I blurted.

First, she looked at me dubiously and then decisively shook her head. "No, it can't be because of you."

It felt so easy to confess I turned out to be an amateur, incapable of working for Europe. We stood up and continued our walk. Alice was listening to me like an attentive doctor. It opened me up. I told her that without Karolina I have been making mistake after mistake and had no clue how to stop this negative spiral. And now my managers started realizing that I was useless, which is why they refused to approve the Diadem assessment. But what is even worse, I lacked the competence to persuade them.

Alice took me at the elbow. It was so charmingly natural, but I forced myself not to think of her fingers lying on my arm. "I have no clue how to work in your agency," Alice said. "But I recall that when we met in VorschungsLab you were well prepared, attentive, and curious. Yinzi and I immediately liked you. Can it be that we are facing an impostor phenomenon here?"

I had no idea what she was talking about.

"People often doubt their skills and talents," she clarified, "but sometimes their doubts are so strong that they explain their success by some kind of deception and become afraid to be exposed as frauds."

"The latter sounds exactly like my case," I replied. "Just there is one little difference: I really don't work well, otherwise our director wouldn't have rejected my assessment of the Diadem. This job is too big for me," I concluded, willing to punish myself.

Alice sniggered. "And what if your director is right, and it's me who is bad? Remember, Doctor Roth, who canceled our presentation on the day when you tested the Diadem? In the beginning, he treated us like any other research project conducted within the University Hospital. But then he became more and more critical. Once Yinzi heard him saying that the Diadem was counter-scientific and that we didn't belong there. He often hinders our participation in conferences and seminars. The one in Frankfurt was a lucky coincidence because the organizers approached me directly and even then, Doctor Roth tried to hinder my participation. And recently he decided to give Yinzi and myself more hospital shifts and less time for our research."

We stopped at another observation point. From here the red roofs of Heidelberg looked like soldiers who came to the Neckar River, to bend their knees to us. I glanced at Alice. There was certain comradeship in the way she smiled and nodded while looking down at Heidelberg, as if at a good old friend. Her profile reminded me of old Romain coins. The sun started getting dark orange and cold.

"And by the way," she suddenly added, "your agency won't be the first to reject us. A couple of other organizations also refused to fund the Diadem. Who cares? As long as we believe in our device, we won't stop. Day after day, month after month... with the inventions like ours even tiny progress costs hours of doubts and years of work."

There was zero drama in her voice, just a strength of spirit. I couldn't resist her anymore. I put my hands on her shoulders. She felt exactly like she sounded: strong and reliable. She didn't move over. I started caressing her warm neck and hair.

"I admire you for what you are. Not everybody would keep up in such circumstances," I said. My fingertip found her silent neck artery. I felt her heartbeat, which was no less rapid than mine. She wanted to look aside, but I was holding her head. I wanted her to keep looking in my eyes.

She took a deep breath. "I'd pay a higher price if I drop everything and all my life keep wondering whether I was right or wrong."

Was it her answer or the way it resonated in me? But I didn't dare to touch her anymore. I took her thin warm fingers and kissed them as if I were her soldier or servant and she – my queen.

We silently walked back. The city was slowly getting illuminated by street lights, and it was full of Friday evening joy. Everywhere people were sitting at the tables under the artificial hitters. The air smelled of fried meat and coffee. On our way back to the Train Station, I was looking for proper farewell words, but everything sounded either dramatic or ridiculous.

Only before entering the train that would bring me to Frankfurt, I finally said, "Alice, you are the last person I would like to disappoint. But I don't have any moral right to get closer to you, not until I am done with the Diadem assessment."

Alice caressed my hair with her warm fingertips. "My disappointment has absolutely nothing to do with your work." She pecked my cheek and went away.

Maxim to Veronika. A risky guess

Nika, privet,

Time to talk seriously. You didn't leave me any possibility to hear your voice, fine. Let's talk in writing. Since we had split, I couldn't stop thinking of you. You became my curse. Even after we have landed at different ends of the world, I couldn't let you go. Although in a new country with a new job, despair still poisoned my soul. And the only antidote was a dream that one day we would be together again. Stupid to hope for it, isn't it?

However, this hope kept me running all these months. I avidly filtered your stingy emails for any details of your new life. Once I even thought of making a surprise visit to Hong Kong and you know what stopped me? The sexual adventures you started sharing in your next emails. Ok, instead of flying to you I decided to date somebody too, fortunately, Barenik provides many opportunities for it. But it's hard to be together with one woman while longing for another. My girlfriends quickly felt it too and left me, to my relief.

After one love didn't drive out another, I took a closer look at your boyfriend. It wasn't just jealousy but also a wish to understand what attracted you. God knows how many hours I spent trying to figure out what he is and whether he is a good match for you. It turned out to be an impossible task: our common friends didn't know anything; your Odnoklassniki[43] account seemed to be dead since you left Moscow; even the company you work for in Hong Kong has a rather barren website.

'What if she on purpose doesn't want to leave any traces?' I asked myself. This kicked my thoughts in a new direction.

For example, I remembered that one day you sent me your picture, and I didn't recognize you. You didn't answer whether it was a wig or you dyed black your wonderful wheat-colored hair. Never mind what you did, but one thing I knew for sure: it wasn't your idea

---

[43] Russian social network launched in 2006

152

because you always loved the golden silk of your hair for the magnetic impact it had on men. Then somebody or some circumstances must have forced you to do so.

Another thing that made me wonder was that pool party you once wrote about. At first glance it sounded like a glamorous phantasy: the pool on the roof, bikini as a dress code, extravagant cocktails. At midnight the party host declared a "free love hour" by taking off your bikini top in front of everybody and kissing you. The next sentence in your email reads: "While I was giving him a blow-job another girl approached us, he kissed her and then turned away from me to fuck her from behind. I put my hands on his shoulders and watched both of them. Only then did I dare to look around and see how others reacted to this show? And you know what? Others were already busy with each other. Despite my excitement, I felt a bit disappointed."

After having read it, I thought it was the party host you were dating. But then you wrote your boyfriend had spent a couple of weeks in Macao repairing something in the Venetian Macao Casino and you could visit him over the weekend and stay in his tiny hotel room. Is a service technician throwing erotic pool parties? That sounded unrealistic. When trying to resolve this puzzle I suddenly thought 'What if the pool party host is not your boyfriend? What if in that ménage à trois you were just an invited number three who is supposed to warm up the couple and then stand and watch?' If so, what made you play this role, feelings? This sounds ridiculous, you are too proud for that.

Plenty of different questions and explanations swarmed in my poor head, which was aching from jealousy. And then I suddenly remembered a very strange talk with Sergey Vladimirovich Kamarinov. I never told you about it before because I didn't want to upset you. It happened when I resigned from the Centrobank and was collecting signatures for my exit clearance list. The assistant let me in. As usual, Kamarinov sat at his massive desk with no computer monitor but therefore with a stone-gray penholder, crystal paperweight, and bronze table clock, - each of these items could look like a weapon in his big hand especially if he were in a bad mood.

"Ah, Reut, come in. Where should I sign?" he said without looking at me.

I put in front of him my clearance list and showed him the place for signature. He signed, said "Ну, бывай"[44] and lost interest in me.

"Thank you very much, Sergey Vladimirovich, all the best," I said and turned away with relief.

"Reut," he suddenly called me back. "Are you aware that we have surveillance cameras in the media monitoring room?" he asked when I approached his desk again.

---

[44] Goodbye (slangy Russian)

154

I shook my head and tried hard to construct a puzzled facial expression. The memory of how we made love there at Christmas flashed in my head. I felt I was blushing. Kamarinov pierced me with joyful satisfaction.

"So that you know: we keep the records as long as we need them. Now hurry up, you have plenty of signatures to collect."

Back then, I thought he just wanted to intimidate me as he always did with all of us. But now it gave me an additional hint. Nika, did you know they had cameras there? Can it be that making love to me in front of the cameras was the last trial you had to pass? Last, because in the first days of the New Year, before the official Russian holidays were even over, you were offered to go to Hong Kong. And if so, you are not working in China just as a simple IT expert!

I will not ask you what you are doing, and I definitely don't want to know who your real employer is. Just give me a sign that my guesses have ground: write a 'vale'[45] or something like this at the end of your next email. That would be enough of a sign for me. I swear it will remain between us forever.

To reassure you that I won't undertake any surprise visits or investigations, let me share with you my plans. There is one assessment I must approve with Carlos, our director. Never was I so sure of the quality of work I have done. I won't exaggerate by

---

[45] Be well (Latin)

saying that my career at InSup and even my whole life depends on this approval. Sending it directly to Carlos would be against our internal rules because I should first get approval from Hilde, my team lead. But tomorrow I am going to jump over her head because she is clueless and showing my work to her would have no added value.

Wish me luck. Maybe later I will explain why this assessment is so important to me.

Feedback from Carlos

An Outlook invitation thrummed into my inbox, making my stomach flip: Carlos. I was invited to come to his office right now. The invitation's subject line was empty. I already knew: if in an EU agency, you are not given time to prepare for a meeting, it's either shit or fun.

Carlos was waiting for me in front of his office. "Surri for the shehrt notice, Maxim," he quacked. "I asked Cristina to schedule this meeting, maybe she forgot." With a gesture reminding me of a king greeting his court nobility, Carlos offered me a seat. "I want to talk about the assessment you sent me in the morning."

"I would like to talk about it too," I replied and the lights of Frankfurt skyline in the window winked at me haughtily.

The long meeting table made me feel smaller. I displaced my chair as far as possible from the table, for this time I couldn't allow myself to be paltry. Carlos sat silently, carefully examining the corner of the table. "I have something impehrtant to say," he finally said. "But fehrst let me ask you one question: what does it mean to you wehrking at InSup?"

"New professional life," I replied quickly, wondering what he was aiming at.

"What else?"

"A chance to support start-ups and their amazing ideas."

Carlos stuck out his tongue as if he had just tasted something disgusting. "Then let me put it differently: to whom is our agency accountable?"

Thanks to him, I knew the answer by heart, for he never missed a chance to slide it into every talk. "We are accountable to European citizens."

Carlos nodded. "Indeed 40% of the InSup budget is provided by the European Commission; the otherr 60% are financed by EU Memberr States."

He paused waiting for my reaction, but I only politely stared at him.

"Maxim, these are not empty wehrds, wehrking for the benefit of all Europeans is in the DNA of our agency. You must remember: every day of our wehrk is paid by Europe and consequently every single thing we do should be conscious and efficient. Do you understand?"

"Yes," I squeezed from myself and imagined how I was smashing his left eyeglass.

Carlos' gaze changed. I followed it. He was looking at my right hand, which I clenched into a fist. "You have nothing to say?" he whispered.

"At InSup we serve European citizens, I understand," I forced myself to pronounce it with maximum conviction while unclenching my fist. For the first time, I felt sick when saying those words. Tonight they made no sense anymore. At the same time, I was getting bogged down in the syrup of all those statements about serving Europe. I bestirred myself. "Carlos, serving everybody is too abstract. With my assessment of The Diadem Project, I am serving those Europeans who suffer from migraine. Especially because the younger generations are increasingly impacted by this disease as compared to 50 years ago. Why was it so wrong to send you the Diadem again? Young Europeans are more biased towards medication than their grandparents, and they would be very much interested in curing their migraine in a non-medical way. The Diadem will serve them well, and so will I!"

Carlos winced as if having a bitter pill in the mouth, which he didn't feel like swallowing. "Let me rymind you, Maxim, that wehrrking in an EU agency means ryspect towards colleagues and robust processes. You sent me the file without Hilde's approval. It is a wehrisome sign of disryspect of our processes and of our carparate culchar. This is unacceptable and I want to pyrsonally tell it to you."

I tossed diplomacy aside. My months-long frustration with Hilde resulted in a theatrical monologue where I described to Carlos all her tricks to avoid steering and decision-making. "In the beginning, I thought we badly understood each other. But now I am sure she simply has no clue how a good start-up assessment should look like," I concluded and drew my breath.

Carlos was silent. I looked at his unblinking eyes behind the round glasses, and a premonition started spreading from my head down to my stomach. I realized that I had just spoken to an emptiness. Suddenly he hissed, "Hilde is an excellent professional, excellent. And your assessment is not good enough indeed."

I gasped. "She doesn't have a single independent idea in her head. She's only excellent in sending emails back and forth."

Carlos' face took a dyspeptic expression, he gazed away. "I don't like your tone, Maxim, you should take crehticism more constructively," he said in a professor-like voice without looking at me. "Blaming others for yo ron puhr performance is not appreciated hirr."

His alleged discernment drove me mad. Be it in the Centrobank, Kamarinov would have been straight-forward: he would have passed the Diadem (in my presence) to another expert saying, that "this braindead woodpecker Reut is capable of nothing." I would prefer such a humiliating resolution to Carlos' swamping diplomacy.

I exhaled and forced myself to try it again. "Listen, Carlos," I said in a mollified tone, "I can complete the Diadem submission very well, really. Just tell me what you are missing, and I'll make it right."

He jumped from his seat as if seeing something disgusting or scary. I stood up too and curdled. Carlos's face changed completely. He looked like a snake that was going to attack: half-open mouth and endless hate behind round glasses. While I stood hypnotized, wondering whether I was going to face a hispanisized, small copy of Kamarinov, Carlos regained his temper. His mouth cramped into something that he probably considered a smile. "So far your assessments have been far below urr stehndards. And yor negativity contradicts the European team spirit."

"I just want to give Europeans an additional way to cure their migraine," I said cautiously, but Carlos didn't listen to me anymore. He seemed to be driven by his inner thoughts. Chest heaving, arms crossed, he shrieked, "I can't afford a toxic climate in the agency. It hinders ur wehrk for the benefit of Europeans. I can't stand it anymore. You... you don't belong here!" Should he have on his enormous table a single item, suitable to throw into me, I am sure, he would have done it.

"Should I resign?" I asked, hardly recognizing my own trembling voice.

"You said it yourself," he squawked.

Stupefied, I didn't remember how I returned to my office, where a new email was already waiting for me.

From: Fadila Ribeiro Villescas

To: Maxim Reut

CC: Carlos de Santos Gomez

Subject: Warning

Dear Maxim,

I would like to warn you that HR received numerous reports about your non-compliance with InSup's corporate rules. It's of utmost importance that you align yourself with our ethics and spirit. HR will follow up with you.

Kind regards,

Fadila

I already got used to the fact that Fadila never expressed herself clearly at the first attempt. I continued staring at the monitor and wasn't surprised when another email from her fell in the inbox.

From: Fadila Ribeiro Villescas

To: Maxim Reut

CC: Carlos de Santos Gomez

Subject: Warning

And one more thing.

Internal rules, procedures, code of conduct and corporate ethics are driving the work of each EU agency. Disrespecting and breaching them seriously harms our efficiency. It endangers our little InSup family, all of us.

Another minute later she sent me a new email.

From: Fadila Ribeiro Villescas

To: Maxim Reut

CC: Carlos de Santos Gomez

Subject: Warning

You are kindly asked to consult all the documents mentioned in my earlier email. They can be found on the webpage of the European Commission. Please ensure compliance!

KR,

Fadila

I felt my stomach drop as I tried to digest my defeat with Carlos and the truth that I turned out to be incapable of working in a European institution. A thought about Alice jabbed into my heart. It appeared that I didn't deserve to be together with her. How quickly and easily could I fail everywhere?! I approached my office window: behind it, Frankfurt looked like a black desert.

Time to admit it: you don't belong here, I said to myself grimly. *Write your resignation letter, be good at least in this.*

"Может, поговорим?[46]," I suddenly heard a voice behind my back.

Girl with contacts

I jerked. *Was it possible that I heard Russian within InSup?!*

It was Isabel. Her face was unusually taut, almost unrecognizable.

"You speak Russian?!"

She hastily waved me away. "Did you send out your resignation to Carlos?"

"I was going to. Wait… how do you know about it?"

She exhaled with relief, sat on the corner of my desk, and flipped her auburn locks. "I was afraid I might be late." I goggle-eyed her without answering. She looked back at me pensively, sighed, and finally said, "Maxim, I owe you an explanation. But for now, please forget resignation and let's get out of here."

---

[46] Shall we talk? (Russian)

Isabel Aquilina grew up in a strict catholic family, which was not so unusual for Malta. It became clear very early that she was too intelligent to blindly believe and obey. At family gatherings, instead of playing with a dozen of her cousins, she preferred to sit at the table with adults and pose them unexpectedly valid questions.

When she grew older, she started reading newspapers, watching documentaries, and having her own opinion about everything. It became a family attraction. The relatives on purpose posed her tricky questions and blew out their cheeks when getting her firm answers. But nobody in the family took her seriously. Her aunts prattled with her mother in lowered voices about arranging a marriage for Isabel as soon as possible - to save the poor girl from becoming a bluestocking.

No wonder right after the school Isabel ran from Malta as far away as possible: to Scotland. She easily entered (with a scholarship!) St Andrews University to study at the Faculty of Art and to have her first serious relationship with a course mate. The latter, by the way, proposed to her. An average offspring of a British aristocratic family, he wasn't an idiot and didn't want to fool away a marriage with a "Bright Maltese" (Isabel's nickname in St Andrews). But she recalled her aunts, decisively refused, and passed the Concours[47] to the European Commission.

---

[47] A multi-layered recruitment competition and examination to select staff to all EU institutions

Only when she became a staff member of the Commission's directorate-general for agriculture, did she, for the first time, visit her family in Malta, where absolutely nothing had changed. The aunts kept talking about marriage; this time because they saw Isabel as a ticket to a pleasant, settled life. But Isabel didn't want anybody to share the European Union's capital with. She returned to Brussels alone. Nobody could fit into the city better than this sharp-minded girl speaking freely almost all languages of "Old Europe": French, German, Italian, and Spanish besides her mother tongues, English and Maltese.

But then something happened that Isabel later qualified as the biggest disaster: a breathtaking love affair with a colleague. After some time, breath was regained, and love began to hurt. No cozy Christmas Eve together, no visits to friends, no romantic evenings in restaurants and other public places, for which Brussels was too small. The married man with four kids belonged neither to her nor to himself. The haut fonctionnaire[48] in the third generation he was everything she loved: curious, vivid, and cheerful. Only one thing she hated in him: he didn't want to change his life. He could offer her only short evenings and long weekends (when his wife brought their three kids to France for family visits).

Happiness and loneliness don't usually match. Breaking up with him was hard, especially because he didn't want (or maybe was too

---

[48] Public servant (French)

weak) to let her go. Every time she left him, he made her return and reunite with him with increased almost suicidal passion. To save her soul, she went far away. The 3-year contract in Moscow, in the EU delegation to Russia, was a timely opportunity, which she immediately grabbed. She invested all her energy in learning Russian and studying the country.

At this point in her story, I had to admit she knew Moscow very well. She dropped some astute observations about the places she had seen; easily operated with the names of streets and metro stations; finally, among her favorite places, she named those I never visited. When her Russian contract was over, she went for another 3 years to the EU Intellectual Property Office in Alicante. There she met Carlos, who searched for EU employees interested in working for the freshly created EU agency in Frankfurt – InSup.

"What about your uhm…French colleague, you never saw him again?" I asked.

Not really. They stopped being addicted to each other but managed to stay friends. Since then, she has met him now and then in Brussels. He is very thankful that she ruined neither his family life nor his reputation while cutting this Gordian knot of their love. In the meantime, he made such a splendid career that she doesn't dare to convey his name to anybody. He thinks Isabel sacrificed her career in Brussels because of him. She disagrees but prefers not to persuade him, for he helps her with so many tricky problems and stands ready to do it again and again.

"Why didn't you tell me you lived in Moscow?"

Isabel faintly shrugged. "I learned to be suspicious of people from Russia. They surprised me too often and not always positively. I thought it wouldn't harm if I waited a bit before telling you."

Isabel brought me to a place called "Hemingway", a café with glass walls. She resolutely went to a little table overlooking the River Main. While I was taking a seat and looking around, she exchanged German greetings with a waiter. The place was crowded but a tiny candle on the table and the inky black mirror of the River Main outside, made me feel snug. Isabel put her hands with locked fingers on the table, freckles popped up on the upper part of her nose and cheeks.

"Please take my words seriously: no way you should resign."

"You still didn't explain: how did you know I was going to?"

She gave me a long measuring look, as if still considering whether she could trust me. Finally, she said, "Since you came to me with the Diadem, I kept wondering about what was going on around this assessment. Recently I finally could explain it to myself, but this is a type of guess I would prefer not to believe in. 'All right,' I said to myself, 'if I am speculating correctly, they will soon move Maxim out from M-Unit. As long as it doesn't happen, the speculation should not be outspoken.' And tonight, Cristina told me about the email you received from Fadila (as Carlos' assistant she sees all the emails that land in his inbox). To me, it smelled not just like changing positions but like resignation. That's why I ran to you."

The waiter brought Isabel's order. While he was placing on our table red wine and little plates with olives, sausages, and something else, Isabel said, "It's a perfect place for business meetings. The tables are far from each other, we can talk undisturbed."

I looked around. Indeed, the tables were occupied by men and women in business suits. I couldn't spot any couples. My eyes alighted on Isabel: one couldn't take her for a romantic date either. Her face was taut; the usually attentive gaze was absent, as if she was recalling something unpleasant.

"Some weeks ago, Carlos asked me to shift my efforts to the Science unit," she went on once the waiter left. "I was surprised because I never worked with S-Unit. My portfolio mostly relates to areas like medicine, sports, and food. 'Why suddenly science?' I thought. Carlos has been rejecting almost every second assessment of M-Unit. Wouldn't it be logical if he asked me to reinforce Medicine and not Science?"

"He thinks I am incompetent and won't be able to make assessments even with your help," I said grimly.

She winced, and the freckles on her pale face became dark gray. "I think the explanation lies in the way InSup reports about the start-ups that got our funding. We only indicate the title and the description, but we don't say, which unit assessed the project. Mind you, S-Unit deals a lot with biotechnologies that are very often linked to medicine. So if InSup reports about biotechnological start-ups, it would look like M-Unit still works."

"I don't follow you. Why to play off the Science work for my efforts in M-Unit?"

Isabel took a wooden pick from the plate of tapas, instantly pinned on it a black olive, a piece of chorizo, and sent it into her mouth. "It's because you don't know Carlos the way I do. He doesn't mean to help you. He wants everything he is responsible for to be perfect or at least look like it. By removing Karolina and forcing you to resign, he would kill M-Unit. However, by shifting me to Science he could still create the impression that the medical start-ups are considered all right."

"But Carlos didn't remove Karolina, it was Broomy," I objected.

Isabel pinned a cube of cheese on her stick. "This is very naive to think that Hilde could remove Karolina, the most experienced and hard-working expert, without Carlos' approval. I was surprised when Carlos made Hilde responsible for the Chinese delegation. Why do so, if this was usually the task of Karolina? But when I saw how it all developed, I became certain that he orchestrated the conflict between two ladies and then simply watched Broomy revenging Karolina for her poor performance."

We went silent. Isabel was fiddling with the stalk of her wineglass with both hands.

"This sounds plausible," I said. "Broomy and Karolina are so different that even I could forecast future tension between them. But, Isabel, you are wrong about me and my resignation. It's me who misbehaved. I jumped over Broomy's head. Today in the morning I sent Carlos the Diadem assessment, once again, without Broomy's approval. Carlos has a right to fire me because I disrespected our working processes."

Isabel laughed. "I think Carlos and Fadila count very much on your ignorance in this question. This is InSup, Maxim, an EU agency. They can't fire anybody after the successful probation period unless it's something serious, a murder, or any other kind of crime, for which you should be imprisoned. Otherwise, they can't even launch an internal disciplinary procedure against you because you disrespected our rules only once, it's not a repetitive act, do you understand?"

I was too stupefied to answer. Isabel's eyes sought me inquiringly. "Let me guess," she said. "It was you who asked Carlos whether you should resign. Then he gave you an answer, which could be interpreted as 'yes' but I am sure it wasn't a clear yes."

I gasped. She took it as a confirmation of her words. She leaned closer so that I felt her perfume, the scent of wet grass. "Carlos hopes you resign now. By the way, the warning from HR came while you had this unpleasant talk with him. You don't think it's a coincidence, do you?"

I scrunched from a spicy prawn I had just swallowed. "Мда, заразили тебя подозрительностью в Москве[49]," I said enjoying that I could talk to her in my mother tongue. "Now when you explained it, I tend to agree they are trying to frame me into voluntary resignation. But one thing I still don't get: why does Carlos want to kill M-Unit?!"

Isabel took a big sip of wine. "This is a ten-thousand-euro question. I don't know why," she said pensively. Then she looked at me and a cold decisiveness flashed in her eyes. "But we could find the answer together."

Conspirator

When an IT expert who usually runs in a pullover or T-shirt suddenly pops up in your office in full business uniform, including a tie, everybody would feel that something important is going on.

"Hello, Cristina, may I disturb you for five minutes?" Ian asked, fidgeting in the jacket, which he wore for the second time since his job interview in InSup. "Did you or Carlos experience in the last days that your Outlook is getting slower or behaves somehow strange?"

---

[49]Well, you got infected with queerness in Moscow (Russian)

Cristina pierced him through her Harry-Potter-glasses, "No, are we supposed to?"

"Hopefully not," Ian said serenely, as IT guys usually do when talking about big computer disasters. "Our vendor warned us that after the recent software update, some of his clients were complaining about their laptops. It made us nervous because half of InSup laptops are exactly from the same lot."

"What were clients complaining about?" Cristina asked while Ian was checking the stock number of her computer against something in the papers he held.

"First, the laptop becomes considerably slower. Then you get a black screen for five to ten seconds. This repeats for days. And then clients get the black screen for much longer. According to the reports, some clients couldn't restart anymore and lost the work of the previous twenty-four hours," Ian said without taking his eyes off the papers. "I take note you don't have any complaints, so no patching is required."

Cristina nodded pensively.

"Could you confirm Carlos has no complaints either?"

The reference to Carlos interrupted Cristina's thoughts. "I would prefer to ask Carlos, but he already left for lunch. Could you come back exactly in one hour?"

"No need, just ask him whenever he returns," Ian replied hastily. "Then just write an email to the IT helpdesk, and one of us will come over. Have a nice afternoon."

He turned away, but Cristina was too experienced to let an IT expert walk out of her office. "Wait a moment, Ian! You mentioned patching, what does it mean? How long would it take?"

Ian batted his ginger eyelashes. "I don't know. I would need to install a program that the vendor sent us. It might take ten minutes, maybe longer. Why...?" He made a step towards the door, which expedited Cristina's decision.

"Wait, Ian. Could you install this program anyway on Carlos' laptop? Just to be on the safe side? Now it's a perfect moment while Carlos is out for lunch. And you could report to your team lead that you fully secured Carlos' computer!"

"Hi, everybody," Isabel popped up in Cristina's office. "Cristina, are we still having our lunch?"

"Of course!" Cristina scuttled. "Look, Ian, I will log in for you on Carlos' laptop. And since you are so very kind, could you install this program on my computer too? I am his assistant, my laptop is in no small part decisive for his work. Please!"

Ian sighed. "Ok, I can do it."

"Du bist ein Schatz[50] as Germans would say. I owe you one," Cristina chirped and joyfully flitted away with Isabel by her side.

Twenty minutes later, Ian was in my office with sparkling blue eyes. "I did exactly the way you said. As soon as I tried to leave, Cristina requested me to stay. She insisted on installing the patch on both their computers."

My plan worked. A model of a personal assistant, Cristina couldn't let Ian go without reinforcing the security of Carlos' computer (as she thought). If only she knew Ian had installed a totally different program; the one allowing him to access Carlos' inbox. It looked like a virus scanner and wouldn't cause alarm, at least not with InSup's IT security.

"By the way I installed the same program on Cristina's computer," Ian beamed. "I know, you didn't instruct me about it, but I thought why not since I am already there? After all, we will use it only if we need it. Once we are done, I'll remove everything."

I couldn't recognize my friend anymore. Quiet, laconic, phlegmatic, he seemed to live in full harmony with the universe. I had doubts he would be ready to take the risk and help me with the investigation against Carlos. But without him hacking Carlos' computer, it would have been way more difficult. So I decided to give it a try.

---

[50] You are a treasure (German)

Choosing the words thoroughly, I told Ian about The Diadem Project. I wanted to observe his reaction first. He listened to me dispassionately and even submissively. For a moment, I thought I'd better not embroil him. But when I described our last talk with Carlos and how I was about to resign, Ian exclaimed, "Something is definitely wrong with this arrogant bastard. I wish one day somebody kicks his ass!"

I stared at him with surprise. "Are you also having problems with him?!"

Ian did. A couple of months ago, InSup hired two external IT consultants to set up the IT security infrastructure. Ian was supposed to coordinate their work. He spent some time thinking of the tasks he could give to these two. He wanted to be efficient and ensure continuity so that the three of them could jump for and support each other. Everything was supposed to work well. Then a scandal came. Both IT consultants were Indians and turned out to be from different castes namely "warriors" and "servants". The one from the warrior caste categorically refused to work with the one from the servant caste. First, Ian refused to believe it. Especially because the Servant told him he didn't care about castes. But soon, both consultants started hating each other and ended up completely blocking the working process. Ian couldn't but report to Andreas Briener, the head of IT unit.

Born in a quiet village in Austrian Alps, Andreas worshipped two principles: stay neutral and avoid conflicts. He never disputed with anybody and sometimes made mutually exclusive commitments just because they were requested by different parties. But this time, Andreas agreed with Ian that one consultant, preferably the Warrior, must go. Since any dismissals of external consultants had to be done upon the permission of the executive director, Andreas scheduled a talk with Carlos and asked Ian to join. That meeting took both aback. Carlos announced that without facing financial implications InSup can't suspend or cancel the contracts with the IT consultants who have already started in the agency. "You must find the solution outside the contractual relationship," Carlos stated, and Andreas immediately agreed.

Ian tried to object and even suggested filing a complaint with the company that had sent InSup such consultants. But Carlos stonily called Ian to respect the beliefs and national identity of colleagues for the sake of European values and made it clear that no more discussions on this would be tolerated within InSup walls. During Carlos' speech, Andreas was nodding like a bobblehead and later came up with a solution that could be good for everybody except for Ian.

As of then, Ian was supposed to take over the Warrior's tasks while remaining responsible for the overall IT security. The Warrior misinterpreted the situation and started behaving like a boss who doesn't accept orders from anybody. The consultants kept ignoring each other, which made them useless for the work that required their mutual involvement. In the situations where they were supposed to interact, it was Ian working for both of them. Since then, Andreas avoided any talks with Ian, even when asking his regular "How are you?" he immediately spluttered out meaningless answers, as if afraid to hear Ian's reply.

"Maxim, am so thankful for your trust," Ian told me breezily. "Carlos made me a victim, I hated him, but even more, I hated myself for it. And now thanks to you this feeling is gone." His icy blue eyes narrowed and he added in a suddenly husky voice, "I want blood!"

Detection begins

"What a neat apartment!" Isabel smiled.

Ian shined like a birthday boy in anticipation of a party. I looked around. Although we lived in the same house, we never visited each other's places before. Ian's apartment had the same cut as mine, but I couldn't help feeling that it looked somehow bigger. In "my" bedroom Ian seemed to do everything but sleep: there was a large computer table, two monitors, and three chairs he placed specially for Isabel and myself. One classical guitar and one e-guitar were standing on the wall; the jeans and jackets were accurately hanging on the Ikea stander on another wall. "My" living room in Ian's flat was a dining room with a table in the middle covered for three persons and looking like a garden with flower-patterned table napkins and plates, shiny silver sugar pot, and cream jug.

The three of us stood hesitantly and silently, not knowing what to start with.

"Is Karolina coming too?" Ian suddenly asked.

I shook my head. "I felt it would be wrong. Can't explain why, call it intuition."

"Right so," Isabel nodded approvingly. "Karolina believes that everybody in InSup is like her. Anything we do against Carlos or even Hilde, she would consider an action against herself."

Her words gave me a hint about how to go on. "First of all, guys, let me tell you one thing, which you will have to accept. I am going to be solely responsible for everything we are going to do. If we get caught, I want you to stay silent and leave everything to me. If you disagree, we will end this evening right away."

Ian confusedly stared at Isabel, who was pensive.

"This investigation is my business. I don't want you to be in trouble because I breached InSup ethical rules."

Isabel finally spoke. "This is very much appreciated. We (she looked at Ian searchingly) accept your terms but under one condition." I opened my mouth to object, but she cut me off with a gesture. "If we get caught as you express yourself, you will not make any confessions before you talk to me, ok? I know this system pretty well. It offers ways of wrapping up shit into a sweetie paper, believe me."

We glanced at each other.

"I can feel the floor shaking and the glass begin to break,[51]" the song of Stealth seemed to come from the kitchen. Ian grinned. "My playlist switched on automatically." The three of us burst into laughter. Encouraged, Ian went on. "Why don't we start, I want to show you what I've got so far."

We took seats around his computer desk.

"I downloaded all the meetings and phone calls from Carlos' calendar and compared them with the data in the transparency register prepared by Karolina. As a result, I got over 200 entries that are not mentioned in the transparency register." Ian said, opening an Excel file.

Isabel moved closer to the monitor and put her hand on the mouse. "I trust Karolina's accuracy. We can be sure all the official meetings are in. Cristina once said Carlos includes private events in this calendar: doctor's appointments, kids' parties and even shopping," Isabel said, scrolling down the list. "Besides suspicious contacts we are looking for, there might be plenty of harmless entries. Let's have a closer look."

---

[51] "Judgment Day" by Shaun Smith, Ross O'Reilly, Stealth (UK)

We read in silence. Many entries comprised a name or just one word, for example, "Coche[52]" or "Tintorería"[53]. "Reminders to pick up a car from the workshop or his shirts from the dry cleaner," Isabel supposed.

The three of us gasped simultaneously as one item stated "Isabel Aquilina."

"This is my birthday," Isabel said after a moment of abashment and pointed at the date column. "See, 30 August. I remember he sent me birthday greetings on this day. It positively surprised me."

"And I have my birthday on 31 August," Ian suddenly said.

Isabel glanced at him benevolently and suddenly exclaimed, "Birthdays! He must include plenty of birthdays in his calendar: staff, useful contacts, maybe even friends. Could you sort them out by frequency, Ian? Birthdays should have a yearly one."

"Good idea. If we take them out, we will reduce our list," Ian agreed while typing. Soon we got quite a long list of names. With some of them, we were familiar. For example, Cristina, Philipe, and Fadila were there too. Karolina wasn't.

"How does he choose whom to congratulate?" I wondered. "Only those whom he likes?"

---

[52] Car (Spanish)
[53] Dry cleaner (Spanish)

Isabel was thinking. Suddenly she said resolutely, "Spaniards, Spanish network."

"Well, you are Maltese, aren't you?" I asked mistrustfully.

"Ok, let me correct myself: he congratulates not only Spaniards but also Spanish-speaking or those who are somehow linked to Spain. For example, I speak Spanish and I worked in Alicante. And I see here a name of the colleague who is German, but I know for sure that he has a Spanish wife."

She scraped back her hair in a bun and fixed it with the pencil she took from the inner pocket of her jacket. She didn't notice Ian watching this manipulation like hypnotized and went on. "Now, let me go line by line through the names. I will delete all those that are familiar to me and by this, we will hopefully shorten the list."

In the next hour, we removed the entries related to birthdays and those that were in the transparency register but misspelled. Initially, we wanted to remove the Spanish words related to the household, but then Isabel changed her mind as we couldn't really know what they meant. This left us with around 50 entries.

"Time for a break, I will serve dinner," Ian announced.

"Happy to help," Isabel reacted immediately, and both left for the kitchen.

I stayed at the monitor and continued analysing the list. There were companies I never heard about. There was a monthly entry "Spanish speaking lunch" that included all the colleagues whose birthdays Carlos had on the calendar. Some entries were very detailed (probably they were made by Cristina) and some on the contrary were cryptic and no doubt made by Carlos himself.

The spring twilight filled Ian's living room with mystery.

"Where do you sleep, Ian?" I asked, looking around for a bed.

"Here," Ian pointed at the room where we were about to sit at the table. "This is my bedroom actually; I enjoy sleeping in the middle of the apartment. And the dining table I just temporarily brought from the kitchen."

Only then did I notice that the table was placed between a sofa, which obviously served Ian as a bed, and a bookshelf with the TV on it.

For dinner, Ian served a verbose set of sushi from the Japanese supermarket in the city center. He radiated hospitality and kept offering us soja sauce, water, or beer as if it were a friendly dinner. Once we finished with sushi, he insisted that we have a dessert.

"I usually try to avoid sweets but wouldn't refuse a cup of tea," Isabel said.

"I bought the cakes in Iimory, the Japanese pastry shop," Ian looked at her piteously.

"How can I ruin such a lovely dinner concept," Isabel smiled. "I will try one then."

She insisted on helping Ian to clean the table. They replaced the sushi plate with a plate of tiny white, pink, and light green éclairs filled with vanilla, strawberry, and match-flavored cream. As a crown jewel of the dinner, Ian erected on the table a teapot with freshly brewed Irish breakfast tea.

"What keeps me thinking," Isabel said taking a matcha éclair, "is the word 'Barcelona' in Carlos' calendar. It repeats and blocks his calendar for three hours in the late afternoon. Any idea what it could be?"

Ian suggested a football game but rebutted himself after having checked that Barcelona wasn't playing on these days. Isabel complemented Carlos as a Real Madrid fan. It couldn't be any traveling because the blocker wasn't accompanied by the flight number as was the case with other trips. The family gatherings or friends' visits contained the names of invitees and addresses, nothing of this was mentioned for "Barcelona".

"I think it's a code name he uses for himself," Isabel finally said.

"Wow, what a guess," Ian sneered, shining like a silver sugar pot on the table. He was clearly enjoying this evening.

"Imagine you both are members of a tennis club and you meet every Friday to play in this club with each other," Isabel went on. "How would you put it in your calendars?"

"Tennis," we both said simultaneously.

"Voilà. And of course, no address, no name because you know it too well. Now," she cracked a sly smile, "let's imagine that tennis is just a pretext. None of you is interested in playing. You just ping-pong a ball for half an hour and afterward proceed to the key reason of your meeting - a cocaine party. What would you put in your calendars in this case, also bearing in mind that your assistant or IT security can always access it?"

"Tennis," we both said and stared at each other with goggled eyes.

"Ian, could you search for 'Barcelona' throughout his calendar?" I asked and the three of us ran to the computer.

In the last 18 months, Carlos turned out to be in "Barcelona" seven times.

"We should go to this place and find out what he is doing there," I concluded.

Audit mission

From: Cristina Tornero

To: All_InSup_staff

Subject: Preparing for the European Commission Internal Audit

Location: Office of Carlos

Dear all,

Carlos would like to meet all the units to discuss the preparations for the visit of the Internal Auditors from the European Commission.

Please ensure that each unit is represented by at least one person.

Thank you in advance for your cooperation,

Cristina

Finally, Carlos' big meeting table justified its existence. It was crowded with one and a half dozen people representing not only the so-called core units - Science, Sport, Nutrition, Ecology, Education, Computer Technology, Construction, Textile - but also what was called supporting services – Corporate Affairs, Finance, HR, Communication, IT, Administration. Carlos sat at the table's head with Fadila and Hilde on his sides. The faces of meeting participants could hardly hide annoyance.

Only Ian looked around with joyful curiosity, although earlier his head of unit had requested him to attend the meeting arguing that "Ian was the least busy staff for he was supported by two consultants". Isabel was there as well, representing Research. She chatted with her neighbor Maarti, the Finnish colleague dealing with Sport-related start-ups. Isabel, Ian, and I decided not to sit together and not to talk much in the presence of other InSup staff. Philipe entered last, sat next to me, and gave me a wink. He smelled of strong coffee and a good mood.

Carlos stood up, the room went silent. Staring somewhere outside the window he croaked, "Needless to say the intehrnal audit of the European Commission is our second important accountability challenge after the hierring in the European Parliament. The Commission finances 40% of our budget, and we must show that every taxpayers' euro is invested efficiently and for the wellfehr of Europe. In six weeks InSup is going to face the fehrst internal audit mission."

He theatrically paused scanning our faces.

I have called you together, gentlemen, to receive a very unpleasant piece of news: there's an Inspector-General coming,[54] flashed in my head. But if in the Gogol's book (and in general in

---

[54] The first line of "The Government Inspector", the theater piece by Nikolai Gogol.

Russia) this announcement usually caused panic, in InSup nobody seemed to be impressed.

Carlos went on. "Soon we will receive a document request and a questionnehrr from internal auditors. Fadila and Hilde will coordinate our reply. Please make all the efforts to support them and provide them with everything they will ask you for."

Fadila and Hilde were nodding and glowing like two proud wives of a sultan.

"Are auditors going to talk to staff?" somebody asked.

Carlos looked at Hilde who looked at Fadila. "Ehhh... actually..." Fadila fumbled, thumbing through the papers in front of her exactly like on my first day in InSup. All three seemed to be lost.

"The Commission never says it in advance," Isabel suddenly said. "That's the challenge of having internal auditors. They can decide ad-hoc about many things."

We all started bombarding Isabel with more questions. Before every answer she paused, waiting for Carlos' reaction, but our executive director and his two sultan wives seemed relieved that somebody could give us answers. "Auditors will not examine all the documents they request. They will randomly pick up two or three dossiers. They will not meet staff without prior notification. They will send their questions in advance. Each mission lasts from two to four weeks," Isabel kept explaining.

"What if we don't convince the auditors?" Ian asked.

Suddenly, Carlos's malevolent hissing filled the room. "They will be happy with us. This is a matter of honorr for the whole Agency. And my piersonal goal is to make this audit successful." His eyes travelled on us, one by one. "And I count on the support of each of you."

Later, Ian dropped me an SMS. It stated, "Carlos has just included in his calendar a new 'Barcelona'. Next week."

Chapter 5 Investigation

In Cristina's office

From: Hilde Rosenbohm

To: Maxim Reut

CC: Carlos de Santos Gomez; Humain Resources

Subject: Compliance with InSup principles

Dear Maxim,

I would like to point your attention that the management of InSup takes seriously the staff adherence to the ethics and high working standards of our Agency. We understand that in your case, there is room for improvement.

Therefore, may I ask you to schedule bi-weekly meetings with me (30 minutes should suffice) at which you will report on your progress? You are also required to provide me with the monthly written reports about your activities in M-Unit.

Needless to say this process is established to protect you and provide an opportunity for your further growth.

Best,

H.

This message was no surprise. Since Carlos and Fadila understood that I wouldn't resign, they put me under stricter control.

Well, in the Centrobank I learned all right how to imitate things: always say "yes"; thank for everything possible and impossible; keep your mind down and focus on your salary. This approach appeared to work well with Hilde. She desperately tried to lure me into another kind of fray, but every time I turned into a colorful, shiny bobblehead. So, she could spot no "loopholes in my adherence to European values" anymore. Probably it's for the sake of cracking my porcelain defense that she requested regular meetings and monthly reports.

"Left the Cider Glass," stated the SMS from Isabel (that's how Frankfurt inhabitants nicknamed – very much to the point! - our cylindrical building). This message changed the thread of my thoughts.

The search for "Barcelona" through Carlos' Outlook calendar didn't bring any results. The only thing we were sure of was that "Barcelona" wasn't a city. We supposed it was a person but to confirm it we needed the contacts book from his smartphone. For Ian, it wasn't insolvable.

"I don't care about the device," he noted. "All InSup smartphones are on the iCloud. If only we knew his iCloud password, I would access it right away and scan for contacts."

Isabel raised a finger. "Cristina told me once that she has all Carlos' passwords somewhere in her office on a sheet of paper. Just in case of emergency."

"I'll get them," I said. The system of my values seemed to comply perfectly with doing so.

On a day when Carlos was on a business trip, Isabel invited Cristina and a couple of other colleagues to a "ladies' lunch". Her SMS meant they were already on their way to a Thai restaurant near the Main Train Station. As of then, I had fifty minutes. After having ensured that the corridor was empty, I slipped into Cristina's office and locked the door from inside. Usually, Cristina locked her office only in the evening but given that Carlos was away, it wouldn't look suspicious. The first part of the plan went smoothly. To my surprise, I kept calm as if breaking in others' offices were my regular professional task.

I looked around. Cristina's working place was furnished with items that could be found everywhere in InSup: a chair, drawers on rolls under the desk, a coat stand, and a bookshelf. On the bookshelves, some colleagues kept all kinds of things: spare shoes, sports clothes, umbrellas. Mine, for example, bore just a couple of dictionaries, which I brought from Russia. Karolina's shelf, on the contrary, groaned under directories and encyclopedias. Cristina's bookshelf looked different than anything in InSup. It creditably presented the files, calligraphically inscribed "Conferences", "Visits", and "Business trips."

On the shelf below stood files entitled "Meetings/Briefings" sorted by months. On the third shelf Cristina placed the folders she didn't use every day: "Invoices", "Bookings", "Interviews and Articles", "Auditors", "Contacts" and "Miscellaneous." The latter two could be of my interest. I took them and sat at Cristina's desk.

"Contacts" contained dozens of business cards accurately filed in plastic holders. Cristina sorted them out by area: science, technology, food, etc. There was a category "Medicine" as well, and I promised myself to look at it if I had time.

"Miscellaneous" also didn't bring any results: Christmas greetings, invitations to social events, and other things that had zero value, but vanity didn't let Carlos get rid of them.

I returned to the bookshelf; its two lowest levels were almost empty except for a couple of folders entitled "Archive". I lost hope of finding anything useful on the shelves and examined Cristina's desk. It was in perfect order. A couple of papers in the in-tray. I quickly glanced at them: a correspondence addressed to Carlos. A penholder with a flip calendar, a bunch of pens, and markers. Even the mouse pad had been placed at a perfectly right angle to the keyboard. Never in all my life did I see such a well-arranged desk! Only a dirty cup of coffee and a plate with croissant leftovers spoiled the picture. Also, Cristina was looking at me from the framed photo in which she was pictured somewhere in the mountains together with a smiling young man, probably her boyfriend. The boyfriend had a shiny self-certain smile while Cristina looked directly into the camera lens, and I felt guilty meeting her glance.

"I don't care about your possessions and will try to forget what I saw," I mumbled to her and started searching the drawers. It was like glancing inside a female handbag. A pair of shoes, a pack of tampons, an umbrella, a big plastic bag in the biggest bottom drawer. The drawer above contained lipstick, Ibuprofen, a couple of other medicines and drops, a tiny bottle of perfume, and a hand cream.

My heart throbbed: in the highest drawer, I saw papers. But soon my hope melted: these were Cristina's medical invoices, training invitations, and post-its with handwritten dates and phone numbers. I felt sick because this stuff was too intimate and no way I wanted to put my nose into it.

Suddenly I heard the door to Carlos' office opening, and a male voice said something in Spanish. *Carlos returned!* I thought. Fearing that he would decide to see Cristina, I jumped behind the coat stand where I could hide behind Cristina's raincoat and especially the long warm shawl she used to protect herself from the air condition in summer. The voice said something else, and I heard the door closing. I couldn't understand whether he was going to enter Cristina's space or not.

The phone in my pocket vibrated. I accurately took it, and another SMS from Isabel stated: "On the way back." I felt panic. My first intention was to run out of Cristina's office, but the possibility that Carlos would enter at any moment paralyzed me. However, there was no movement behind the door. Probably it was not Carlos but one of those colleagues with whom he had close relations and who entered his office not via Cristina but directly. I calmed down. And at this moment, near the "archive" folders, I noticed a transparent yellow file. It was visible only because I was sitting on the floor. I took it. Bingo. It contained only two lines: a combination of letters and symbols. I made a picture with my smartphone without taking the list out of the plastic file. Then I took a deep breath, rushed to the door, unlocked it, and immediately went away, leaving the door the way Cristina always had it in the middle of the working day - wide open.

Barcelona

The next days I immersed myself in the M-Unit assessments, leaving the investigation to Ian and Isabel. On the appointed evening, I was waiting for them in Barenik. On Mondays at five Barenik was usually half-empty and quiet. Kirill was out of sight doing paperwork. His staff were cleaning desks. This "dead hour" as Kirill called it, was a perfect time for confidential talks.

When Isabel and Ian finally entered, I felt like I hadn't seen them for long. Probably it was because now we avoided each other within the Cider Glass so as not to attract attention. Ian seemed to have changed though. He shook away his phlegmatic glance and looked present and excited. Isabel, true to herself, exuded reserve and irrevocable elegance in her mint-colored pencil dress with three-quarter-long sleeves. Kirill couldn't take his eyes off her when he popped up at our table. He greeted Ian and me and turned to Isabel.

"I am delighted to welcome new guests," he addressed her, holding out a hand. "I am Kirill."

"Isabel, their colleague."

"Kirill is the owner of Barenik and a wholehearted supporter of artists in Frankfurt," I explained, startled at the way he kept Isabel's hand in his, a touch longer than he should have.

"I like your handshake, Isabel," Kirill said. "Will you stay for the evening program?"

"What kind of program are you having tonight?" Ian asked with a sudden tautness to his voice.

Kirill looked at Ian with surprise as if seeing him for the first time; then glanced again at Isabel and finally proclaimed, "Fado music. Two guitar players and a singer. The singer is Brazilian, she is a student at the Frankfurt Conservatory. And the guitarists are German and Swedish, a lovely combination, isn't it? They met here, in Barenik," he added not without pride.

Kirill seemed to be in a chatting mood, but one of his staff called him away. Isabel and Ian exhaled with relief. They could hardly wait any longer to tell me about their findings. To start with, Ian hacked the private email of Carlos.

"How did you get his private email?" I asked.

"My hint," Isabel explained. "I suddenly remembered how once he was on holiday and messaged me from his private email account. He often emails me little requests about statistics, historical facts, and all sorts of questions. I suspect he does it when he wants to impress somebody and show how quickly his staff can serve him. I imagine him sitting with somebody in a bar, saying 'Let me ask my staff', heedlessly dropping me an email and five minutes later receiving my answer."

After getting access to Carlos' corporate and private emails, Isabel spent the entire weekend in front of Ian's computer, reading Carlos' emails, sorting them in different ways, trying to find possible hooks.

Later I realized Ian was also working hard by offering Isabel meals and multiple "coffee breaks" in cafés and parks. Both of them were rewarded for their efforts. The Bright Maltese appreciated being taken care of and fished from a sticky information flaw in an email sent by a certain "De Goya". The email contained only one line in Spanish: "Los detalles mañana[55]."

"Not that it looked suspicious, but the email wasn't sent as a reply to Carlos' question. Strange, isn't it?" Isabel said. "So I checked Carlos' calendar and – here we go, "tomorrow" coincided with a meeting in Barcelona!"

---

[55] Details tomorrow (Spanish)

Later, she discovered more emails from "De Goya", which irrevocably matched the dates when Carlos' calendar was blocked for Barcelona. But none of them included an address or even a description of a meeting point.

"Let's sum up then," I said. "'De Goya' and calendar blockers 'Barcelona' seem to be linked, but we still know neither the purpose nor the place of those meetings. Do we know who 'De Goya' is?"

"Carlos' phone book doesn't contain any de goyas," Ian shook his head. "The internet search wasn't successful either. Spaniards always have double family names and 'Goya' appears in too many searches. Same with social media."

Isabel went on. "Since there are no emails about ticket booking, I am sure 'Barcelona' is somewhere in Frankfurt."

"Barcelona is 10 minutes from here," said Kirill, disposing of our order and keeping his eyes on Isabel. "If you stay for a fado evening, I will tell you the address."

We all stared at him.

Isabel offered Kirill a charming smile. "Happy to listen to a beautiful fado music. I dare to say so on behalf of the three of us," she added, glancing at Ian searchingly.

Ian immediately nodded in response.

"And another little condition," Kirill continued, "may I introduce you to my friend Jens? Maxim knows him too. Jens is looking for a modern incarnation of a Botticelli woman. When he sees you, I am sure, he will stop his search."

I suppressed the smile. Indeed, Jens mentioned something, but at this moment Kirill didn't seem to scout for the sake of contemporary art.

Isabel diplomatically smiled. "Are you sure your friend wants to find one? What if such a search is part of his artistic manner?"

I rarely saw such an open admiration on Kirill's face. "I see your point, no further conditions," he said. "Barcelona are my competitors. In fact, their name comprises two words 'Bar,' and 'Celona.' I am quite allergic to them because their food offer is richer and healthier. But if you want to spend a wonderful evening and get to know interesting people, you should come here. Bar Celona simply can't beat me!"

Maxim to Veronika. Need help

Nika, privet,

Your last email means so much to me. I swear your reply will stay between you and me forever.

I hate to admit it, but you were ten times right. European values turned out to be a system of coordinates that is alien to me. Like a transplanted organ, which my body rejected. Broomy and Fadila force me to report every week about my progress in becoming a truly

EU employee. This is called "disciplinary monitoring". I assiduously write reports about mutual respect, procedural accuracy, and sincere cooperation. But I don't believe anymore in what I am writing. Broomy finds this circus credible. Every time she beams in a buttery smile and says, "I see progress, but you are not yet there," I recall the words of Isabel "EU institutions always believe in what they like to hear."

Recently, I went further than just faking enthusiasm and commitment. I started gunning no less than for Carlos. I admit, I had personal reasons for that, but it looks like something is indeed wrong with him.

I have just returned from a restaurant Bar Celona where Carlos meets somebody whom I suspect to be part of the corruption scheme, which I am trying to reveal. The place was full of after-work drinkers and eaters. For a moment, I thought I was mistaken. It was hard to imagine Carlos having any secret meetings in such a crowd. I made myself to the round bar in the middle and asked for Tolya.

In a couple of minutes, a young man came to the counter from the clients' side: "Haben Sie nach Tolya gefragt?[56]" Tolya looked like a copy of Kirill, the owner of Barenik: blond tail, bright blue eyes. Only younger and less charismatic. I thanked him for his time,

---

[56] Did you ask for Tolya? (German)

but he impatiently waved at me. "I owe one to Kirill. He asked me to meet you, so how can I help?"

Happy to be as business-like as him, I opened on the smartphone the InSup official webpage with Carlos' picture and brief biography. "Have you ever seen him in your bar?"

Tolya took my smartphone and frowned. Some minutes later he said, "I don't think he ever entered Bar Celona, but I saw him twice outside."

"Outside?"

"I can show you if you like."

He brought me to Bar Celona's backdoor and took out a cigarette. I looked around. We were on a quiet street. Tolya pointed at the next door. "When I had my smoking break, I saw this guy entering here."

"Do you know what kind of place it is?" I examined the decent two-floor house and three doorbells, each containing a German surname.

"I do, it's a brothel."

I looked at him mistrustfully. He shrugged and expelled cigarette smoke from his nostrils.

Nika, you might ask me what I am going to do with this information. Honestly, I don't know. I am like a shark that smells blood several kilometers away and can't stop swimming towards it. Unfortunately, I'm a shark with no jaws. I need equipment and guidance. And I have only a couple of days left before Carlos enters this brothel.

I want to see what he is doing there, and I need to record it.

Such favors are not provided for free. I understand and accept in advance any conditions. As your debtor, I might be even more attractive than as a former lover.

Ian's headquarters

On a warm April night, I knocked at Ian's door. Isabel was already there. I had a feeling that Ian's apartment changed, but I couldn't put my finger on anything concrete.

"Isabel prepared the Ceasar salad for us," declared Ian, taking from me my dinner contribution – the bottle of red wine.

"I want to offer you something healthier than Barenik's пельмени и пирожки[57]," Isabel said taking off a snow-white apron with a forget-me-not pattern. "Some romaine lettuce and a piece of roasted rabbit would do you good."

"Rabbit?!"

Isabel sneered. "Maltese traditional meat. We have eaten rabbits for thousands of years since the Phoenicians brought them to the island to ensure fresh meat. It's cheap and trust me - very healthy."

---

[57] Dumplings and pastries (Russian)

Behind the apron she turned to wear a silk caramel-colored dress, making her wavy hair look ginger.

Suddenly, I understood what was making Ian's apartment different this time. It was a new touch that Isabel brought to Ian's lonely place: the apron, the crispy salad... I was certain that even a bunch of chamomiles on the dinner table was her idea.

Hardly did we touch food, Ian announced, "I checked the number that Isabel gave me and have some results." He was trying to suppress a smile, but managed poorly.

"Don't you mind starting from the beginning, I have no clue what you are talking about," I begged.

Ian made his own little investigation. He recalled that the Cider Glass' IT department was in charge of the staff's telephone numbers, both stationary and mobile ones. Every month, Ian's team received invoices for each phone number from the telecommunication provider, just a monthly total, nothing informative. But in case this monthly amount exceeded 100 euros, the provider sent to InSup the detailed information about each telephone number used during that month and the length of each conversation."

"I didn't know it," I mumbled, thanking my common sense for not using my corporate phone for private purposes.

Ian shrugged. "I don't think the agency cares. We usually file those invoices and forget. Sometimes we ask staff to tell us why the hell the amount is so high, just to make them feel under control. But it's just a formality, we never follow up on it. But then I discovered that on his private email, Carlos receives every month two more reports from our telecom provider."

"When Ian told me about it," Isabel went on, "I thought that Carlos certainly knew that his corporate phone might fall under scrutiny and asked Cristina to gather for him another phone number, which he could use for private purposes."

"Ian mentioned two reports," I reminded her.

"I presumed the second is the one of Silvia, his wife."

Ian analyzed those monthly reports for the last fifteen months, since the InSup creation. The first number looked very active and had calls from different countries. The second one was much smaller and comprised either calls to or from Spain and a very limited number of calls across Frankfurt. Isabel checked some Frankfurt numbers: doctors, hairdressers, restaurants.

"So it looks very much like the wife," Ian concluded. "And then I checked the phone number Isabel gave me."

"Wait a moment," I interrupted, "how did you, Isabel, get this number?"

"I've got a bright idea to search in the deleted items of Carlos' private inbox. God bless his habit of cleaning his bin so rarely! And I was lucky: I found one email from 'De Goya' with just one line: 'Try with Paco Pelenzuela Peres' and this phone number."

"Isabel forwarded the number to me and... bingo," Ian grinned, "it was in the telecom reports. Just it's not Carlos but his wife who calls Pelenzuela Peres. She does it regularly, minimum once a month."

Isabel already conducted research on Mr. Pelenzuela Peres finding out he was a doctor. A neurologist who works not just as a practitioner but also as a researcher, publishing articles on Spanish medical platforms and magazines.

"The doctor of the wife," Isabel summed up. "Intuitively, I feel it is something for us. However, I want to share with you one much more important thing. It's about a Barcelona brothel. I chatted with one of my local contacts. She says it's not a brothel." Observing our disappointment, she added, "Or better to say, it's not a simple brothel."

Its business model was indeed unusual. It was just one apartment that could be used only once per evening: a client received the keys ahead of the "visit" and afterward put them in the postbox.

To me, it sounded unrealistic. "In Russia, the owner would have never trusted the keys to a client. Where is the guarantee that clients don't make a duplicate or simply forget to return it and use the flat again?"

Isabel shook her head. "The clients of this place are trustworthy. Many of them are quite famous people in the city. I think it's a perfect place for business meetings, for example, with those people you don't want to be seen with, and especially, whom you prefer not to include in the EU transparency register."

"The next Barcelona meeting is already after tomorrow," Ian reminded us.

"We need to go there as soon as possible," I said. "Do you think I can rent it as a client?"

"I am afraid even my connections won't be enough to get you in. You need to know the owner personally. But even if we manage to enter it, what would we do?"

She rested her eyes on my face. I held her gaze. "I will get us the equipment. But please promise you'll never ask me where it comes from," I said decisively.

Isabel glanced at me as if expecting such an answer. She nodded contentedly. "Then I have an idea how we can get in." She raised her glass of wine. Above the scarlet drink, her smile was tough and confident.

Who is "De Goya"?

Philipe curiously looked around. "I thought I knew it all in Frankfurt. How come I have never been in this club?! Is it new?"

I invited him to Barenik and intended to make his evening unforgettable. "It has existed for some years now. But you won't find it in any city guides because it's neither a restaurant nor a club: it's a snack bar, an "imbiss" as they say in German."

Philipe was turning the menu in the hands. "Imbisses offer currywurst[58] and French fries. Here they eat more sophisticated, although strange. I don't understand a thing."

I explained that Barenik served fast food from the former Soviet Union and a blend of events that otherwise would take place in a gallery, nightclub, or library. That's why almost every evening something was happening here. "Kirill, the owner of Barenik, has an agreement with the city's administration: they allow him to function according to imbiss rules, and in exchange, they proudly extend their reports about Franfurt's cultural life by mentioning the items from Barenik's evening programs."

"He seems to be very successful." Philipe surveyed the surrounding crowd: all tables were occupied and a sizeable group of guests was standing in front of the stage.

Tonight, Barenik was hosting a concert. Philipe once told me he wanted to become a rock musician and before getting kids used to travel across Europe to listen to his beloved bands. When I invited him to a rock concert in Frankfurt, I knew he wouldn't refuse. That was part of my plan.

---

[58] German fast food consisting of a sausage and curry ketchup

"I hope you like tonight's music. It's a folk rock and in the second part they will perform whatever the audience wishes," I said.

Kirill brought us beer. I introduced them to each other. "You have a great outfit," Philipe was consuming with eyes Kirill's white shirt and leather vest with embroidered red and yellow flowers. I couldn't agree more. Handsome, Kirill radiated Nordic certainty and extreme embeddedness. A real star appeal.

"It's because I am performing together with the guys," he said amiably and turned to me. "Will Isabel come?"

I said I didn't know.

"She would have liked it. With her quick sightedness, I thought she would have guessed I was going to perform a Maltese song specially for her," Kirill unsuccessfully tried to hide his disappointment.

"Is he talking about Isabel Aquilina?" Philipe asked once Kirill had left. I admitted. "Let's do him a favor and summon her here!" Philipe suggested and before I answered, took out his smartphone.

Neither Isabel nor Ian knew I had invited Philipe to Barenik. I was happy we couldn't see Isabel's face when Philipe dialed her and joyfully told her that Kirill was longing to see her at his concert to which he, Philipe, was invited by me. "She said she has other plans for the evening but asks to send Kirill her greetings," Philipe told me after having hung up. "Pity, I wanted to see her face when your friend sings a Maltese song! Never mind, I anyway look so much forward to this evening, it's a great place!"

Philipe liked a dinner I chose for us (vareniki with mashed potatoes, mushrooms and sour cream generously covered with fresh parsley). During the concert, he was applauding warmheartedly the musicians and when they switched to the orders from the audience, he sang the songs together with everybody "Smoke on the Water", "Born to Run", and other age-melting pieces.

"It has been an evening like I didn't have for long," he said when the concert was over, and we were drinking our last beer. His gaze became astute as he went on. "Such great evenings shouldn't remain for long without a return service. So let me put it straight: is there anything I can do to thank you?"

I drew in a breath, embarrassed that Philipe discerned my plan so quickly and openly, for I intended to approach him only the next day.

"Go on, Maxim," Philipe encouraged me, "in EU institutions two-thirds of your success depend on the evenings like this."

"Ok," I finally said, "I am looking for information about one person. He is called De Goya. Do you happen to know him?"

My heart beat quicker. By his reaction, I could see that it was not the first time he heard this name. He watched me for some seconds. "De Goya," he finally said, "is not a person. It's a network."

"Network?!"

"Yes, founded for highly educated, wealthy, or simply powerful people. Spanish people, of course. They named the network after the painter Goya, But God forbid you think it's because they are such art lovers. I am sure the only thing they envy is the prominent position Goya could achieve at the royal court and his friendship with Bourbon's aristocracy, of course. The non-members can't be aware of De Goya network, because they find out only once they are offered membership."

"Like Stevenson's 'Suicide Club'," I said with mock bitterness. "You can enter it only if another member brings you in."

"Never heard about such a depressing club." He drank a big sip of beer without taking his eyes off me. "May I ask: how did you find out about De Goya?"

"I was hoping to approach him regarding one of the start-ups in my enormous pipeline," I gave a prepared answer.

"Unless you discovered some Spanish background in your rich family history, I wouldn't be able to recommend you. It's for Spaniards only," he said.

"Are you a member?" I asked shocked.

He rolled his eyes. "Of course, I am, or do you have doubts I am a valuable Spanish professional?!"

"I thought you were half-French..."

"Fifty years ago it could have been a good reason not to let me in but now, my friend, even De Goya is getting global and even a little connection to Spain is already enough. By the way, I recommended my wife to the network. She is Mexican, but they decided she is connected to Spain through me."

"So how does De Goya network function?"

Philipe was proud to explain. All members were initially connected to the central account. If one member needed anything, he sent a request to the "center", which channeled it to the relevant contact. Members were keen to fulfill incoming requests. The more and better you help others, the more you can count on the same support towards yourself.

"Maybe as a member of De Goya, I can help you?" Philipe suddenly asked. He looked straight into my eyes and his glance encouraged me to tell him about The Diadem Project and my attempt to understand why Carlos was critical of this start-up.

"One of my trails is a neurologist from Madrid, Paco Pelenzuela Peres. De Goya recommended him to Carlos. I need to find out why."

Philipe went silent for so long that I started feverishly doubt, whether it had been a good idea to tell him everything.

"Ok," he finally said, "I've never heard the name, but via my channels, I think I can find it out for you."

Cleaners

Isabel was already waiting in front of the brothel. She had her usual business look and, unlike me, wasn't nervous at all. "Did you bring water?" she asked right away.

I did. As requested, I brought two big bottles of still water and two bottles of sparkling water. Isabel nodded approvingly. "Kasia will be happy that this time she doesn't need to carry those heavy bottles upstairs because there is no elevator."

Isabel pressed the doorbell, and the entrance door was immediately unlocked. When we arrived at the second floor, a big blond woman was already waiting for us in front of the apartment. She smiled widely, as if meeting dear guests.

"Guten Morgen, meine liebe[59]," said Isabel.

"Hallo, hallo, kommt bitte rein[60]," Kasia replied.

Isabel warned me that Kasia was Polish and spoke only German. I politely shook Kasia's plump hand when Isabel presented us to each other. Otherwise, I just stood by Isabel, silent, faking a barely veiled boredom.

"Kasia is going to show us the apartment now," Isabel pronounced in a boss-like voice turning to me. "Maxim, please look

---

[59] Good morning, my dear (German)
[60] Hi, hi, please come in (German)

around, if you have any critical observations, let me know." I nodded. "Kasia, wir sind bereit. Maxim wird die Räume fotografieren[61]," Isabel said.

The apartment looked ordinary: white walls, faceless furniture, zero design, although neat and comfortable. Kasia was saying something, Isabel - translating into English, but even without those explanations everything was clear. From the antechamber, one could proceed on two sides. On the right lay a living room, which led to a bedroom; on the left - a large kitchen. The only thing that surprised me was the bathroom with no bathtub but a large walk-in shower behind the glass doors like in luxury hotels. "Kasia says that the bathroom takes most of her energy because the water in Frankfurt contains much too much calcium; it constantly covers all the glass and metal stuff with white calcium spots," Isabel translated to me. She kept chatting with Kasia as if it was her best friend. "Ok, Maxim," she said finally, "please picture the rooms but from a different perspective than the apartment owner gave us so that we have an objective view. Don't forget to picture the view from all windows. The more details we get, the better it is for the management. In the meantime, I will help Kasia in the bedroom."

I nodded and took out my smartphone. After Kasia showed us the apartment, I got some ideas about where to plant the cameras.

---

[61] We are ready. Maxim will make photos of the rooms (German)

The kitchen looked to me like a perfect place for negotiations: a large table in the center with four chairs around. Near the big coffee machine, I saw a jag full of coffee capsules, so I replaced it with mine, which contained a hidden camera. I assumed Carlos would spend most of the evening in the kitchen and was tempted to plant the second hidden camera there too. But then I remembered Nika's guidance: only one camera per room. Isabel and Kasia were still in the bedroom, so I called Ian. "All fine," Ian replied without saying hello. "I can see you standing near the kitchen table. Don't forget about the sound check."

"Maxim, you brought water, didn't you?" called Isabel from the bedroom where she was helping Kasia to exchange bed laundry.

I brought them the water bottles. It was a signal to Isabel that I was done with the kitchen. The bed looked fresh and impeccable. "Wow, like in a hotel," I said without faking my admiration.

"I work in hotels, always work very well," Kasia tried to explain in broken English. She was pleased with my reaction.

Isabel jammed the dirty laundry into a portable laundry bag. "Uff, Kasia, das ist kein leichtes Job[62]," she said. "Maxim," she took again a business-like tone, "Kasia says it shouldn't be noisy to sleep here in the night, but I would appreciate your view as well." She

---

[62] That's not an easy job (German)

took water and went with Kasia to the kitchen. The living room and the bedroom were at my disposal now.

The living room had everything one needs to spend the evening comfortably: a sofa, a TV set, a coffee table, and even a shelf with books to make the client feel intellectual. So, the moulage of Goethe's "Faust" with a second hidden camera went perfectly well on the bookshelf.

The bedroom looked like a place for two: one king-size bed, two night tables with lamps on both sides; a little writing desk in one corner, and a big built-in cupboard in another one. The cupboard was empty. The room couldn't be used for business talks. I felt that leaving here a camera would be a waste. But Nika's guidance was implacable: a camera in a bedroom is a must. I placed it, hidden in a framed picture of Frankfurt, on the writing desk. Then I sat on the bed and said, "The bedroom looks superb. I wonder what my friend Ian would think of it." An SMS from Ian immediately clanked: "Ian would hope Carlos won't use this enormous bed." It was a confirmation that the sound check was successful. I went back to Isabel and Kasia, who were placing water in the fridge.

"So, how do you find this apartment?" Isabel asked me in the preoccupied tone of a buyer who was going to make a purchase of the century. "In my view, it's nicely located and clean. A good option for somebody who doesn't enjoy living in a hotel for several days."

"Agree," I replied copying her intonation. "And the price looks reasonable. Maybe the landlord can even give a discount."

Isabel nodded and looked around pensively. "Then, if you are ready, let's go. Just please take the trash bag, I promised Kasia we would throw it away." She thanked Kasia in German and they warmheartedly said goodbye.

"Thank you for help," Kasia said to me.

"I told Kasia that we would show the pictures to our boss and might come back if he has more questions. I said the person for whom we want to rent this apartment, is very important for us," Isabel said.

I couldn't suppress my admiration of her naturalness.

"It was easy. Kasia is my cleaning lady," Isabel explained after we had left the house. "She knows who I am and where I work."

I couldn't believe my ears.

Isabel just made a lucky guess. She "inherited" Kasia from the previous tenant of the apartment she moved in after she got the job in InSup. Soon the standard "how are you"-talks developed into closer relations thanks to Isabel's curiosity and openness. One day, Kasia mentioned that her sister also worked for the same cleaning agency. In particular, Kasia's sister every day had to clean one apartment in the city center. The apartment sometimes looked like a catastrophe, but most of the time remained rather clean and even deserted. Including the exchange of bed laundry, it had to be cleaned every day, literally, without weekends and holidays; so Kasia, from time to time, had to replace her sister. Neither of them had a clue what kind of apartment it was. They thought it was a flat on booking.com.

"I could match the dots together only after you had spoken to Tolya from Bar Celona," Isabel grinned. "The rest was easy. When I understood that this was 'our' apartment, I said to Kasia we would like to rent it for a couple of weeks but wanted to see it live and not just as pictures on the internet. To do me a favor, Kasia replaced her sister to show us the apartment. Ian would call it a luck of the Irish!"

I couldn't agree more. It was our investigative score, and right before Carlos had a meeting in Bar Celona tonight!"

"Tomorrow Kasia will come to clean it again. I will return and discreetly pick up the cameras. I spotted the mug in the kitchen. What about the other two? Where did you place them?"

I explained and mentioned that my biggest hope was the kitchen. It looked like a comfortable place to hold illegal business talks. Isabel raised her eyebrows in surprise. "If I had to use this boring apartment, it would be for the sake of its bathroom - the best place for making love." She caught my half-distrustful and half-terrified glance and expertly added, "What? I would have put all three cameras there!"

Carlos

Ian opened the door, the intense blue eyes rolled in a comic horror. "Come in. He is already there."

Isabel and I ran to take the seats in front of the monitor. Carlos arrived at the Bar Celona flat straight from the office and now was moving from one room to another, appearing in sequence on all three screens that transmitted signals from my hidden cameras.

"He seems to inspect the apartment," Isabel said. "Hopefully, not checking for spy equipment," she mumbled.

I pretended I didn't hear her last words, for there would be no better reaction, at least not to my knowledge.

In the bedroom, Carlos folded back the bedcover, opening the dark lilac bedsheets without a single wrinkle. Then he returned to the living room, sat on the sofa, typed something on his smartphone, and put it back in his expensive leather briefcase.

"Since nothing is happening, and you both are anyway on watch, I'll get us a snack," Ian said. He went to the kitchen, switched on the music, and started clanking dishes.

In the meantime, Carlos carefully hung his jacket in the antechamber and put the briefcase in the wardrobe. He brought from the kitchen a bottle of water and two glasses. "He is expecting one visitor," Isabel commented. Carlos already was tilting the windows and closing thick, dark gray curtains. Because of the darkness, the vision deteriorated, but the cameras were strong enough to adjust and we kept seeing him relatively well. He went back to the living room.

"He seems to know well the apartment. Just look at this: not a single unnecessary move," I said.

Isabel nodded. "And it's not the first time he is going to meet his counterpart. He seems neither nervous nor excited. With the same facial expression, he makes himself a coffee in our kitchenette."

Carlos stretched on the sofa and closed his eyes.

Tah-taaah. Ta-dah-daaah dah-dah dah-dah.

Tah-Taaah. Ta-dah-daaah-daaah

In the kitchen, Ian switched on his favorite Dire Straits song. "Now look at them," Ian crooned. "That's the way you do it… play the guitar on the MTV"[63]

The doorbell rang, and Carlos left the living room. He returned together with a breathtakingly beautiful girl. Both Isabel and I reflexively moved closer to the monitor - to get a better look. The first thing that attracted me was the scarlet lipstick that made her irresistibly seductive and dangerous even in the dim light and through the hidden camera.

"Buenos tardes, mi Señora," Carlos babbled, looking at her bottom-up.

---

[63] "Money for nothing" by Mark Knopfler, Sting

She answered something with a dark, gruff voice. "Shut up, I didn't allow you to speak. You will be punished," Isabel translated.

Carlos sat down and put his hands on his knees like a schoolchild. The woman started unbuttoning her trench coat, which finally slipped on the floor.

"Recoger[64]," she commanded, and Carlos almost jumped on the floor and took the coat in both hands as if it were a valuable exhibit item. While he was hanging her coat in the antechamber, she stood still like a statue. He returned and sat down again.

"You sat down twice without my permission. You will be punished," Isabel translated.

"Sí, mi Señora."

"La-la-la-la, microwave ovens and custom kitchen deliveri-i-i-ies," Ian kept humming.

"Shut up. I haven't said you can talk. My bag!"

Carlos ran again out. Usually unhurried like a king, tonight he was all a fidgety obedience. The abject facial expression subtly changed his face, so that I sometimes wondered whether it was really him.

Señora stretched long legs in dainty overknees on the sofa. I blew out my cheeks: she had an ideal body underlined by the

---

[64] Pick it up (Spanish)

sophisticated construction of heavy leather stripes her dress was made of.

"Cool boots, but these stilettos scare me," Ian popped up holding a plate full of bread triangles, each topped with creamy cheese, ham, and a slice of fresh cucumber. "Is Carlos still there?" We didn't need to answer because Carlos already appeared again in the living room. "I feared something like this," Ian sighed. "I am not sure I want to see what is going to happen." The last sentence he pronounced half-piteously, half-inquiringly. Isabel seemed to have spotted it too, for she looked away from the monitor, glanced at me, and subtly nodded.

"Of course, Ian," I replied. "You already did so much, have a well-deserved break."

Actually, Ian's wish was well in line with Nika's guidance: never forget that your investigation might come to light every moment. So the fewer people see the video from your hidden cameras, the better for yourself.

Once Ian happily withdrew to the kitchen, I turned to Isabel, but she didn't let me even start.

"Spare your words, I am staying. If the entire evening leaves us with the conclusion that Carlos likes playing submissive, I would be even more relieved! But my intuition tells me this story smells much worse, unfortunately."

In the meantime, Carlos brought to Señora a stately leather bag and took again a slave-of-the-lamp pose.

"Ponerlo en el suelo. Desvestirse."

"Put it on the ground. Undress," Isabel translated.

Without clothes, Carlos looked even smaller, and his face – more round. Instead of pants, he had a black leather construction high waist but (to my horror) with open butt cheeks.

"Ḥaqq Alla[65], I think I will never be hungry again," Isabel grumbled, putting an unfinished sandwich back on the plate. "One thing is comforting me, however," she grinned, "So far Carlos behaves like a blameless EU employee. His ehm… preferences are not so exciting actually."

At that moment, I envied her. She seemed to be observing something ordinary and as easily forgettable as a wind blow in spring. Unlike her, I was fighting against a nauseous feeling of unease. If we were in Moscow and the hidden cameras caught Sergey Vladimirovich Kamarinov the way they caught Carlos, I would have feared for the careers of all of us, including Veronika who was far away. Kamarinov would surely spot what we did and find the pretext to fire everybody involved, even Ian who refused to watch the video. While Carlos' capacities in this regard were unclear to me, I felt that "Barcelona" not only threw our inquiry off the scent

---

[65] Goddamit (Maltese)

but foisted Carlos' dirty washing on me. Knowing this side of my executive director for the rest of my life in InSup (however long it will be) made me sick.

Señora continued giving him orders. "Get up!"

Each command of hers Carlos obeyed like a soldier echoing every time "Sí, mi Señora."

For a long time, Señora was observing him naked in front of her, his face down.

"Legs wider," Isabel said and turned to me. "Don't you mind if I stop translating this porno? I would be happy not to watch it, but since they might say in Spanish something that would give us a hint, I am staying – God forgive me – till the end."

I didn't mind. The translation was needless. Carlos anyway followed each order of his Señora with a zealous precision.

"Hands behind your back."

He obeyed. She took another long minute to observe him.

With the command "Aprender[66]" he put on his four.

"Raise your head."

She sat down and opened her legs wide.

"Acérquese[67]."

He approached, his head being hidden from us between her legs. Señora closed on him a leather neck collar that perfectly fitted

---

[66] Learn (Spanish)

[67] Approach (Spanish)

Carlos' leather pants but was in such a contrast with his round four-eyed face that I burst out laughing. Isabel hid her face in the palms.

In the meantime, Señora took out of the bag a flogger and paddler. She started "punishing" Carlos. He was saying something different than "Si, Señora".

"Are they saying anything of our interest?" I asked.

"Not at all, Señora explains what she slams him for, and he says how he must behave in the future, a typical BDSM practice. I start thinking there will be nothing else."

Isabel was right. I would have lashed Carlos myself, but no way when he had such panties. Soon Isabel and I got bored. In the meantime, Señora ordered Carlos to the bedroom where she fixed him with leather hand bands to the bed and sat on his bespectacled face while keeping paddling his crooked legs and stomach. There was a second when she looked directly into the camera and moaned in a hoarse voice, "You serve well," which made my skin crawl.

"I am sorry you have to watch it," I said to Isabel, avoiding looking at her.

"You don't have to," she echoed. "Inscrutable are the ways of 'De Goya'". Suddenly she chuckled, "And I would be sorry if we had never found what 'Barcelona' means, although it looked like a more serious mystery."

Señora stood up and went to the kitchen where thanks to the hidden camera we saw her close up: stretched facial contours, long noble nose, and black smoky eyes. What surprised me is that while making herself coffee her scarlet lips were slightly open as if never dropping her role of a dominant although Carlos remained handcuffed on the bed and couldn't see her. She made herself a tiny espresso cup, drank it in one gulp, and left. In the living room, she appeared already in the trench coat. She started packing her bag.

"Is she going to leave without freeing him?" whispered Isabel.

"I wouldn't mind if he stays here forever," I mumbled.

"Cierra los ojos[68]," Señora declared before entering the bedroom.

She opened the handcuffs and started moving her puddle along Carlos' body.

"¿Te gusta servirme? habla[69]."

"Si, Señora Tais."

"She said she didn't allow him to call her by name and next time she will punish him for it," Isabel translated.

Carlos held the bed's headboard and continued lying with closed eyes. Señora Tais turned her back to him and left the apartment. Carlos didn't move.

"What is going on there?"

"She ordered him to hold the headboard and stay like this for 1000 seconds," Isabel explained.

"Seriously?"

She only shrugged with a facial expression "These-BDSM-guys-have-wild-phantasies."

---

[68] Close your eyes (Spanish)

[69] Do you like serving me? Speak! (Spanish)

Carlos appeared to be fully obeying his dominatrix even in her absence. For the next fifteen minutes, he remained motionless showing the camera his round stomach with pinkish marks from the paddler. Isabel used the pause to go to the kitchen and bring us coffee. Afterward, Carlos stood up, dressed, and left the apartment.

"Perfect timing," Isabel said with a certain respect. "They finished exactly at eight o'clock and in half an hour he will be at home, 30 minutes before Silvia serves him and children dinner."

"May I ask you: what the hell was it?" Ian asked after having ensured that the hidden cameras didn't show anybody anymore.

"I have two observations to share with you," Isabel replied serenely. "First, Philipe was subtle when he described you De Goya as a business network. It seems to fulfill all kinds of its members' needs. And second, Carlos could impeccably hide 'Barcelona' from everybody; pity that our brilliant investigation didn't bring us a millimeter further.

We paused. It was a dangerous moment. I could feel their disappointment and despair. It was time to recall Veronika's advice "You must have an appetite to find out more and you must maintain this appetite in others."

"All right, guys," I tried to sound firm and not overenthusiastic. "Now we all are clear about De Goya and Barcelona. Let's bury this evening deep in our memory. That's not what we were looking for. But there is another trail we still have to follow, namely Paco Pelenzuela Peres. Philipe promised me to shed light on this doctor."

Chapter 6 Showdown

Silvia

I savored the warm May air while walking along Bockenheimer Landstrasse and admiring creamy pyramids of chestnut trees on both sides. This long and wide street was surprisingly quiet. The twilight plummeted. I easily found the café with a sign "Bistro 66" on the facade. Philipe was already waiting inside at the window. Despite a demonic name, the café looked sweet. The glass counter advertised culinary treasuries: chocolate cakes with raspberries, apple strudel, and tartlets with nuts. *Ian could spend the whole evening here*, I thought.

"I know why this place has '66' in its name: it smells of seduction," I said, taking a seat at Philipe's small wooden table and savoring the blended scent of coffee, cinnamon, and vanilla.

"My poetic friend!" Philipe grinned. "The postal address of this building is Bockenheimer Landstrasse 66. I guess the owner didn't thrash hard his phantasy… To be honest, I am not a fan of this coffee shop. It's sickly sweet for a cynical guy like me. But my wife is unwell, and Bistro is simply close to my home. So let me be quick because my kids won't be busy with their homework for very long. He cocked his head to the side like an eagle observing its spoils, "You recently posed a question. My answer is 'no', Paco Pelenzuela Peres has no business with Carlos." Philipe paused while the waiter was serving our order: a latté for me and an espresso for him. Then he went on, "Pelenzuela Peres is the doctor of Silvia, Carlos' wife."

Before I could open my mouth, he cockily added, "Don't thank me, I didn't need to do an extensive research. My dear wife and Silvia happen to be good friends."

How could Agustina and Silvia not become friends?! They were too similar not to notice each other among the Spanish parents of the European School of Frankfurt. Well educated, once having a good job in Spain (Silvia - as an accountant, Agustina - as a history researcher), willing to have an active life but having little chance for both spoke no German.

They met in the school that was created in Frankfurt after the city had become a host of the European Central Bank. In fact, every city hosting an EU institution or agency must have a European School, where EU employees' kids could study according to the curriculum of their home countries. The "mother" of all European Schools, which was located in Brussels, of course, contained the language sections of all EU member states. But the European School of Frankfurt was much smaller and could offer education only in English, German, French, and Italian. That's why the parents of Spanish kids had to organize themselves and arrange for their offspring Spanish-speaking afternoon activities. Agustina's son was in the same class as Silvia's older twins, while the daughter was the classmate of the younger twins. Both ladies jointly (and enthusiastically) organized for Spanish schoolkids what normal parents fear as the devil fears holy water: class trips, readings, concerts, and stuff like this. No wonder that both of them were invited to join the European School Parents' Committee.

"So how come such an active parent needs a doctor?" I asked.

Apparently, it was no secret. Many mothers in the school knew it too. Silvia suffered from headaches, so sudden and strong that they sometimes made her behave strangely. One day, Agustina prepared the cake for the school fair, to sell in pieces to collect money for one of those "European-Children-for-Africa-initiatives". Silvia came around to help prepare the cake stand. When the cake was cut, Silvia took it and… dropped it. She claimed she wanted to place it right in front of the poster "Spanish delicacies", but Agustina could see that she missed that table by a good half a meter. Agustina even thought that Silvia had dropped the cake on purpose because it looked much better than hers. But some minutes later Silvia became pale and miserable. She had to leave the fair without seeing the school performance of all her twins, which no Spanish mama would miss. So Agustina's offense died out.

Another day, Agustina witnessed how those headaches could become real torture. "Since she saw it, she envies neither Silvia's two housekeepers nor her jewelry, nothing that a woman can be jealous about," Philipe exultantly concluded and sipped his espresso.

One day, Silvia brought the older twins to a birthday party. She was upset because one of their housekeepers had quit with immediate effect. Actually, those girls constantly kept leaving because handling two pairs of twins in a set with Carlos would be too much, even for Mary Poppins[70]. Whenever these girls had a chance, they complained about having to combine babysitting with cooking, shopping, ironing, and other household tasks. On that day, the most long-term one lost her nerves, packed, and left without saying a word. The necessity to look again for additional help upset Silvia tremendously.

After confirming with the parents of the birthday kid when they should pick up the children, Agustina and Silvia stepped out onto the street. Suddenly, Silvia's face got pinched with disgust. "This entire house smells rotten fish; how can they throw a children's party there?!" she exclaimed. Agustina didn't notice any smell but preferred not to dispute with a bad-tempered Silvia who jumped on the next topic and started complaining about her life in Frankfurt without sun, friends, job, and the Spanish language. To stop this miserable buzzing, Agustina asked whether Silvia would come to a reading evening for their younger kids. "I wish I would never have to bother myself with all this," Silvia snapped. "Why can't we let the school do its job?" Her face creased and her voice got louder, "I hate listening to all the kids talk. It can be interesting only to their parents,

---

[70] Magical nanny created by the Australian-British writer Pamela Travers

although I wouldn't mind skipping what mine are prattling too. I have enough of that at home." Agustina paused uncomfortably.

Suddenly Silvia reeled; her upper body lurched toward her feet, and she vomited explosively. Agustina was helplessly running around her, patting Silvia's shoulder, offering to bring her back to the party house. But Silvia ignored all the efforts. She seemed to be somewhere far away, in a world of pain and consternation. And so did both stay for quite some time.

Finally, Silvia came round and handed Agustina her smartphone, "I have one of my usual headaches and can't drive. Please call Carlos, he will pick me up." And in a voice full of hate, she added, "It's all his fault. I've got these since I became a mother."

Agustina dialed Carlos, who didn't seem to be surprised. He briefly asked where they were and arrived in ten minutes. By then Silvia looked like a dead person: pale, with violet circles around her eyes, and bluish lips.

"And then came Doctor Francisco Pelenzuela Peres."

"Why 'Francisco'? The doctor I am interested in is called 'Paco'!" I gasped.

"All Spanish Franciscos are usually called 'Paco'. When you meet more Spaniards, you'll get used to it," Philipe explained. "So, Paco is a good doctor indeed," Philipe concluded. "Silvia once even told my wife that he had made her life more predictable."

Philipe pushed away the coffee cup, ready to leave.

"Last question, Philipe," I said, "do you by chance know when Silvia started getting treatment from doctor Paco?"

"Around last summer holidays," Philipe replied.

Right when I joined the Cider Glass, I thought.

Isabel makes a phone call

"Are we still InSup?" I gasped when entering Isabel's office.

She wore headphones with a foam microphone at the mouth, which fit better in a cockpit. Ian with sparkling eyes and similar headphones was busy settling something among the accurately sorted files on Isabel's desk. He looked like a board engineer getting ready for his first flight.

"I am going to make a phone call to Paco Pelenzuela Peres," Isabel replied. "And Ian is going to record it." She glanced at me unseeing, took from her desk a pencil, and plugged it into her hair bun.

"Why would Silvia's doctor talk to you?"

Isabel pressed her lips. The freckles on her pale upper cheeks and nose became dark, matching the shade of her mouse-gray vest suit, which she wore next to the skin. "I will tell him I am Carlos' assistant. Cristina is on a whole-day training today, so no chance our calls cross."

Ian appeared to be finished with the cables. He sat opposite Isabel and opened his laptop. "I was monitoring Cristina's telephone," he explained to me. "Her last call to this doctor was quite some time ago, before Christmas. Isabel's call won't look suspicious."

I nodded. The plan sounded good. We needed tangible evidence. Carlos' numerous emails, in which he rejected the Diadem without proper explanation, wouldn't serve as sufficient proof.

Ian darted his look from me to Isabel. "I am ready to start," he finally said.

"So am I," Isabel responded, plugging the second pencil into her hair. "Let's get it done."

"Consultorio del doctor Pelenzuela."[71]

"Buenas tardes, esta es la oficina de Carlos de Santos Gomez[72]," Isabel started in an unfamiliar, high-pitched voice.

After a brief exchange, she was asked to hold a line. A minute later, another voice asked in English, "How can I help you?"

"I am so glad you speak English, my Spanish is terrible," Isabel chirped. "I need to track a delivery to the spouse of my boss, Mr. De Santos Gomez. The spouse's name is Silvia Molina Alvarez. Could you help me, please?"

---

[71] Office of Doctor Pelenzuela (Spanish)
[72] Good afternoon, this is the office of Carlos de Santos Gomez (Spanish)

The person on the line readily replied, "Let me see... Anti-Mig... (Isabel gave both of us a meaningful look and scribbled something in her notepad). Yes, delivery in ten days."

"Strange. Do you see whether the previous delivery arrived?" Isabel asked.

"Yes, it did. Shipment is done directly from the US," (Isabel sent us another look) "but we usually get a delivery confirmation."

"You are amazingly well-organized. Do you have a confirmation from the previous month?"

"Yes."

"And from the month before?"

"Yes, the notifications punctually come in the first week of every month."

"This is really, really strange," Isabel went on chirping. "Maybe Anti-Mig was delivered when no one was at home, and it is still waiting for Ms. Molina Alvarez in the post office? Such things often happen in Frankfurt, you know."

Her vis-à-vis seemed to be glad that Isabel found herself an explanation. When asked to forward the previous notification, she readily asked to which email address.

"Do you have the address of Cristina, another assistant of Mr. de Santos Gomez?"

"Cristina Tornero?"

"Yes, please forward it to her. We are working together. She is aware of the problem too."

"Sure, I understand. Ms. Tornero has just got it."

Ian checked something on his monitor and gave us a thumb-up.

"Hi, guys." Philipe was standing at the door, his eyes traveling on us. He made a comically terrified face and switched to whisper, "Sorry to disturb… Isabel, I need you but I'll come back later."

I rushed towards him, hoping he wouldn't pay much attention to Ian's equipment. "Isabel helps me with a new assessment," I hissed.

"And Ian is working his way towards a superior caste?" Philipe hissed in response.

I glanced at Ian while spasmodically thinking about how to justify his presence, especially the headphones. But my concerns were unnecessary. Ian held a wire that mysteriously appeared in his hands as if fixing something under Isabel's desk. He didn't seem to pay attention to us. Isabel scribbled something on the paper and showed it to Philipe: "In 15 min. by you."

"Take your time, not urgent," Philipe whispered and turned away.

Soon after he had left, the call was over.

"It looks like the gossip of Agustina makes sense," Isabel declared, taking off the headphones.

Ian was already disconnecting the recorder. "I forwarded to myself the doctor's notification and deleted it from Cristina's inbox," he said. "It's a simple shipment notice containing the name of Silvia and her address, but of course no name of the medication."

Isabel shrugged, "Not a problem, Anti-Mig was mentioned twice in this phone call: once by me and once by the assistant to Pelenzuela Peres, we will provide the exact timecodes. This is a solid proof."

"Actually I didn't get it," Ian admitted. "Why is this medication a proof?"

"Look at this." Isabel beckoned us to her monitor. There was a scan of an article entitled "Exciting news for migraine patients" authored by Francisco Pelenzuela Peres and even containing his little picture (a typical doctor's beard-and-glasses look). "My contact in the European Medicines Agency sent it to me. They have a database of all the medical magazines in Europe," Isabel explained.

Apparently, doctor Pelenzuela Peres took part in the research program conducted by the American Neurological Centre California. The research aimed to develop and test a new medicine on volunteers suffering from different types of migraines.

"Migraine," I gasped. "Carlos' wife suffers from migraine! How could I not understand it before? Temporary loss of orientation, phantom smells, and mood swings. Obviously, she has a very heavy form."

Isabel nodded approvingly and went on. "The article states that the Neurological Centre has got volunteers from all over the world. I guess Doctor Pelenzuela Peres included Silvia in the testing group and the treatment did work for her. Now look here," she marked with a cursor the sentence *US Neurological Centre in California is undergoing licensing and registration in the US and intends to start the same procedure in the EU Medicines Agency.* "Do you understand what it means?" Isabel exclaimed. "They haven't come to the European market! Not yet. But before doing so, they would like to assess their chances and those of the potential competitors."

"And the Diadem is their competitor," I said.

Isabel victoriously tossed her head, which made pencils fly out of her auburn hair bun. "Omm Alla,[73] were all these in my head?!" She gaped at Ian, who already jumped on the floor to collect the pencils. Then she turned to me, "You got it right, Maxim. From what I saw in the Diadem dossier, Alice and co-founders were presenting their invention in conferences, were publishing articles about it, so the Neurological Centre California is aware of the Diadem. But an invention by a couple of junior doctors can become a real competitor only if InSup or anybody else provides them with funding. And on the other side, we have a wife of the InSup director whose life became so much better thanks to Anti-Mig."

---

[73] Holy Mother of God (Maltese)

"And to keep receiving this medicine for his dear wife, Carlos needs to do only one thing: reject the funding for The Diadem Project and any other start-ups, which the Californian Centre sees as competitors," I concluded.

Isabel shrugged. "A safe way. He only needs to move an experienced analyst out of M-Unit and claim that the new young project analyst made poor work that doesn't meet InSup quality standards. Who would pay attention? The European Commission usually screens the projects that were approved for funding, they don't care about the rejected ones."

I approached the window and looked down at the River Main promenade. Wrapped in the spring green, the water invitingly winked at me under the sun. "So I was like an annoying bee for Carlos, bringing him The Diadem assessment again and again. No wonder he killed plenty of other assessments too; otherwise, the rejection of the Diadem wouldn't have looked credible," I bitterly laughed.

Isabel poured water with slices of apples into three glasses. "Carlos could have rejected your work again and again, for long months." She handed water to Ian and me. "But then you made a mistake. You sent him the assessment without Broomy's approval, so Carlos got a pretext to intimidate you. I think he counted very much on your resignation and now will try to punish you for not doing so."

"Can we stop him now when we got him pinned?" Ian asked gingerly.

Isabel raised her water glass, we followed. "No, we can't. Nobody can fire Carlos. The Executive Director of InSup is appointed by the European Parliament, and only the parliament can fire him." She cast her eyes from me to Ian and back. "But we have a proven conflict of interest. It suffices for the Commission to launch an internal investigation and recommend Carlos to reassess the Diadem."

"Is that all?" Ian mumbled in dismay.

"For a European institution that's a lot!" Isabel replied vehemently. "But I feel with you. The extent, to which the EU bureaucracy tolerates grubbiness, is startling."

New task from Carlos

From: Cristina Tornero

To: All_InSup_staff

CC: Carlos de Santos Gomez; Isabel Aquilina

Subject: Coordination of the internal audit submission

Dear all,

Please be informed that Carlos has appointed Isabel Aquilina as a coordinator of the package to be provided to the European Commission's internal auditors. Therefore, before sending it to Hilde, please first show the documents to Isabel. She will check the content and formatting and might require you to make amendments. Please note that Isabel's "green light" is necessary before sending the documents to Hilde.

Thank you in advance for your cooperation,

Cristina

"Hi, Maxim, would you be available for a coffee?" quacked Carlos, poking his head into my office. He stretched his lips as if somebody squeezed his balls, but I already knew that in his mimic vocabulary, it meant a friendly smile.

"Ye...yes." Pretending that I was busy with something else would be no option, for Cristina always checked our calendars for him.

Not knowing where he was going, I followed him to the elevator and then out of the Cider Glass towards the Main Train Station. All the way I kept my distance and hunched my back to look smaller. I remembered Isabel's advice, "God forbid you to talk to him while walking, this would force him to look at you bottom-up. Not his favorite, given that you are two heads taller than him. Just walk silently behind like a slave."

Still without saying anything Carlos suddenly opened a shabby door and ducked into a dim room that turned out to be an unspectacular coffee shop with a wooden counter and a few standing tables.

"Buenos Dias," said a girl at the counter.

She looked familiar. Probably it's in Barenik that I saw this glossy black hair and a stretched facial contour. She and Carlos exchanged greetings in Spanish before she politely asked, "Was darf es sein?[74]"

"They have excellent coffee here. The best in the city if I may," Carlos said switching to a whisper by the end of each sentence. For the next one, he obviously didn't take enough air. "What are you having?" he croaked. It sounded like a point-blank shot rather than an offer.

I remembered how once Sergey Vladimirovich Kamarinov invited my team to the special canteen for Centrobank's top management. Naturally, it was much smaller than our staff canteen. But the respectful silence and the presence of some board of directors' members intimidated us. We sat at the table covered with a snow-white starched tablecloth and froze.

"Ну, шо будете?"[75] Kamarinov said archly.

---

[74] What would you like? (German)
[75] So, what are you having? (Russian)

We had no idea. There was no menu card on the table and no food could be seen in the entire place. Kamarinov watched us with a semi-smile. The three of us helplessly looked at our team lead Slava.

"Same as you, Sergey Vladimirovich," Slava jabbered.

"Right," Kamarinov said contentedly and took the menu card from the hands of a waitress, who had just approached.

"Same as you, Carlos," I mumbled.

Carlos nodded and said something in Spanish to the barista. "Muy bien," she replied.

When I took out my wallet, Carlos raised his palm. "It's on me." He meant to make a royal gesture of generosity, even if he almost hit me in the nose. We received two tiny cups of espresso and went to a tall coffee table. Suddenly, Carlos appeared to be taller than usual. (Later I noticed that our table was placed at a stair on which Carlos stepped).

"The best coffee in the city," Carlos repeated looking at me expectantly.

I swallowed an unbearably bitter liquid that knocked down my receptors. "Very tasty, thank you, Carlos."

"My pleazur."

Under his gaze, I sipped my espresso again.

"I want to share with you my concehrns, Maxim," he suddenly said in his usual tone, looking somewhere behind my shoulder. "The upcoming internal audit is crucial for the agency. We must be very well prepehrd for it."

I studiously nodded.

"However, our files are not yet in the state I would like them to be. I need somebody who will enhance the quality of our documentassion. And I was thinking of you."

"Of me?!"

He tilted his head and closed his eyes as if tired of talking about something unpleasant. "I think we both agrrree that your assessments are weak and so is aderrrens to European values. Isn't it?"

After I squeezed a "yes" out of myself he went on. "You could be of benefit to the Agency."

"How?"

So far, internal auditors were interested in what Carlos called a "quantitative report": the number of start-ups that got funding, the number of rejections, the number of business trips, the number of recruitment campaigns, and the number of meetings the Agency hosted. The disaster could happen once they arrive at the Cider Glass. On-site they could request any (at this word Carlos' eyes behind glasses got rounder) additional information. Nobody knew what they would decide to look at and why. "We should be suhr in each and every document. The problem is that some files are currently not satisfahctory. You should restructuhr and if need be redraft them," Carlos concluded.

"Sorry, but why can't colleagues arrange the files themselves? Isn't it logical?"

Carlos listened to me with the mouth shut but he made a face as if trying to touch his nose with his tongue. "Colleagues have much more important things to do," he finally answered.

"So do I!"

"Not anymore. Maxim, I am kindly asking you to make this task your highest priority. Assessments can wait." He gazed at me, and for one second I saw my own distorted reflection in his round glasses. "I am afraid we can't discuss it anymore. I trust you will be fully committed to this task. Rrremember you sehrve Europe, we all sehrve," at these words, he glanced at the barista.

I flinched for I finally recognized her. In a uniform of apron and without her scarlet lipstick, she looked neither dangerous nor seductive. But it was her, Señora Tais from Barcelona.

Back in the office, I found my inbox flooded with new emails from Fadila. These were the documents to be brushed up: technical specifications for procurement, minutes of meetings, and project assessments done by other units. Dozens of emails with bold black subject lines and several attachments each. After their number reached 40, I stopped counting. Now I could easily imagine what Cinderella felt on the evening before the big ball.

"Lovely familiar files." Isabel was scrolling down those documents after I had told her about my coffee with Carlos. "I bounced them back to their senders because they are terrible. Broomy and Fadila turned out to have no idea how to conduct the quality assurance of audit files. That's why Carlos asked me for a personal favor to jump in."

Isabel took the mouse and paged the documents again. "Interesting. I returned many more poor files, but not all of them are here," she mumbled.

She took one of her pencils and wrote something down. "Look," she finally said and showed me the names she had just written. "These are the names of colleagues whose documents you should improve. Do you notice any logic?"

I read her calligraphic letters - Fadila, Diego, José-Luis – and fetched a bitter laughter. "All Spaniards. In one go, Carlos blocks me from doing assessments and offers a nice little service to De Goya network members from InSup."

At Alice's home

In Russia, my Fridays finished at a quarter to five. InSup had no "shortened Fridays". I followed Karolina's example, who worked longer hours five days a week because she didn't want to postpone anything to the next week unless it was unavoidable. Later, I noticed that not everybody in the Cider Glass treats Fridays like Karolina. Philipe always disappeared after lunch, although still checking his emails and answering the urgent ones. Many colleagues commuted and had to catch a plane or a train home; therefore, they declined meetings on Friday afternoons.

On that Friday, I left the office in a commuter-like hour to go to Heidelberg. At VorschungsLab I spotted Alice's bike. I took a seat in the opposite café from where I could watch the entrance door. Alice had no idea I was around. Calling her didn't feel right. I preferred to wait patiently for the end of her working day. Like Karolina, she didn't seem to have shortened Fridays. The waiting time allowed me to think once again about what I was going to do, namely to send European ethical rules to hell.

Finally, I saw Alice leaving VorschungsLab. In jeans and a white polo shirt, she looked thin and fragile. To my surprise, instead of picking up her bike, she walked in the opposite direction. I ran out of the café and followed. She was in no hurry, watching vitrines and enjoying a warm evening. Suddenly, she sped up and disappeared around the corner. I rushed after her, but she dissolved in the air. Confused, I went along the street and noticed an inner court where Alice probably had turned. It was a quiet place. A two-floor house and a couple of cherry trees hiding behind their dollishly pink crowns.

"Maxim," Alice said, emerging from the trees, her mobile phone in her hand. "How come you are here?"

"I wanted to see you. How come you are playing spy games?"

She shrugged. Some funny things happening in the last days summed up in something vexatious. Days ago, Yinzi noticed a man near VorschungsLab. Actually, rather his backpack. Not too big, it seemed to rest comfortably on the back of its carrier. Yinzi adored even the color: dark brown with a thin blue stripe striking it diagonally. She even wanted to ask who produces such lovely backpacks, but didn't dare.

Even more was her surprise when she noticed the same backpack near the University Hospital. This time she decisively went to the owner to ask about the brand, but when she came closer, she saw again the man from around VorschungsLab. This time she took a closer look at him: young, with an unremarkable face and average constitution. He was difficult to remember, but she recalled that it was his cold and unfriendly glance that had stopped her from asking about his nice backpack. Yinzi laughingly complained to Alice about such a misfortune. Alice supposed that the "dream of a backpack" together with its owner belongs to the University somehow. But then she noticed it... near her home (with no chance to identify the carrier). And today from the window she saw somebody walking around her bike (with no chance to spot the backpack). So, she decided to do a trick and catch him.

"I just wanted to take his picture and report to the police. But it was you. Maybe I became overly suspicious," Alice laughed.

We left the courtyard and walked back to pick up Alice's bike.

"I was indeed after you," I said.

I felt relieved that finally, I could explain to her what was really going on with The Diadem Project. The bike she was pushing was between us, but I could feel we were getting closer. I put my hand on the wheel. It allowed me to touch her warm fingers.

When I told her about my talk to Philipe, she interrupted me. "Neurological Centre California? You know they approached us. They seemed impressed, but it didn't work because they didn't want to invest in us. They just wanted to buy the idea and to have all the co-founders out."

I gasped. But Alice said it wasn't anything extraordinary. Many start-ups frequently get similar offers. Alice and her partners refused and forgot about this story.

"Can you find out the name of the person who approached you?" I asked. "It could be an important supplement to my investigation and a pressure on Carlos."

Alice stopped and looked at me the way I secretly dreamed of. "I am so touched by what you are doing for me."

"What if I do it for myself?" I couldn't help putting my hands on her shoulders. We were alone in the entire city. Only at the end of the street, a bike popped up.

"I hope you don't risk your job because of me," Alice whispered.

I didn't answer. Nothing was more important at this moment than the pulse on her neck under my fingers. The bicycle was coming closer. *Crazy how he drives on the sidewalk with such a speed*, I thought. The next moment, I acted intuitively. I kicked Alice's bike and simultaneously pulled her in my direction. She screamed in pain and fell on me. My back scraped the ground, making my skin burn. The cyclist spun and disappeared around the corner.

Alice was lying on me, eyes closed. "Are you all right?" I asked.

To my relief, she nodded without opening her eyes and stretched her lips to smile. "These insolent cyclists."

I helped her up. She was shivering and looked haggard. The right knee of her jeans was covered with an augmenting blood spot. "I'll lock your bike and call us a taxi," I mumbled.

Once I finished the manipulations with the locker, I noticed Alice was sitting on the pavement. When she raised her eyes to me, they were like dark cold stones on her greenish face. "My migraine has just started," she whispered. "Please bring me home."

All the way in the taxi, she was breathing through her mouth. In front of her door, she grabbed the keys and, without opening her eyes, gave them to me. When I opened the door, she took me by the hand and brought me inside. Then she handed me her mobile phone. "Please call Yinzi and ask her to bring the Diadem. She will understand." While I was explaining to Yinzi what happened, Alice lay on the bed like a cut flower.

"Yinzi is in the hospital. She can come in half an hour or so," I said in a low voice.

"Please feel at home. I'd better not move and not talk to you now."

I looked around. The apartment was neat, modest, and cozy. I imagined how Alice has breakfast in a large kitchen and how she sits on a sofa in a living room. Her bedroom was fresh and well-lit. Only Alice in her dirty and bloodstained jeans looked like a wrong element. Afraid to touch her, I covered her with a blanket I found in a living room.

Yinzi looked older than I remembered, maybe because of her unicorn hair being tied up in a bun. She said hello and immediately went to the bedroom. I heard her talking quietly to Alice. Finally, she entered the kitchen. I silently put in front of her a cup of green tea.

"I turned the Diadem on the strongest regime," she explained in an educative tone doctors speak with the relatives of their patients. "It's a rare opportunity for us to test it during an acute phase. Usually, when a sudden attack happens, patients prefer to rely on their medication. But Alice remains a scientist and an experimentalist even in pain."

Yinzi was going to check on Alice every half an hour. She hoped that in a couple of hours, Alice would feel better.

"What would she need then?" I asked.

"Hot tea with sugar would definitely do her good. Let's think of us now, we also need to survive the next hours."

It was past eight o'clock, and I ran to the closest supermarket. Then together with Yinzi, we prepared a dinner. Yinzi's moves were quick; she knew where to find what in Alice's kitchen.

"Is this a reason she invented the Diadem?" I asked when we were eating the freshly prepared noodle salad with tomatoes and green beans.

Yinzi nodded. "Her mother also suffers from strong migraines. In her childhood, before any party or family event, Alice used to pray that her mother wouldn't get it because those attacks often started in the morning and the family had to cancel all their plans right away.

"Today it happened in the middle of the day. Why?"

"Maybe because of a sudden fall or because she was tired. There are still many things we don't know about migraines."

"I don't want to scare you, but I have the impression this bicycle crashed into us on purpose," I said. "He was driving straight at us."

"Did he, by chance, have a brown backpack?" Yinzi asked.

"No, he didn't. Probably he decided to change the outfit after Alice had spotted him near her home."

Yinzi looked at me suspiciously. "You know, we have a very strong bicycle lobby in Germany. They are trying to get as many bike lanes as possible. Some cyclists might drive into you just because you happened to step into their lane. They are really mad about defending their space."

I shook my head. "I think somebody, a big company, would like to stop the Diadem research. Have you heard about the Neurological Centre California?"

"Yes," she immediately replied, "I was sure they like us and want to become our partners. But then they offered us to sell the patent on the Diadem. It was a generous offer…But we rejected it, for we wanted to develop the Diadem ourselves." She cast a distrustful look at me, as if deciding whether to go on. "They contacted me afterward," she finally said. "Offered me a job if I persuade others to sell the patent. I declined, of course, such games are not for me."

"Did they offer the same to the others?"

She shook her head. "I don't know… never spoke about it to them."

In two hours, Alice got better. Pallid and wary, she drank tea and even wanly smiled when Yinzi declared that the fourth regime works exactly as expected and that "the night will finish the recovery process."

"I guess I can leave you alone with her?" Yinzi asked me. "I disinfected the abrasion on the knee and helped her to put on her pajamas. She is going to spend in the Diadem the entire night. Call me in case of emergency." Suddenly she smiled mischievously, "Otherwise, I hope you have a calm night."

Alice fell asleep. I washed the dishes in the kitchen. The only place I could sleep was a sofa in the living room. It felt unreal to be going to bed in Alice's apartment just like this, having Alice sleeping next door. While diving into sleep, I thought that although I saw this apartment for the first time, I immediately felt at home. And everything here - the teapot, a fresh towel I found to take a shower, a blanket I took to cover myself - felt like mine. Everything here was so welcoming: the bookshelves in the living room, the pot with basil on the window. And behind the glycine-cloaked window was Moscow, quiet and deserted. A car stopped in front of the house. I could barely see the driver's face, but somehow I knew he was looking up at me through the windscreen. He carried danger. I wanted to get out of the window but couldn't move. I knew he saw me. He switched on the headlight, painfully bright, shooting straight into my eyes, and started the engine. "Good I am on the first floor," I thought and suddenly noticed that I was not. I was already outside, and the car rushed straight forward. Alice stood next to me. I pushed her as far away as possible. But the driver turned and targeted her. I rushed towards Alice, but she was gone. The car turned to follow her. The driver sped up. I was too far away and knew that something bad was going to happen.

"Maxim," Alice whispered.

"Alice, run," I told her and woke up from the sound of my voice. Alice was sitting next to me. She smelled shower gel. "It was just a bad dream and an uncomfortable sofa," she said.

"Are you feeling better?"

"Yes, it's gone." Even in the morning twilight, I could see that she was smiling. It filled me with joy.

"You must lay comfortably, otherwise you will have a headache too," she said, drizzling water on me from her freshly washed hair. She radiated energy. "I have just changed the bedsheets. Why don't you lay on my bed and try to fall asleep again?"

"Only together with you," I said, taking her in my hands.

It was early morning when the black velvet of the sky started blanching and the city birds started singing because that was the only time when they could hear each other. It was an hour when no words were needed. We broke each other's boundaries. The only thing I wanted was to stand still in time together with her and soak up every touch.

Shadowing and robbery

I returned to Frankfurt only the next day after having accompanied Alice to her night shift in the hospital. The memories of being together with her were filling me up like a balloon. Unable to lock myself in the apartment, I took a walk. For the first time since I split up with Nika, I felt like I had a girlfriend. Not a one-night stand, not a sex partner, but someone with whom I wanted to be outside the bed, too.

The evening was warm and lilac, and so was my mood until I noticed a man. It could have been a student, but something in him made me anxious. It was neither his outfit, nor appearances, but the way he walked. He was exaggeratingly moving his head as if admiring the city. We were in the narrow street of Goethestrasse: full of fancy boutiques, good for window-shopping, but otherwise nothing to admire so euphorically. I recalled I saw this bloke ten minutes ago when I stopped to admire the Alte Oper Square illuminated in peach-colored shades. Back then, he rushed past the Alte Oper fountain, and I even thought that he must be a local who had long ago stopped noticing the beauty of his city.

The idea he might be after me filled me with nausea and a wish to run. I forced myself to slow down, as if distracted by my own thoughts. While checking for cars before crossing Kaiserstrasse, I could inspect my possible shadow. Older than me, with short mousy hair, scruffy jeans, and a gray hoody. I took out my mobile phone, pretending to have received a message. It allowed me to slow down naturally. Twice on my way, I discreetly turned back. He augmented the distance between us but was still around. Alice and Yinzi were right, it was hard to remember his face. The backpack with a blue stripe also wasn't there. Instead, he carried a bumbag on his starting belly. During my last attempt to examine him, our eyes met. He held my gaze with a poker face, but his eyes didn't seem to have alighted on me accidentally. He knew who I was.

Our weird saunter continued. I was frenetically thinking of where to bring him so that he would lose sight of me. The sky turned dark blue. I stepped on the brightly illuminated bridge to cross the River Main.

Shoot me… shoot me[76]

There are always street musicians on Frankfurt bridges. No wonder. Tourists love walking there, as they offer a wonderful view of the skyline. But for tourists, it was too late. I stopped near two musicians who didn't seem to care they had almost no audience and generously spread their voices over the river, "*Come together right now over me!*"

I glanced over the shoulder. He came very close. In the street light, I could see well his face. Looking straight at me, he screwed

---

[76] "Come together" by John Lennon, Paul McCartney

his face into a smile. *He is trying to scare me*, I thought and hurried from the bridge.

Shoot me... shoot me

On the other bank of the city, I felt more familiar. Here I had more options to bring him to and shake him off. We went further in Sachsenhausen and came closer to a little art gallery my ex-girlfriend, Gayane, and her friends used for their get-togethers. The gallery had an external staircase leading to the little balcony where visitors could smoke. I planned to climb there and take a picture of my shadow while he was sniffing around in the courtyard. I turned to the street on which the gallery was located and ran as fast as I could. Some minutes later I was on the balcony, the gallery was closed. From my hidey hole, I had a perfect view. My follower appeared soon. He poorly pretended to have a walk, but by his heavy breath, one could see he had been running. He slowly walked around, pretending he was interested in the building, but his eyes were scanning everything around, quickly but thoroughly.

"Ладно, дома увидимся[77]," he suddenly said and left.

His words paralyzed me. It was like in spy movies, but worse because it was real. I don't remember how much time I sat without moving. Finally, I sent the photos and video to Ian and climbed down.

---

[77] Ok, see you at home (Russian)

The rest of my way home was clear to go. I even started wondering whether my shadow indeed had said something in Russian or maybe it was just my fantasy. But then something felt wrong about my flat's entrance door. I stopped and tried to understand what was bothering me. I found the answer quickly: my doormat was missing. *Coincidence,* I persuaded myself and put my key into the lock. The door cracked open without me turning the lock. Sweating in fear, I entered. The flat was dark. I went in and switched on the lights in one room after another. Finally, I could exhale with relief; the apartment was empty. I glanced again across the living room and my blood curdled.

"Maxim," somebody called from outside, "are you there?"

It was Ian. Isabel stood next to him. "We had a walk when we received the pictures and a video. We felt that something was wrong and ran home. What happened?" Ian gave me a measuring look. "Are you ok?"

I silently beckoned them to enter the living room and pointed at the coffee table. There was an open bottle of beer on it. It was empty because its content covered the table and the floor nearby with a smelly, sticky layer. My door mat also laid on the coffee table. I raised it with two fingers to find my InSup laptop under it, open and smelling beer.

Isabel got everything immediately. "They entered the apartment and spoiled your laptop the way everybody would think you simply dropped the beer bottle on it."

"Did they do anything else?" Ian asked.

I shook my head.

"What about your private iPad? It's where you keep all the files for our investigation, don't you?" Ian asked.

I ran to the bedroom with little doubt about what I would find there. The night table where I usually kept my iPad charging was empty. The charger wasn't there too.

I returned to Isabel and Ian. "It's gone."

"Strange that they didn't steal your InSup laptop too. Why just spoil it? Nowadays, the files can be easily restored," Isabel said pensively.

"I think I know why," Ian answered instead of me. "A stolen corporate computer is an operational incident because there is a risk that it contains confidential information, which becomes available to the external world. It should be included in the InSup operational incident report. And if somebody poured beer on the laptop, it doesn't classify as an incident but just as a technical accident, which we don't need to report."

"I don't get it," I said.

Isabel sighed. "The robbers didn't want InSup's incident report to get longer because it's Carlos who bears the ultimate responsibility for all such incidents. That's why they simply poured beer on it. It means they were sent here by Carlos."

Ian nervously tumbled his hair. "But then, Carlos knows about our investigation?"

"Yes, he does, but I don't understand how he found out," I replied, thinking that Nika would have been much better in keeping it a secret; probably that's why it's her and not me whom Kamarinov offered the job in Hong Kong.

"I know how," Isabel suddenly said, her face flushed with anger and the freckles on the upper cheeks became bright ginger.

In the cinema

From: Isabel Aquilina

To: Contributors_to_IAC_mission

Subject: Kind reminder - Submission to EC Auditors

Dear colleagues,

The deadline for submitting the documentation to EC Auditors is approaching. Please look at the table I created with the overview of those parts I am still missing from you.

Please send me those parts asap. If you have questions, don't hesitate to ask me.

Thank you in advance,

Isabel

From: Philipe Fernandez

To: Isabel Aquilina

Subject: Re: Kind reminder - Submission to EC Auditors - WAF??

I have just seen that I must prepare an "external engagement report". I had no clue about it. Could you meet me and explain?

I snuck into a cinema room. Isabel and Ian were already there, in the last row, right next to the lane. Ian held a king-size pack of popcorn.

"A German social drama, seriously?" Ian hissed. "Especially when in the room next door there is a thriller?!"

"The other room is crowded, impossible to talk," I replied. "It's much better here. I have bad news, guys: somebody has just attacked Yinzi."

Tah-tah. Tah dah tah-tah. The main theme from *Mission Impossible* switched on. It was publicity for the new movie coming soon.

Isabel pressed fingers against her open mouth. "Is she all right?"

"Yes, but terrified. Alice says the attacker had taken her handbag, which he dropped 200 meters away with all the contents untouched. No doubt it's the same guy or one of those who crashed into Alice and broke into my apartment. If they see us together, they will be after you two. That's why I asked you to come here."

Even in the dim light of the cinema room, I could see their aghast faces.

"They might attack you again. You shouldn't be alone," Isabel whispered.

"Don't worry about me. I will be all right. And I would definitely feel better if you stayed out of sight."

"But this terror should be stopped, Maxim." Isabel became so loud that the rare volunteers to watch a social drama started turning their heads. "Let's go to the police," she suggested in a lower voice.

I shook my head. "There is only one way to stop them. We should complete our investigation and send it to internal auditors. Once it's out, there will be nothing to browbeat me for."

Isabel frowned. "How can we complete it if they took your iPad?" she asked.

Ian answered her instead of me. "I have everything safe and sound. After every update, Maxim sent the file to me. That was Maxim's idea."

"Wow." Isabel pecked Ian on the cheek. "Then tonight I can finalize it and send it out to the internal auditors."

"No, not you," I interrupted her. "The report will go from my email. Neither you nor Ian should be associated with it. After all, it's my assessment."

They were shaking heads distrustfully, searching for the arguments to persuade me. Both looked lost.

"Spiderman returns," said the screen, "ab 18. August im Kino[78]."

"Guys, I am sorry I got you in trouble. But I promise everything will be good again," I said, and before they could answer me, slipped

---

[78] As of 18 August in the cinema (German)

down the staircase. I was afraid they would notice that everything went out of my control.

On the same day in the evening, I received a call from Alice. The supervisor of research projects, Doctor Roth, persuaded the University Hospital to close The Diadem Project. Alice and Yinzi got time until 30 June to complete the ongoing tests. Afterward, they planned to rejoin other Diadem co-founders in Berlin. She begged me to stop fighting windmills and not to risk my career. In a voice she thought sounded self-assured, she described plenty of opportunities waiting for the Diadem in the German capital. I don't remember what I answered. Her words were bubbling in my head, and only one thought was straight and clear: Alice was leaving Heidelberg forever.

Maxim to Veronika. A whistleblower

Nika, privet.

It's me, writing from a new email account. This platform has a well-done encryption of messages, but I will be still avoiding details.

I want to confess: before I found your idea to write emails repulsive. I thought, if Nika wants to keep me at arm's length, why wouldn't she simply say so? I accepted your rules through gritted teeth, but ever since my iPad was stolen, I have been blessing our emails every day. The burglars won't find a single trace of yours: no

WhatsApp chats, no reference in the contact book. Even our emails won't be found because I was permanently deleting them, as well as my answers to you from the "sent" folder. Exactly like you requested!

Your second piece of advice was a blessing too. You know, before watering my working laptop with beer, they hacked it. I am smiling when I think of their puzzled physiognomies: they couldn't find a single relevant file because there was simply none! Each new bit of information I meticulously sent to the Upper Guitarist and then deleted it from my C-drive. Probably out of fury, they destroyed all my files with a virus.

My iPad looks pristine as well. All the files were deleted long time ago as if I were preparing for sale. See, I've been an assiduous pupil of yours and I am in your hock for this lesson.

Oh, there is yet one more thing you turned out to be right about: Carlos is now after me. He appears to be linked to an American company, the competitor of the Diadem. While Carlos is intimidating me and the inventors, Americans somehow forced the University Hospital to close the Diadem. The Bright Maltese believes that the only way to stop them is to disclose the complete case to the internal audit of our parent organization.

Can you imagine doing something like this in the Centrobank?! If I ever leaked any details of our work to media or even internal security, Kamarinov would have thrown me out with zero severance and a "*волчий билет*[79]" for the rest of my days. But apparently in Europe, they even encourage people to squeal by offering them confidentiality and protection. Instead of calling such guys a spy or a sneak they invented for them a pious term – a whistleblower. They even set up a special channel for whistleblowers through which I will forward the results of my investigation. Carlos will never be told who denounced him. We are expecting the internal audit mission soon and I hope they will arrive in Frankfurt already armed with the information from me.

So here is the outcome of my first year in Germany. Instead of becoming a European professional, I became a whistleblower. It feels right and I want to bring it to an end, even if I have to resign afterward. I don't care. Instead of a sparkling, refreshing drink, the Cider Glass turned to contain quite some acrid booze.

Nika, there is one more favor I still want to ask you, although I probably don't deserve it. Is there a way I can protect the Diadem inventors? My pursuers wrongly think that the inventors help me with my investigation. Is there a way to track those blokes and scare them somehow? I must confess that the Diadem team means something to me. Maybe not as much as you do, but for their safety, I am ready to give anything you would ask me for.

---

[79] Russian idiomatic expression that can be literally translated as "wolf's ticket" and means to be blacklisted

Chapter 7 Conspiracy

Philipe

Isabel had her usual "Vitamin- triple C-look," as I called it: Calm, Certain, Concentrated. But when I came closer, I noticed grayish freckles on her nose and upper cheeks. Her tense face was in an unhealthy contrast with her outfit: a joyful tangerine jumper put over the white shirt with large cuffs. Unseeing, she fiddled with one of her pencils. I felt embarrassed to distract her, but it was she who had texted me to come.

"Isabel," I called, sending her a questioning gaze.

She sighed heavily. "It's not going to be pleasant, but you should hear this nevertheless."

"So, my dear Isabel, here I am." Philipe entered Isabel's office. He was in a good mood, as usual. "Oh, hi, Maxim," he added, noticing me. Not without irritation as I could feel.

"Carlos made Maxim responsible for the quality check of some reports. That's why I asked him to join," Isabel explained.

Philipe sent me a morose gaze. "This internal audit will stay forever in the history of InSup."

In response, I made a helpless gesture to show that this is by far not my choice to be here and in charge of anything. He didn't seem to be persuaded. "Even if there are five quality checkers, I don't understand shit. What is an "external engagement report"? Since when it's me who must deal with this animal?"

"Du calme[80]," Isabel replied tossing her auburn head. "It's a new reporting standard that was introduced recently. You know, the Commission always changes those requirements. Carlos told me that as a press officer you are the best-placed to do it."

"Carlos didn't speak to me about that," Philipe objected with aspiration.

Isabel shrugged. "He trusted I will bring you bad news. But who am I to stop you from talking to Carlos? Feel free to tell him you don't care about the new Commission's requirements." She paused a second, watching Philipe glowing. Satisfied so, she added, "If you are interested, I have an idea. We could approach it pragmatically."

Philipe's attitude changed immediately. He grinned. "Now I recognize you. I am all ears."

Isabel smiled charmingly. "Please have a seat." Philipe readily plopped down. Isabel on the contrary, stood up from her desk and approached him. "Before I offer you my solution, let me pose you a minor question." The smile trickled away from her face. "Did you tell Carlos we investigate his conflict of interest with The Diadem Project?"

---

[80] Calm down (French)

Her question sent me into a tailspin. Trying to hide my shock, I was observing Philipe. He drew in a breath, gazing from Isabel to me and back. "I have no idea what you are talking about," he forced out.

Isabel brought her face closer to Philipe's. "Let me help you. You didn't know it was supposed to be a secret?"

He shook his head. "I always respected you for being smart, wise, and all, but you are going too far. Mind with whom you are playing your games."

I felt like I saw him for the first time. He raised his shoulders, and his face changed as he narrowed his eyes and looked at Isabel with disgust. Even his voice sounded unpleasant.

Isabel didn't seem to notice this change unless she always saw him this way. She stretched her lips in a wide smile, her eyes remaining cold and indifferent. "I don't play games. I am just posing a question. If you have nothing to say, I'd rather let you hurry with producing the external engagement report."

Philipe jumped out and ran to the door. I wanted to run after him, but Isabel raised her snow-white arm while still glancing at Philipe's back. Before opening the door, he turned to us. Instead of the joyful eagle, a blood-thirsty carrion was looking at us. "What do you want from me? Maxim didn't say it was a secret," he shrieked.

Isabel raised both hands in a surrendering gesture. "Fully understand. Then what happened next is not a secret either. Why don't you tell us everything?"

Indeed, Philipe had a chat with Carlos. A harmless one. Carlos complained that M-Unit was underperforming. And Philipe – for the sake of persuading him – said that Maxim was keen to complete one assessment because he's in love with the inventor who submitted it. And love helps move mountains. It was a kind joke to entertain Carlos, nothing more.

"How did Carlos react? Did he ask you anything else?" Isabel narrowed her eyes.

Carlos did. A week later he complained to Philipe that I keep harassing him, and while having full respect for my Russian origins, he fears for the security of his family.

"What?!" I couldn't help screaming.

Isabel ignored me and nodded to Philipe to continue.

Carlos asked Philipe for a favor to talk to a security expert who was supposed to protect Silvia and the kids. Of course, Philipe agreed. Soon, this expert, a very polite man, by the way, called. He said he wanted to make my psychological portrait and asked Philipe to meet me in Bistro 66, at the table near the window, which he already reserved.

"I was sure he sees you and understands that no way you are a psychopath!" Philipe said, for the first time looking me in the eyes.

"So, back then, in Bistro 66, you first told me about Silvia's doctor and afterwards you reported to Carlos that... I know about Silvia's doctor?!I can only admire your quick wits," I snorted.

Unjust reproach. Philipe didn't say a word. Carlos got it from Paco Pelenzuela, personally. Paco was surprised when Carlos' assistant called his office, claiming that Silvia hadn't received the medication for the previous month. And Carlos wasn't stupid. He immediately assumed that it was Maxim who had made the call. The only thing he couldn't understand was which woman would agree to play his assistant. To this question Philipe had a half-joking answer: the girl from Heidelberg, the Diadem start-upper of course! It was just meaningless gossip, which Philipe invented to entertain Carlos.

Isabel turned to me. "That's why they stalked Alice."

"Stalked?" Philipe's eyes searchingly traveled from me to Isabel. "Guys, I couldn't imagine it going that far. And by the way, why don't you ask about things I didn't tell Carlos?"

We simultaneously turned to him.

He simpered. "I didn't tell him, my dear Isabel, that you are behind this investigation. I understood it when Kirill, the barman from that funny imbiss, asked about you. We all know how much Carlos trusts you. Just think how disappointed he would be if he found out. But I didn't say a word because whatever you may think of me, I am always on your side."

Isabel gave him a long, level stare. "This conversation never happened," she finally said. "And you won't need to produce an external engagement report. I am going to delete it from your tasks."

Philipe beamed. "Thank you, my dear, I knew I could always rely on you… And you can rely on me as usual," he added after a pause. Isabel looked away. Philipe nodded to me and stumbled out.

"Honestly, I always considered Philipe a weak chain in our investigation," Isabel told me when the three of us met later in Ian's apartment. "He belongs to the system, much too much to turn against it."

"I still can't believe it. He was always so sarcastic and critical towards the Cider Glass," I objected.

"Towards the Agency, but not to its top management. Have you ever heard him complaining about Carlos?" Isabel smiled. "Do you know why? Because he will never be critical of people who decide about his promotion and workload! Just the contrary, he is keen on doing his boss a favor, for example, by warning him about an investigation like ours."

"I can't get it. Why did he help us then?" Ian asked. "After all, everything we know about the De Goya network and doctor Pelenzuela, we know thanks to him!"

Isabel sighed. "Philipe is smart and efficient. He despises endless tolerance towards lazy and incompetent senior managers the EU institutions are stuffed with. Believe me, he saw plenty of them after he had passed the Concours to the Commission. That's why he often sounds sarcastic. But never - and I mean it - *never* would Philipe miss a chance to benefit from circumstances. Revealing your intentions to Carlos was his chance to win his trust and gratitude. He couldn't resist it."

Ian looked at Isabel anxiously. "But now you have to do his job and produce this external engagement report for auditors?"

Isabel tossed her head, and her auburn hair made a soft wave. "I invented it. Or better to say I exaggerated: auditors ask for such a report from bigger agencies, from InSup they wouldn't need it, an extract from our Annual Report would be enough, but Philipe is too ignorant to know it."

Both Ian and I looked at her with admiration.

"Then may I ask you one very personal question, Isabel?" I said cautiously. "Why are you helping me? Philipe is right: because of me you risk losing Carlos' trust and sympathy."

Isabel pursed her lips.

Once, the Bright Maltese worked in Brussels. She had to prepare an Annual Report for her directorate general. After several weeks of chasing people over the quality of the provided data and reminding them about deadlines, she finalized the publication. The European Parliament and other stakeholders expressed satisfaction; her director was proud; and Isabel believed she had done an outstanding job. But then the director summoned her to his office to say that he had several complaints about her behavior. Colleagues complained she unnecessarily stressed and even humiliated them with her reminders. The director didn't disclose names, but Isabel understood the complaints were raised by those people who produced the worst contributions, on which she had worked the most trying to improve them.

"I saw too many EU employees, incompetent but highly paid, who were pursuing only their interests and giving a shit about Europe. Our investigation is my revenge on those EU parasites," Isabel said dismally.

Rock around the work

From: Hilde Rosenbohm

To: Maxim Reut

CC: Carlos de Santos Gomez

Subject: Your performance and way forward

Dear Maxim,

On behalf of Carlos, I would like to invite you to discuss your performance. We want to know how you took into account the guidance about European values and ethics. Please prepare a detailed report with examples, observations, and a list of your achievements.

Looking forward to a fruitful discussion.

Best,

H.

My head was filled with fog. A usual result of short nights, which I faced increasingly often. Nevertheless, looking back at the last three months, I was satisfied. I found a way to cope with Carlos and Broomy. First, I sorted out all start-ups into two groups and focused my efforts on the first group - those projects that, as I could judge, deserved the EU funding. The other group comprised weaker start-ups, which I would anyway put on hold or even reject. I was assessing the latter ones according to the same methodology, but superficially and, therefore, quicker. The trick was in the sequence I was sending my work to Broomy and Carlos: one "good" start-up after 2 or 3 "worse" ones. It seemed to work. Broomy gave up guessing what Carlos would say and started forwarding him my assessments with the same ambiguous sentence: "I see certain progress, but not sure about the overall quality. Would welcome your view." To maintain my image of a poor analyst, Carlos rejected every second and third submission, but thanks to my trick, he still approved those I wanted him to.

The only nuisance was that I had to prepare assessments in my free time because during working hours, I had to write reports about how well I worked and how nicely I behaved. In addition, Broomy was flooding me with her typical flippant requests: "Did you already make the planning for the next month? If not, please do so before lunch"; "Please prepare a memo on how you improve the quality of files for internal auditors"; and my favorite "Please make a briefing note on how you inform yourself about the necessity of start-ups". Each email ended with the usual "Best, H." that felt like a smack in my face.

Broomy's favorite reaction to my assessments was, "Did you already ask another unit for their view? In EU institutions we always try to collect different feedbacks, maybe colleagues offer you the view from another perspective..." Earlier I would have rushed to do what she said. But I wasn't the InSup newcomer anymore. Now I acted differently. As a first step, I activated my "I-won't-do-a-fuck" mode and put each Broomy's request aside. The longer the better. Afterward, I emailed my assessment to other units while putting Broomy in copy. The challenge was to formulate my request for the "new perspective" in such a way that nobody would understand what I really wanted. Therefore, my emails abounded with smarmy figures of speech but never came to the point. I made it unclear whether I was asking for input or just sharing something for information. As a result, other units ignored my emails. I didn't insist on them answering, and Broomy didn't keep track of this exchange. From time to time, I reported to her that the feedback was provided orally and "was neutral". She never bothered to check. *Is this how one should work for Europe?* I asked myself sometimes. But as long as I could get at least a dozen start-ups funded, I was ready to play this game.

Carlos and Broomy were already sitting at the table when Cristina whispered, "Good luck" and let me enter. Both looked like bureaucratized versions of Agents Smiths: white shirts, gray suits, and morbid gazes behind optical glasses.

"Come in, Maxim, take a seat," Broomy said in a teacher's voice.

Carlos nodded to something above my head and stared at the table.

"We organized this meeting to discuss with you the way forward as regards your work in the agency. To start with, could you please share with us your impressions and thoughts?"

Amazing how well Isabel knows them, I thought. "They will first let you speak," she said, when preparing me for this meeting. "They need to test the ground and to feel your mood. Confuse them, make them think you forgot about the past conflicts."

"I am very excited to work in InSup. Interesting work, nice colleagues, and most importantly a sense of mission. It's an opportunity to learn every day." These words physically tasted in my mouth like spinach cooked without salt. Isabel's instructions appeared to work because Broomy nodded and even Carlos stretched his lips in something that could be interpreted as a positive reaction.

"Then you will definitely appreciate the new task we'd like to give you. It's another chance to learn," Broomy said, looking at Carlos as if for support. Carlos was staring at his round face reflected

276

in his round watch. Isabel told me not to interrupt them and not to ask questions until they allowed me to. I constructed a politely curious mien.

"This task is very important for the agency and demonstrates our trust," Broomy continued. "You should create a database of rejected and pending applications we have had since the very beginning of our existence. It should be accurate and detailed: the reasons for rejections, external communication, names of assessors, - everything should be there."

My stomach dropped, but I kept following Isabel's guidance to stay silent as much as I could.

"You must start as soon as possible so that we can show the auditors that we are already working on this database," Broomy added.

"But the auditors arrive next week already, it's a shell game! Can I start with this database later, after you find a new project analyst for M-Unit?" I couldn't control myself despite Isabel's warning that any objection I express will return as a boomerang.

Broomy offered me a yellowish smile as if she was waiting for something like this. "Your style and your working ethics are a second thing we would like to discuss with you. Your career in the agency depends on this," she declared triumphantly.

Isabel knew it would come. She said it's their favorite topic because all my counterarguments would prove they are right. "There is only one trick that can work," she told me.

"I already offered my apologies to all the colleagues involved. We clarified all the misunderstandings," I said, trying hard to show how preoccupied I was.

Broomy kept showing me her teeth, but her eyes had no expression. As Isabel expected, she didn't understand which people and which misunderstandings I was referring to, but she couldn't admit it. "Oh, this is very good. We are glad that you took our guidance seriously," she mumbled.

"Of course, I did, I want to maintain our ethical culture and to learn from everybody." I tried to sound passionate.

Broomy nodded and looked at Carlos. She didn't know how to continue this talk. I considered myself a winner of this round. But suddenly Carlos put a piece of paper in front of me. "Look here," he grumbled. Broomy seemed to be surprised. She craned her neck, but Carlos' hand was still on the table and hindered the view.

I looked down. It was a print-out of an email.

Dear Carlos,

We recently received this whistleblowing report from an InSup staff member. Given such short notice, we can't include this topic in the upcoming audit mission, but later on, we might come back to you and ask for explanations.

Looking forward to meeting you in Frankfurt.

InSup Internal Audit mission

Below this message was my report to auditors; however, anything that pointed at me (my signature and email address) was removed.

"We both know the ahuhtor," Carlos hissed.

I looked straight into his face and said, "I am not sure I understand you."

"You don't understand?" For the first time, I heard emotion in his voice. It was hate. Broomy seemed to feel it as well. She so intensively tried to see the paper on the table that her face came too close to Carlos' arm. No wonder he hit her in the face. Broomy's glasses slipped to her nose.

"Oh, I am...," Carlos flinched and went silent. Unlike me, he obviously saw for the first time her glasses-free face with one squinted eye. "...sorry," he mumbled, folding the print-out and putting it back in his pocket.

I kept looking at him with a poker face.

Carlos turned to Broomy who hastily erected the glasses back on her nose. "I received a report from the IT who recently had to replace Maxim's laptop. They say the laptop stopped working because somebody puhred bierr on it. Doesn't matter who it was, but I think you and Maxim would agree that we in InSup handle responsibility for every item within these walls that is paid by European taxpayers," he explained.

"Oh, of course." Broomy intensively nodded. "Beer? On the laptop? Well, I think now Maxim should work even harder. And the database of rejected cases is a very good opportunity to immediately show your commitment to taxpayers, Maxim." She seemed to be relieved by the new turn of our talk. "Maxim, do you recognize the importance of the agency to be accountable to European citizens?"

Although her words were getting increasingly meaningless to me, I sighed and constructed a sad face expression. "I am so sorry for my clumsiness," Isabel told me that in EU institutions it's safer to admit the fake guilt rather than to prove your innocence.

"Unethical and unprofessional behaviourr in our agency has a high price," Carlos said, looking somewhere at the ceiling. "We expect the first draft of the rejections database in two days. Focus on this task, please."

"Will do. However, I can't start immediately working on it," I replied. Both blinked at me with annoyance. "My new laptop was infected with a virus, so I need to recover it first," I explained. Then I looked straight at Carlos, wanly smiled, and pronounced the words I had rehearsed for quite some time last night: "BDSM pleasures in Barcelona." I articulated each word and tried to sound affirmative.

The result left me satisfied. Behind the glasses, Carlos' rounded eyes stared back at me with horror. He opened his mouth as if he was about to say something, but no sound came out.

"I beg your pardon?" Broomy said.

I turned to her. "BDSM pleasures in Barcelona (I slightly raised my voice when pronouncing it again) is a very annoying computer virus. It has affected some systems of InSup." I looked back at Carlos, who seemed to have frozen. "It dominates you. Dominates all your programs. Never heard about it?"

Carlos swallowed a lump in the throat but remained silent.

Broomy shrugged. "There are so many viruses."

"This virus was designed by a Spanish hacker group. They call themselves De Goya and sell the best coffee in the city. I thought you might know them," I said, without taking my eyes off Carlos. "There is a risk that BDSM pleasures (Carlos' pursed his lips) will end up in every laptop in our agency and all our employees will see..."

"You can return to your regular work for now," Carlos interrupted me.

As soon as I left Carlos' office, I sent Ian an SMS with just one word: "go". Good timing mattered more than ever.

From: Ian Murphy

To: all_InSup staff

CC: Carlos de Santos Gomez

Subject: WARNING - "BDSM pleasures in Barcelona" - VIRUS

Dear colleagues,

You may have received or probably will receive an email that might intrigue you. The pictures attached to this email look plausible and the cover text looks relevant. (The email is usually tailored to each user individually, that's why we prefer not to provide you with an example, since those texts significantly differ from each other).

Please be informed that this email bears a virus called "BDSM pleasures in Barcelona". Some of our colleagues have already been affected by this virus. If you receive such an email, please don't click on any links and report to IT Helpdesk.

Thank you in advance for your cooperation.

Ian on behalf of the IT unit

Ian's concert

This warm, smoke-blue evening I was on my way to Barenik, happy to take a break from everything. The city put a friendly sundown on my shoulders. Being alone but not lonely felt good. Alice and Yinzi went to Berlin to present the Diadem at a Medical Fair. Their train left from Frankfurt and Alice for the first time spent the weekend at my place. I couldn't suppress a smile, recalling how I was preparing for this weekend. Isabel sent me Kasia, her cleaning lady and our Barcelona-opener. Ian brought the stand-alone light so that in the evening the flat would look more intimate. Then he took me shopping and insisted I buy plenty of vegetables and fruits.

For the first time, I felt I had not only worked in Frankfurt but also had a life. Two days with Alice were like a dream I had when I just arrived. It took me one year to reach it, not so bad. It was as natural and lovely as being with her in Heidelberg. We suited each other.

I sped up to turn around the corner and suddenly returned, pretending to read the name of the street on the plate as if I got lost. The trick worked: my shadow immediately slowed town so that I could notice him 20 steps from me. It was a new lad. I noticed a brown carrying sling on his scruffy pullover. Probably it was the owner of the blue-striped backpack, which had attracted so much of Yinzi's attention. I suppressed a wish to approach him and shout into his face, "Bad work!" But Nika said under no circumstances I should show that I identified him.

Together with my shadow, I went to the metro and soon was standing in front of Barenik. He didn't immediately follow me, probably hoping that after one drink I'd leave. Bad luck for him, not tonight.

Barenik bustled with people, my usual table was taken, and I felt like a homeless person. But the next moment Kirill waved at me from the counter.

"Сколько лет, сколько зим[81]!" he said joyfully when I approached to greet him. (It was ironic because I was here with Alice one day ago). "Where is wonderful Alice?"

"In Berlin, at the conference."

"Now I understand why Isabel and Ian told me to send you to their table." I followed Kirill's finger as he pointed. Isabel and Ian were waving to me from a table in front of the stage. I waved back. "I hope you distract Ian a bit. He is like a frozen fish among penguins," Kirill quickly added and went to serve another guest.

Isabel looked glamorous in an emerald spaghetti dress and rocky eye make-up (dark green with glitter). Some of Barenik's guests were staring at her, which made Ian even more pale and reserved.

"Is your shadow around?" Isabel asked.

"He followed me tonight and will soon enter, I guess."

"I am concerned that you are still on their hook, although the results of our investigation are already in auditors' hands," she spluttered out. I didn't want to spoil the evening with the answer and just shrugged my shoulders. "I think tonight you can openly sit with us. We will just enjoy the music together. Why would your shadow

---

[81] Long time no see (Russian)

suspect that it's us who are involved in the investigation?" Isabel added.

I nodded. "Agreed. All we need tonight is a break and delightful music!"

We simultaneously looked at Ian. His antsy gaze traveled from me to Kirill's counter, from the stage to Isabel. He opened his mouth to say something but changed his mind and only shook his head in response. He looked hapless.

"Ian, I've never seen a friendlier audience than in Barenik," I started. "And believe me, I know what I am talking about; playing here is just like... like entertaining your friends."

The light went dim, a usual signal before the start of the performance. Ian jumped to his feet.

"Wait." Isabel softly put her hand on his arm, and he sat down again.

Kirill hopped on the stage. He wore ideally cut baby-blue jeans and a long black jacket with sparkles. "Dear friends, I am happy to present to you a big music lover who is going to share his talent with us tonight. It took me several months to find out that he is a brilliant guitarist, and then to persuade him to prepare this program. Ladies and Gentlemen, I give you... Ian Murphy! "

Applauds were warm and encouraging, but Ian looked like a condemned criminal in front of the guillotine. He ascended the stage on stiff legs.

"His guitar," Isabel whispered.

Ian left the instrument standing at the wall. I grabbed it, ran to the stage, and passed it to Ian with a deep bow. "Thank you, Maxim, a nice attempt to join, but better not," Kirill said, and the audience laughed and applauded again.

The concert started, and I stopped recognizing two guys on the stage. I already heard Kirill singing rock songs, but this time, he sounded different. What exactly was new - the melody, the rhythm? I couldn't spot it. And in this new interpretation, Kirill's voice sounded more dramatic and intimate than usual. He even looked different: vulnerable, serious.

But a much bigger metamorphosis happened to Ian. He was no longer a short-spoken and shy boy. On stage, he was a free man, passionate and self-confident. His emotions were infectious and easily spread over the audience. When they sang in the duo "Tears in heaven" I somehow felt like it was Ian who had just lost his son. And whatever he was doing – taking a sip of water, nodding to Kirill, tuning the guitar between the songs – it was simply interesting to look at him. *Artistic charisma?* I asked myself and glanced at Isabel to check whether she saw the same as what I did.

Isabel seemed to see much more. She was slightly smiling. No doubt tonight her eyes were on Ian only and these were the eyes of a woman in love. *Из наслаждений жизни одной любви музыка уступает,*[82] I couldn't help saying.

"Не поняла[83]," Isabel looked at me questioningly. I returned a wide grin. She blushed.

After the concert, Kirill sat down at our table, which turned into the center of a human whirlpool. Everybody talked simultaneously, congratulating Ian and Kirill, and patting all of us, Isabel and myself included, on the shoulders.

"Interesting arrangement of well-known compositions, congratulations from my side as well," Isabel finally said.

Kirill pointed at Ian. "Please meet the author of the awesome interpretation!"

Although the concert was over, Ian still looked like a stage star. "Thank you for this opportunity, Kirill. I'll never forget it," he said.

Kirill raised his eyebrows, "You don't think it was a one-off show, do you? I plan to have it five or six times a year. You'd better start preparing for the next one!"

After Kirill went back to the counter, I for the first time felt uncomfortable being alone with Ian and Isabel. Something new was being born between them, and I felt that no third eye should watch

---

[82] Of life's pleasures, music yields only to love. (free translation of A.Pushkin)

[83] I didn't understand (Russian)

it. "Guys, let's be cautious. I'll get out so that my shadow - if he is here - doesn't pay too much attention to you."

It was a smart pretext to leave. They didn't mind. After having assured Isabel that I'd be cautious, I slipped away. On my way back, the metro and the night streets of Sachsenhausen were clear, nobody followed me. My shadow seemed to have taken time off. The song of Shivaree was turning in my head – already in Ian's interpretation, acoustic and bluesy.

There's a nail in the door and glass on the lawn.[84]

Suddenly two people grabbed me from both sides. "Веди себя тихо, и все будет хорошо[85]," one of them said. And so, we walked liked three drunken friends past my house.

While they were marching me somewhere, I calmed down and tried to remember which way we were going. It was easy: soon we went exactly to the same courtyard where I pictured one of them on a robbery day.

"Хорошее место ты нам показал, видишь еще раз пригодилось[86]," said the same lad. He spoke Russian without an accent. His companion was silent, probably not understanding a

---

[84] "Goodnight Moon" by Ambrosia Parsley, Duke McVinnie

[85] Be quiet and everything will be ok (Russian)

[86] Nice place you showed us, it's come in handy again (Russian)

thing. He was half hugging me around the shoulders. None of them had a blue stripe backpack as far as darkness allowed me to judge.

"Came from Russia and think you can blackmail honest people like this. Think you will be allowed to? Что ты там грозишься разослать?[87]»

He came closer and hit me in the stomach, not too strong. The other held me tighter, blocking my arms.

"Because of this, you two are wasting your evening?" I tried to sound amused.

"Think of your own evening and try not to spoil it, ok? Answer the question."

I tried to depict boredom. "Нет у меня ничего. Сделал простейший фотошоп, надеялся взять его на испуг. Shall I show you?[88]."

"Go on."

I took out my phone and showed him a picture that I had prepared the night before my talk with Carlos and Broomy. (It was another advice of Nika to have a fake photo at hand in case of such a turn). The picture was a mediocre BDSM snapshot from the

---

[87] What are you threatening to send out? (Russian)

[88] I have nothing, made the simplest photoshop. Just wanted to give him a scare (Russian)

Internet where the man had a photoshopped Carlos' head (from his portrait on InSup's website). It looked comical rather than credible.

My chaser laughed. "Говно работа[89]."

"I said you are losing time with me."

"Listen to me," he turned serious. "If you ever remember that there is such a word 'blackmail', you'll wake up in hospital with broken legs and without one eye. Got it?" Without waiting for my reply, he hit me in the stomach with all his strength. Everything grew dark in my eyes. I choked but couldn't fall because the other lad held me tight. "Your Jewish bitch won't be the better off too," I heard through a hot fog. The thought of Alice splashed cold in my head.

"А она-то тут при чем[90]?! I rapped out, and from the last forces kicked the knee of the guy behind me. He groaned and loosened his grasp on my shoulders. I felt he had shifted his weight to his front leg; it was the right moment: I grabbed him and hip-rolled on the ground as I used to when practicing unarmed self-defense. At this very moment, the Russian punched me in the jaw. My mouth was immediately filled with blood. He took me by the lapels while his partner got on his feet and painfully twisted my arms behind the back.

---

[89] Shitty work (Russian)
[90] What does she have to do with it?! (Russian)

"It's a matter of two: this motherfucker Carlos and myself," I said with effort moving my broken lips.

He breathed into my face fury and expensive tobacco; I felt like vomiting. "И не надо на меня тут зубами щелкать. Ты сам эту кашу заварил. Короче [91], if your boss complains about you one more time, blame yourself."

With a barely noticeable move, he hit me with the edge of his hand between the ribs.

"Fuck," I moaned and spat blood into his face. He raised the hand to hit me again, but the other guy suddenly freed me and stamped away. It looked like a signal because the Russian followed him without glancing a single more time at me. I felt I couldn't stand on my own. I collected all my forces while watching them leave. Once they disappeared out of sight, I allowed myself to fall on the ground, in a comfortable dark unconsciousness.

La-la-la...until I say, "Goodnight, Moon."

Computer diagnostic

From: Isabel Aquilina

To: InSup Internal Audit Mission

CC: Carlos de Santos Gomez

---

[91] Don't clench your teeth at me, you are the one who stirred up trouble. In brief (Russian)

Subject: InSup Documentation

Dear IA colleagues,

On behalf of the Executive Director of InSup, I am sending you the documents that you requested earlier.

Should you have questions, please do not hesitate to contact us at any time.

Kind regards,

Isabel

List of attachments:

1. Filled in self-assessment questionnaire

2. Organizational chart of InSup

3. Budget expenditures

4. List of procurements

5. List of recruitment campaigns

6. List of approved applications (with short descriptions)

7. List of rejected applications (without descriptions)

8. Minutes of Board meetings including voting results

9. List of meetings with external parties hosted by InSup.

From: InSup Internal Audit mission

To: Carlos de Santos Gomez

Subject: Re: InSup Documentation

Dear Carlos,

Thank you for the timely submission of documents, which we are already consulting. We have a question about the whistleblower report, which is not directly relevant to our mission but is still something we should keep an eye on. The whistleblower claims that The Diadem Project was never granted the EU funding, but in the Attachment 6 (list of approved assessments) the Diadem is mentioned. Have you recently approved it? If so, could you share the rationale for this decision as well as the detailed decision-making process?

Thank you in advance for your cooperation,

Audit mission

From: Carlos de Santos Gomez

To: Isabel Aquilina

Subject: Fw: Re: InSup Documentation

Do you have an explanation for this?? To my knowledge, Diadem just couldn't be on the list of approved projects. Why was it in the attachment 6??

Late in the evening, Ian knocked at my door. "What a shitstorm it was," he started without any introductions. I pulled him into the kitchen, where we sat down with two bottles of beer and without turning on the light - not to attract attention to my windows.

First Carlos called for Isabel. She came with the laptop and showed him the list of approved projects she received from him (the Diadem was in it). To prove that the list came from Carlos, Isabel opened the email he sent and showed that it was indeed the email with the attached list of approved projects, including the Diadem. Carlos couldn't understand shit. Neither did she, Isabel admitted, and suggested summoning somebody from the IT Unit.

Ian came with a well-prepared mien of being-amazed-by-mess-non-IT-people-can-create. He pretended he didn't immediately get the point. After Isabel explained again, Ian said he needed to conduct a full diagnostic of Carlos' laptop. He suggested doing it during Carlos' lunch break as it would take over one hour. They agreed, and after lunch, Ian met both of them again. He started describing a six-step diagnostics he had just conducted. Carlos got bored after step three and asked Ian to go straight to the conclusions. So, Ian said exactly what he had rehearsed.

"Rehearsed?"

"Of course. Isabel says rehearsing is the best way to prepare if you want to sound natural and not forget any important points," Ian replied in the voice of a troubadour in love.

In a well-rehearsed manner, Ian explained that Carlos' Outlook was infected, which meant that any files he sent as attachments could potentially be corrupted. Ian could see that the file Carlos was asking about, was manipulated but couldn't spot what exactly was done. Ian didn't forget to mention several times that the firewall and security system had been updated and the computer was safe now. Then he did another rehearsed thing: he shut up, counted to five, and asked whether Carlos opened the virus email "BDSM pleasures in Barcelona." Carlos' face changed color to one of a rain worm and he rushed to end this meeting.

"So, the issue was closed," Ian declared wily. "He is sure that the file was corrupted because of his own mistake, which he will never dare to disclose. I was on his computer when I sent him 'BDSM pleasures', he did click on the link in the email. I think the whiff you made when meeting him and Hilde worked well: Carlos really thought it might contain his pictures. Now Isabel is cleared from the suspicion that it was her who included the Diadem in the document for auditors." He went silent and for the first time sipped his beer.

I sniggered. So far everything was going according to my plan.

"I don't understand your plan," Ian suddenly said. "Carlos suspects you know something about Barcelona, which won't make you friends. And by faking the list for auditors, you won't get funding for Alice. What the hell are you doing?!"

I beamed (although Ian couldn't see my face anyway in the darkness), but I knew it would help me sound certain. "I rely on Carlos' Pharisaic gut."

Carlos changes his mind

"Are you busy, Maxim?" a familiar voice quacked above my ear. Without waiting for my answer, Carlos was already tiptoeing into my office. "Enjoying quietness? Good for concentrassion?" he asked, sizing up Karolina's empty desk.

I opened my mouth to say how much I hoped Karolina would return but interrupted myself. There was no need to prolong the small talk Carlos was trying to make. "This is ok," I said stiffly.

"I would like to ask you," he got serious, "about The Diadem Project. Where do you stand with it?"

Behind the round glasses, he was looking straight at me. I returned a level stare. "As far as I remember, you sent it back to be."

He winced. "I retehrned it with my comments. Have you already addressed them?"

"Now I am very much confused." I shook my head, as if trying to sort out my thoughts. "Are you saying that all these weeks you were waiting for the amended assessment of The Diadem Project?"

I stood up to look down at him. He made two steps backward. I quickly passed by him and stopped at the door.

"I promise this conversation stays between us," I said.

He looked around as if seeking support. The blue enamel sky was observing him through the window. And so was I. Then I on purpose loudly locked the door with the key, I had had stuck in advance into the keyhole. Carlos was motionless and probably even breathless.

"You kept the Diadem pending because you didn't like my assessment. Now you are asking me to finalize it. Why did you change your mind, Carlos?" I asked.

Without taking his eyes off me, he backed down to the window. "We must pehrmanently improve the quality of our wehrk for the sake of European taxpayers," he finally squeezed out of himself and looked at the prostrated River Main. "You addressed my concehrns. I also made an extra effort and reconsidered your assessment. Now I'd like it to be finalized. We all undergo such an evrrry day progress."

I shook my head. "It doesn't work with me anymore. All these casts of sentences about the sake of taxpayers or daily progress are just bullshit you use when you don't want to disclose your real goals. I am waiting for the truth."

He jerked as if punched.

"Maxim, European values are our driving force," he mumbled.

"You cure your wife's migraines in exchange for blocking a European start-up. How does this fit European values?" I interrupted him. His glance mixed shock with hate. "I know you are blocking the Diadem to keep receiving the medication from the Neurological Centre California. And I know you hired a local private security agency to browbeat me and the Diadem inventors. I know the name and the address of this agency, I have a video and witnesses. So, the poem about European values you can soon declaim to the German law enforcement."

My last words seemed to refresh his reactions. "It wasn't me," he shrieked. "I complained out loud that you were harassing me with the same assessment, don't riehmember who was present, don't know anything."

"Fantastic statement. Are you sure anybody would believe it? Especially after I prove that I improved three times the same assessment before sending it to you. Do European values qualify this act as harassment?"

"This start-up is not European, it's an Israeli one. EU taxpayers don't have to finance anything coming from this occupational state," he bleated after a pause.

Probably he hoped to stupefy me with his statement. But thanks to Isabel I knew that Spain had the highest anti-Israeli attitudes among Western European countries. As a proud De Goya member Carlos was flesh of Spain's flesh.

"Keep your antisemitism for yourself and don't even dare to move our discussion as far from yourself as possible. Three out of four Diadem co-founders are EU citizens. It's a European start-up, which you tried to kill for private reasons."

His mouth turned into a crack, contorting his face. He wanted to say something, but I cut him off. "I know your plan well. You removed Karolina because you wanted the Diadem to remain unassessed. Instead, you got me, and you thought you could impregnate me with an inferiority complex about my work and compliance with European values." He opened his mouth again, but I went on. "Teaching me European values while having a proven conflict of interest... you are ridiculous!"

His glasses fogged up, his forefront got covered with beads of sweat. He took off his glasses and started cleaning them with a wine-colored handkerchief matching his tie. "I had to protect my wife, my family."

"All family fathers say so," I echoed. "BDSM games with Señora Tais (I tried to imitate his voice when calling her name) at the Bar Celona restaurant do belong to this protection."

I held his gaze full of rancor. It was easy because he disgusted me more than I feared him. And in turn, I had more trumps in my pocket.

"I don't need you to admit that I am right," I finally said, "because I know I am, and I can prove it. I offer a deal: I recall my whistleblower report with apologies for being mistaken about you. (Internal Auditors would be pleased to have one issue off their desk).

Then I send you the completed Diadem assessment. In return, you call off your stalkers and ensure the safety of the Diadem team in Heidelberg. We forget everything and move on."

He turned his back to me and froze again. I returned to work, demonstrating that I completely lost interest in our discussion. In reality, I was typing again and again just one sentence that came into my mind: "Tempest in the Cider Glass is blowing itself out. Tempest in the Cider Glass is blowing itself out". After I had filled half of a page with this sentence, Carlos turned and squawked, "Ok."

"Thanks, very much appreciated," I replied, without stopping to type.

He went to my desk. "When will I have the pleazur to get the assessment?"

His round eyes were traveling somewhere above my head.

"Tomorrow first thing in the morning."

He winced. "I'd like to see it by close of business today. I will cancel my evening plans to approve it tonight and reply to the auditors."

I could hardly suppress a victorious cry when he had left. The assessment was finalized a long time ago, and I could have sent it out immediately. But I already learned that showing speed in EU institutions makes you look suspicious. I had to exhibit patience.

Striking out Blue Stripe

Ian was fidgeting in his seat. In the inner mirror, I could see him turning his head, opening and closing his laptop.

"Isabel has a nice car," I tried to distract him.

"Nice" was too strong of a word. The car was barren: no decorations on the front glass; no items on the back seat; just the scent of wet grass after rain reminding me of the car's owner. Out of curiosity, I opened the glove compartment: a little pharmaceutical box and a pocket of paper handkerchiefs. I smiled. Everything was accurate and rational, like Isabel herself.

"Why does it take her so long?" Ian was smoldering.

I turned to him. "She plays well her role: pretends she needs time to understand whether this private detective agency is the right one for her and probably asks them a million useless questions."

"Makes sense." Ian nodded. "But what if she fails to get into their Wi-Fi?"

"Nothing dramatic. We will stop everything and try it another way."

My smartphone jingled; it was a message from Isabel.

"Ian, she is already in. Here is the name of their network."

"Got it." That was the distraction I needed for Ian. He became decisive and concentrated. A couple of minutes later, he said, mesmerized, "I can't believe it. With the program you gave me, I am already inside their network."

Obviously, Nika cracks much more serious things with this program, I thought.

"How many devices do you see?"

"One big computer, one laptop, three smartphones, of which one is Isabel's."

The composition that I had awaited. "Let's exclude smartphones. They might hold them in their hands, and we don't need injuries," I said.

Soon Isabel left the agency and called me. She wore unusually bright makeup. Although the car was 10 meters away, I could see her scarlet lips moving simultaneously with the words I heard on the phone. "It's them. The agency does many doubtful things. Two detectives are in. One spoke to me in a 40 square meter office. He has a laptop and two mobile phones. The other one sits in a room next door. I couldn't really see how big it is."

"Did you see a stationary computer anywhere?"

"No... I don't think so."

I expected this answer. They probably used the stationary computer for the back-office needs. Very good, such computers are always more important than the front-office ones.

"Then we go on." I put down the phone. Excitement started bubbling somewhere in my throat, causing a slight nausea. I turned to Ian and tried to sound calm. "Let's target first the big computer and then the laptop. Don't rush. Wait for the signal from Isabel."

I left the car. Blood was throbbing in my ears. Everything around turned blurry. The only thing I could see was the entrance door of the detective agency and Isabel in front of it. She was still talking on the phone and didn't even look at me.

I pushed the door and kept staying there holding the door hanger behind my back. A blond man stood up to greet me. "Guten Tag, wie kann ich Ihnen helfen[92]?"

"Privet, recognize me?" I bellowed. My loud voice hyped me up. At the same time, I needed to attract the attention of the second detective. It worked. A second man popped up from the other room. It was an old acquaintance of mine, the Russian. Both looked at me as if they had no clue what I was talking about.

"My name is Maxim Reut, two weeks ago your people broke into my apartment in Frankfurt." I glanced straight at the Russian and scathingly added, "А с тобой мы еще мило побеседовали, да так, что я полчаса потом блевал[93]."

The blonde stared at me incredulously. The Russian smiled wanly. Neither moved, obviously awaiting my next steps.

---

[92] How can I help you? (German)

[93] And with you we had a nice talk so that I was vomiting for half an hour afterward (Russian)

I tilted and closed back the entrance door as if I were nervous. It was the signal for Isabel.

"For your own sake, leave alone both girls in Heidelberg, that's my advice." (At home I trained to pronounce this sentence in 5 seconds). Right afterward, something flopped in the neighboring room. The Russian ran there, screamed something in German, and started blasting a fire extinguisher. The air filled with a smell of burned wires.

The blonde lost his cool and looked around as if for complicity.

"Your colleagues, just a couple of levels more professional than you, say hello. Do you understand what I mean?" I asked him.

He didn't reply.

"Ask yourself how I found you and how I got into your computer. Ask yourself what else I am capable of." I fixed my gaze on him. Finally, he nodded. "Don't dare to face down my friends in Heidelberg, do you hear me? And I want back the iPad you had stolen from my apartment," I said.

Suddenly, the entrance door pushed me painfully in the back. The person entering carried a brown backpack with a blue stripe. It was the same guy who was shadowing me for the very first time after I had returned from Heidelberg. "Guten Tag." He looked at me in irritation, which converted into surprise when he recognized me.

I didn't count on the appearance of the third person behind my back. I didn't know how to proceed. "Last warning!" I screamed into his face - rather from despair. He recoiled – rather from surprise.

"Herr Pietke, eine kleine Frage hätte ich noch[94]." Isabel entered the room, almost pushing both Blue Stripe and myself away. She glanced at us arrogantly and went straight to the blonde. She kept chirping in German when the laptop on the blonde's desk exploded. Isabel screamed, "Ach du meine Güte?![95]"

I suppressed a smirk. Isabel was ok. She always used this German expression as a joke. If she were really shocked or scared, she would have screamed her usual "Fox kollox[96]." I got the point. She was giving me a chance to escape. While three men ran to Isabel, I slipped away.

Later, Isabel and Ian picked me up in the neighboring block.

"Why did you decide to return?" I asked Isabel.

She offered me a dazzled scarlet smile. "I just understood that Blue Stripe blocked the entrance door, and you won't be able to give me a sign anymore. Waiting too long for the next explosion would spoil the impression. So, I told Ian to start the attack exactly in one minute, which he did with a royal precision." She sent Ian a tender glance in the mirror.

---

[94] Mr Pietke, I have another little question (German)
[95] Oh my God (German)
[96] Fuck everything (Maltese)

"I can't believe you could design a new plan in seconds," I sniggered.

"She is such an actress!" Ian laughed. "She imitated shock so well that all three lads forgot that their equipment had just been burned and started running around her with water and whatnot. In the end, they all fell in love with her, I think."

Isabel cunningly raised an eyebrow. "I was glad to get out of my research desk and finally act on-site, and you know what? I liked it tremendously!"

Epilogue

"Guess what I found in front of my door? The stolen laptop!" I declared.

"We scared them!" Isabel sounded semi-interrogative and semi-delighted.

I didn't want to disappoint her. Not a single moment our little show scared them. What really made them think, was the virus that had burned their hardware. "They will find out who produces such viruses and will back down," Nika promised me. "They will understand who helped you find their shit of an agency and will opt for not crossing your path anymore."

"Let's celebrate!" Ian suggested.

The three of us were in Barenik. It was getting crowded. For tonight Kirill organized readings of a young German fantasy writer. As a tribute to his books, guests came dressed in T-shirts with whimsical printouts: medieval knights with punk haircuts and high-tech gadgets instead of swards.

"Let's wait for Alice. She and Philipe should join us soon," I said.

"Philipe?!" Isabel and Ian exclaimed simultaneously.

"They are meeting Silvia, Carlos' wife. Now, when the Diadem got EU funding, Heidelberg University renewed its research permission. Alice and Yinzi will continue with the tests for the Diadem, and Alice has an idea to invite Silvia to the experimental group. Remember the Christmas party when Silvia and Karolina crashed into each other? Alice thinks Silvia suffers from the Alice-in-Wonderland syndrome, a type of migraine when people misjudge distances. Silvia could be valuable for her research. So, I risked to benefit from Philipe's bad conscious and asked him to introduce Alice and Silvia to each other."

Isabel shook her head dubiously, making an elegant wave with her curly auburn hair. "'Risked to benefit' is exactly what it is," she said.

"Didn't you tell me that EU institutions praise networking more than integrity?" I asked in return.

She sighed. "You are right. If Alice wants another test participant, then Philipe is the best to help her get Silvia on board." She moved her chair closer to mine and without stopping to smile at Kirill, who was passing by our table, mumbled, "Before Philipe joins us, will you tell us what did you do to get Carlos' approval for the Diadem? I thought our goal was to report Carlos to the Commission's internal audit. But it looks like you had another plan."

I looked around. Karolina was supposed to join us too, but since she still wasn't there, it was a suitable moment to give Ian and Isabel the explanations they deserved. "After everything you told me about Eurocrats in Brussels, I thought reporting Carlos to the Commission would be a poor option."

I recalled Cristina's emails, in which she, on behalf of Carlos, harped about how perfect everything should look like in front of the auditors. After the fifth email, I knew what I should do.

"I think I understood Carlos' biggest phobia," I said. "He is afraid that people will see his mistakes. That's what triggered my plan. I became certain that once he sends the auditors the list of approved projects, he will never admit that this list contained a mistake. I needed auditors to ask him why on earth he had listed the Diadem among the approved projects, despite the whistleblower report. That's how Ian came into play."

Isabel gasped. Ian looked at us. Once phlegmatic, his eyes were full of energy and naughtiness. "That day I spent more time in Carlos' inbox than in my own," he said. "Right after he had sent to you, Isabel, the approved documentation for auditors, I recalled this email and sent from his inbox the new one, in which the list of approved projects contained the Diadem."

"Ok," Isabel was digesting what she had just heard. "But internal auditors are usually quite slow. Was it a coincidence that they so quickly noticed the Diadem in the list? Or did you anonymously point their attention at it?"

Astute Isabel. The Commission's auditors didn't notice a thing, of course. And they didn't send Carlos any emails. It was us! I composed a fake email and Ian sent it from the email account of the auditors. "Hacking generic accounts is the easiest job." Ian gave Isabel a wink.

She slowly nodded. "Why didn't you tell me?"

I replied instead of Ian, "We needed to divert suspicion from you so that Carlos doesn't think that you were in cahoots."

That's why we invented the entire story with "BDSM pleasures in Barcelona". It wasn't just to chafe Carlos. We wanted him to keep the BDSM email in his inbox as long as possible, trying to understand how genuine it was. We baited the hook, and he swallowed it. Carlos was busy with this email for quite some time.

"When I told him that his computer might be corrupted, he believed that the list for auditors was manipulated through the BDSM virus and could blame only himself for not deleting it immediately," Ian laughed.

The rest of the plan realized itself automatically. Carlos ran to me. He wanted to approve the Diadem hindsight and as a bonus, he hoped to discredit my whistleblower report.

Isabel had more questions to ask, but somebody put their hands on her shoulders.

"Here we are," declared Philipe. Alice stood next to him. "Guys, it was amazing," Philipe exclaimed, hardly he and Alice took a seat. "I rarely saw how simply and quickly a doctor can build trust with a patient. And with Silvia it's not so easy, believe me. My compliments, Alice."

Alice shrugged shyly. "I know too well how she feels."

She wore a refreshingly white dress with a cherry pattern. I've got a wish to hug and keep her only for myself. Philipe looked at Alice with admiring eyes. I couldn't help recalling how he agreed to organize this meeting. He puffed out a smoke and grinned. "If Alice helps Silvia, Carlos will be grateful to me for the rest of his life. To me and not to you because it's me who found a worthy alternative for his wife, even if it's not the truth."

"And if the Diadem doesn't help her?"

"Nevertheless, Carlos will be thankful for my attention and attempt to help. I am the winner anyway. And of course, I will owe you another one, my friend. Benefits first and nothing personal, that's how we tick in EU institutions."

"Did Silvia agree to join the experimental group?" I asked.

Philipe looked at me reproachfully. "You have doubts after everything I have just said?!"

"I simply can't explain to myself why Carlos didn't rush to approve the Diadem and get his wife into the experiment right after Karolina had shown him this project. Couldn't he see his wife would be the first to benefit from it?!" My eyes traveled from Isabel to Philipe and back. They were silent. "I lost count of him saying that InSup is working for the good of EU citizens. Doesn't he consider Silvia one of those?"

Philipe sniggered. "Trust me, he considers her much more important than any of those!"

Isabel darted me a sullen look. "I tend to agree with Philipe. Carlos has zero faith in "the high-quality work InSup is delivering for Europe. The babbling about our accountability towards Europeans he leaves for inside the Cider Glass. And outside he only believes in De Goya network."

"I brought you someone else," declared Kirill, accompanying Karolina to our table. While everybody was greeting each other, I ordered his best wine and a big variety of Georgian khinkali. A minute later, Kirill returned with wine glasses. "Looks like a celebration. What happened?" he asked.

"My start-up has just received funding from InSup," Alice said, blushing.

She sent me a glance for which I would have done everything once again and again. My bruises and my career prospects in InSup didn't matter at all. Only her flourishing face did.

Alice raised her glass. "My entire team, we are so thankful to all of you. I know you did more than needed and probably more than allowed. And I promise you that you won't regret it. For you!"

"I have been in this system for over ten years, but I have never felt more right than now. Prost[97]!" Isabel clanked her glass with Alice.

"And I want to raise my glass for Karolina," I said. "You were the one who told me the Diadem should get EU funding because it has a big future. And then you produced such a precise transparency register that allowed me to… to persuade Carlos."

Philipe laughed. "The power of your persuasion exceeded all our expectations."

Isabel sent him her usual disapproving gaze. But Karolina didn't notice anything.

I decided to change the topic. "There is another thing I want to tell you. I am moving to Heidelberg."

"Two hours by train every day? That's tough but not impossible," Isabel said pensively.

"I'll buy me a motorbike," I chuckled.

Maxim to Veronika. See you?

Nika, privet,

Another EU institutional summer break is over, and autumn starts throbbing in every office of the Cider Glass. I spent August in

---

[97] To your health (German)

Germany, traveling across the Rhein-Main area and for one lovely week I went to Berlin. I must confess, the German capital reminded me of Moscow of my childhood before crazy buildings of business centers and malls started growing all over. Berlin still has plenty of Soviet-style houses but it's not the only thing that made me feel at home, it's the endless spacy avenues and the well-measured rhythm of a city that doesn't want to become an aggressive megapolis, exactly like Moscow in the late 1980s. Maybe I got sentimental simply because I wasn't alone and saw only the positive in everything that surrounded me?

Nika, I hate to admit it, but you were right as usual: neither an EU passport nor the new job could make me a European. Our HR still has me under surveillance for my non-compliance with European ethics. But it doesn't upset me anymore. I know I will never be in line with an obsolete sense of justice and a blind submission to the shitty rules. I won't adhere to such values and will pay a high price for it. I know Carlos already looks forward to refusing the extension of my contract. But before it happens, I still have one year and a half in the Cider Glass and I intend to do my job well and serve Europeans according to my understanding.

Since I am back from my Berlin holidays, a couple of weird things happened. A stranger approached Ian in front of our house and asked whether Maxim Reut lived there. Ian said he didn't know. Out of fear that the stranger spotted the lie, Ian avoided eye contact

314

with him and as a result has zero recollection of his appearance. And yesterday I received an empty postcard with the sculpture of the Frankfurt Lady Justice (the one that has open eyes, unlike the typical sculptures with a blindfold). The postcard came to my office address: my name was printed in the addressee line and the sender. Otherwise, the card was empty, leaving me guessing. Ian and Isabel think that the Neurological Centre California didn't drop the idea of browbeating me. But I think somebody was trying to figure out whether I am still working in InSup or the postcard will return to its sender.

Can it be that our common friends had lost me? I understand their plight: I recently moved to Heidelberg, so officially I don't reside in Frankfurt anymore and my name is nowhere to be found across databases of Frankfurt authorities. Probably they grew alarmed that I would disappear from their view?

Nika, I confirm I am ready to atone for the photo frame with secret, smoky computers, and all your guidance. I will never forget how I begged you for help and got it with no interrogation. I won't back down. But it must be your request, and unlike your colleagues, you know where to find me. I won't talk to anybody else. Pass it on to Sergey Vladimirovich together with my regards.

Printed in France by Amazon
Brétigny-sur-Orge, FR